RAVAGED THRONE

A RUSSIAN MAFIA ROMANCE (BOOK TWO OF THE SOLOVEV BRATVA DUET)

NICOLE FOX

Copyright © 2022 by Nicole Fox

All rights reserved.

No part of this book may be reproduced in any form or by any electronic or mechanical means, including information storage and retrieval systems, without written permission from the author, except for the use of brief quotations in a book review.

❦ Created with Vellum

MAILING LIST

Sign up to my mailing list!
New subscribers receive a FREE steamy bad boy romance novel.

Click the link below to join.
https://sendfox.com/nicolefox

ALSO BY NICOLE FOX

Solovev Bratva

Ravaged Crown

Ravaged Throne

Vorobev Bratva

Velvet Devil

Velvet Angel

Romanoff Bratva

Immaculate Deception

Immaculate Corruption

Kovalyov Bratva

Gilded Cage

Gilded Tears

Jaded Soul

Jaded Devil

Ripped Veil

Ripped Lace

Mazzeo Mafia Duet

Liar's Lullaby (Book 1)

Sinner's Lullaby (Book 2)

Bratva Crime Syndicate

*Can be read in any order!

Lies He Told Me

Scars He Gave Me

Sins He Taught Me

Belluci Mafia Trilogy

Corrupted Angel (Book 1)

Corrupted Queen (Book 2)

Corrupted Empire (Book 3)

De Maggio Mafia Duet

Devil in a Suit (Book 1)

Devil at the Altar (Book 2)

Kornilov Bratva Duet

Married to the Don (Book 1)

Til Death Do Us Part (Book 2)

Heirs to the Bratva Empire

Can be read in any order!

Kostya

Maksim

Andrei

Princes of Ravenlake Academy (Bully Romance)

Can be read as standalones!

Cruel Prep

Cruel Academy

Cruel Elite

Tsezar Bratva

Nightfall (Book 1)

Daybreak (Book 2)

Russian Crime Brotherhood

Can be read in any order!

Owned by the Mob Boss

Unprotected with the Mob Boss

Knocked Up by the Mob Boss

Sold to the Mob Boss

Stolen by the Mob Boss

Trapped with the Mob Boss

Volkov Bratva

Broken Vows (Book 1)

Broken Hope (Book 2)

Broken Sins *(standalone)*

Other Standalones

Vin: A Mafia Romance

Box Sets

Bratva Mob Bosses (Russian Crime Brotherhood Books 1-6)

Tsezar Bratva (Tsezar Bratva Duet Books 1-2)

Heirs to the Bratva Empire

The Mafia Dons Collection

The Don's Corruption

RAVAGED THRONE
BOOK TWO OF THE SOLOVEV BRATVA DUET

My husband doesn't know about our son.

But that won't be enough to keep him safe. Because our little baby boy is the heir to two thrones.

And there are a lot of bad men out there who want to stop him from reaching them.

So I ran into the mountains.

Into a nightmare of my own making.

I thought I'd gotten away…

But I was wrong.

Even there, in the freezing cold middle of nowhere, Leo found me.

And when he did, I lied to keep my baby safe.

But I should've learned a long time ago:

Leo Solovev knows everything.

Except for how this story will end.

RAVAGED THRONE is Book Two of the Solovev Bratva Duet. Make sure you've read the beginning of Leo and Willow's story in Book One, RAVAGED CROWN, before beginning this one!

1

WILLOW

I am not who I thought I was.

"Willow Powers" is a lie.

But the truth? That doesn't feel right, either.

I guess that doesn't stop it from being true. Nor does that stop it from driving me insane. It's been on an endless loop inside my head for the last week. *Viktoria Mikhailov. Viktoria Mikhailov. I am Viktoria Mikhailov.*

The name still doesn't ring any bells. The woman to whom that name belongs is a stranger.

Me? I'm nothing.

I look down at my ravaged fingernails. I tear at them when I'm nervous. One nail in particular has an ugly, jagged edge. It looks dangerous, like it could do some damage if I put my mind to it. But the moment I apply pressure, it folds like a piece of tissue paper.

I'm pretty sure that's a sign of malnourishment. It bothers me only because of the child I'm carrying. A child I thought had been born out of something real. True love. Happily ever after.

What a fucking joke.

It was all a farce. If I hadn't been so naive, I would have seen it much earlier.

"Dreaming about your beloved husband again?"

Her voice sends a shiver down my spine. It carries a dusky quality that promises all sorts of pain.

I turn from the barred window and watch Brit glide into the room. Her beauty always seems excessive, ethereal. Like someone layered too many filters on a photo.

But as I've learned, Brit is very, very real.

She's dressed in dark jeans and a tight white blouse today. Her blonde hair is loose, falling around her shoulders. She looks as flawless as she has from the moment I first saw her.

In comparison, I haven't showered in six days. My scalp itches. Over the last week, I've been losing progressively larger clumps of my once-thick black hair.

Time has warped for me inside this cage. I only know it's been a week because she tells me so. But in my head, it's been a lifetime.

"I don't dream about anything," I tell her quietly. That's the truth: in the few restless hours of sleep I'm able to get each night, I see mostly darkness. It's still preferable to this hell.

"No?" Brit asks, coming forward. "You look like the kind of girl who never stops dreaming." Her tongue slides over her bottom lip as though I'm her next meal.

Before I can stop myself, I glance down at my arm. She grabbed me two days ago and left behind three long claw marks. It looks like I was mauled by an animal.

"Pretty Bratva princess," she hisses, reaching out and grabbing a lock of my hair. I wrench away from her and her nose wrinkles. "You don't smell like a princess, though."

"Whose fault is that?" I snap, before I can will myself to bite my tongue.

Her eyes go wide and her head jerks towards the door as though she's just heard something. There are moments when I wonder if there's not something seriously wrong with the woman.

Apart from the obvious, of course.

When no one comes, she tightens her grip on my hair and pulls down hard, yanking me towards her. "He wants you dirty," she tells me. "He likes his women dirty."

I shudder, but I'm pretty sure she doesn't notice. She jerks her head towards the door again.

I haven't seen Spartak Belov since he dragged me out of that warehouse. I haven't seen Leo, either. Not in person, at least. But sometimes, when I close my eyes, the shadows converge…

And I see him.

Leo's broad-shouldered silhouette against the dark sky beyond. The last glimpse of him I got before I was taken away.

He wasn't even looking at me.

He has the power to move mountains. The power to take life at will and walk away without a mark on his conscience. He has the kind of power men chase their entire lives and never achieve.

And yet, he simply let Belov strut away with me in chains.

That's the part about my sleep I don't mention to Brit: when I don't dream of darkness, I see the harsh lines of his unmovable face. So handsome and so cold.

I remember those quiet moments between our combined breaths. When he was inside me, and I felt whole.

Did I imagine that? Did I imagine the way he looked at me, with something warm and real in his eyes? Did I imagine all of it?

No. I can't have imagined everything. If nothing else, one thing remains real.

My hand almost flutters to my stomach, but I squelch the instinct.

This is not his baby.

This baby is mine and mine alone.

Leo Solovev only ever saw me as a weapon, and he'll view the baby as the same—if he gets the chance.

"So pretty," Brit says, tugging on my hair again, bringing me back to my bitter reality. I wince at the pain and she smiles even brighter. "So very pretty."

"Please," I whisper. The word tears from between my lips, mostly because when I'm docile and subservient, she's a little less cruel to me.

"Please what?"

"Please… master." I spit out the word like a piece of rotten fruit.

Brit's eyes glow a little. She looks like a snake. "Who would have thought that Viktoria Mikhailov would call me master," she says, delighted. "It's wonderful."

"You've got the wrong girl." I've been saying it over and over again, trying to make someone understand. I don't know who Viktoria is. Whoever they want me to be, I can't be her.

"You're a disappointment, I'll give you that. But that doesn't make you any less a prize." She leans in close, her minty breath fanning over my face. "Whoever holds you, holds the key to the Mikhailov Bratva. So I'd say you're very much the right girl."

My stomach twists again. *The key.* Leo called me that, too.

The night we met at that restaurant was no accident. He knew who I was. He came with the intention of taking me. Whether he'd come with the intention of fucking me in the booth, though, I can't let myself consider.

It doesn't matter. Either way, I played easily, naively into his hands.

To be honest, a part of me was almost relieved to finally understand it all. It always seemed impossible that a man like him would be interested in someone like me. The truth was brutal, but at least it was the truth.

"I'm no key," I whisper.

She smirks at me. "The little princess wants to turn back into an ordinary girl, huh?"

"My parents," I say. "Where are they?"

She shrugs. "Don't know. Nor do I care."

I keep asking, but she won't tell me anything. I look for the guilt in her eyes, trying to see if she's done something horrible to them—but then again, I'm not sure she's capable of that emotion. I'm not sure she has a conscience at all. God knows there's no soul behind those shimmering eyes. Only pain—both hers and mine reflected in them.

"You killed them?"

"Did I?" She shrugs again. "Perhaps. I don't keep track."

"It's one of the qualities I appreciate most about you," someone else croons.

Spartak Belov's slick voice cuts through hers. I feel my body clench. I want to cave in on myself and disappear altogether.

I've grown used to her claustrophobic presence. But the two of them together? Nauseating.

I jerk away from Brit so fast that she loses her hold on my hair. She gives me an irritated look, but thankfully, she's too distracted by him to keep inflicting petty pain.

"I thought I heard someone lurking out there," Brit says.

He stalks into the room and goes straight to her. "Nothing gets past you, does it?"

He grabs her around the waist and pulls her possessively forward. Their bodies slam together. The kiss that follows is heated, passionate. But they aren't lost to it. It's meant to be an exhibition. They're nothing if not performers.

I watch as their tongues war with one another. And it is definitely a war. They both seem to be fighting for the upper hand. I'm willing to bet half of their attraction is tied up in their struggle to be the more powerful one.

It's a hollow battle, though. Even I know that Brit's struggle for dominance is relegated to their bed.

And in this case, my cell.

When they part, Spartak keeps his arm around Brit's waist. But he turns towards me, licking her off his lips.

"Why haven't you let the girl shower?" he muses as he looks at me.

I glare at Brit. She smiles in return, no shame about her lie being discovered. "I wanted to see what it would take to make her beauty wilt."

"My jealous little kitten." Belov laughs and then licks the side of her face like an affectionate cat. "You wanted to see if you could make her repulsive to me."

She shrugs again. "Do you still want to fuck her?"

He eyes me carefully. "As badly as ever."

She stiffens, but her expression is detached. I wonder if it's all just an act. She seems too good for this man. Like she could swallow him whole and spit out his bones if she wanted.

"Is it because she's beautiful?" Brit asks. "Or because she's the Mikhailov princess?"

"Do I need to choose?"

Brit wriggles out of his grip. He lets her go. Mostly because he's focused on me. When he takes one predatory step in my direction, I scurry backwards. My skin is already crawling, my stomach churning. I don't know what I'll do if he touches me.

"She's got some new scars," Belov remarks with an appraising eye.

Brit rolls her eyes. "A few scratches. Nothing significant. If she's going to be a part of this life, she'd better grow a thicker skin."

"I want no part of this life," I croak.

Belov's mouth tips up in an amused smirk. "You don't have a choice, darling." He sidles closer and runs two fingers down the side of my face.

A scream lodges in my throat. I want to fight back.

But I wasn't meant to fight back. It wouldn't help, anyway. My life has prepared me for this. I'm made to survive. To endure and take pain lying down. To swallow my screams.

Belov's fingers flutter from my face to my chest, and I tense. But even when he curls his hand around my sore right breast, I don't do anything.

"If you want to fuck someone, choose me," Brit blurts. She'd never do something as pedestrian as blushing, but her eyes do churn like she regrets having spoken up.

"Jealous, my beauty?" Spartak asks her, even as he never takes his eyes off me.

"She's nothing," Brit says. "You need a real woman."

Finally, he releases me. I'd be relieved, if it weren't for the anger narrowing his eyes.

"Your husband made a bold move in taking down two of my buildings," he snarls. "It was reckless, considering everything I could do to you in retaliation."

I shiver. But it has nothing to do with Belov this time. Leo doesn't care about me. He never did. My suffering means nothing to him.

So if Spartak wants to take out his anger on me?

Well, Leo won't lift a finger to stop him.

"He knows I need you alive, pretty princess," he says. "But I don't need you whole."

Suddenly, I twist away from him and dry heave. If there was anything in my stomach, it would have come out all over his shoes.

Belov lunges backwards. "Leo Solovev is going to pay for his hubris."

"You're the one with hubris." I wipe my mouth with the back of my hand, looking up at him from the floor. I'm in the weaker position, but I can't hold back anymore. "You should have known that Leo makes good on his promises. If you'd given me back to him, you wouldn't have lost half your men."

"Men can be replaced," Belov snaps. "And I can rebuild."

"But how long will it take? And at what cost?"

I know I've gone a step too far when his eyes grow cold. He reaches under the hem of his shirt and pulls out a blade.

Brit says something, but I don't know what. The sight of the knife has stolen all my other senses.

Is he going to kill me now?

Is he going to cut my baby out of me?

Why didn't I just keep my mouth shut?

Snarling, Spartak grabs my hair and forces me onto my knees. He dances the knife over my jaw and down my exposed throat like he's looking for the best place to start carving.

The blade is cold, but I fear that if I shudder, it'll tear into my flesh. I squeeze my eyes closed.

This is not my world.

This is not my life.

He pulls the knife away from my skin, and I wait for the sting of pain. For the warm drip of blood down my neck.

Instead, I feel a rush of air against my cheek as he slashes downward. There is no pain, though, just a distant slicing sound.

When he's done, he drops me to the floor again. I open my eyes and see the dark strands of hair littering the floor. I look up and see the same dark tresses in his hand.

I lift a hand to my head. My fingers tremble as they traverse this alien territory.

He's cut off at least a foot of my hair. It falls just past my ears now, the edges jagged.

"Ha!" Brit cackles. "Not so pretty anymore."

Belov turns and walks out of the room without another word, but the she-devil stays.

I crawl back until my spine hits the wall just beneath the barred window. The dingy light comes through the thick slats and lands on Brit, illuminating her as she moves towards me. She drops to her hands and knees and comes in so close that I can see the blue lines radiating out from her irises.

She's as beautiful as she is terrifying. An angel of death, sent to torture me and me alone.

Her hand lashes out and tightens around my neck. My mouth opens, but this time I can't scream because she's blocking my windpipe. It's not the first time she's made me fear for my life since I was locked in here. But judging by the look in her eyes, it might be the last.

Then something weird happens.

Her other hand finds mine. Our entwined fingers are squeezed against her chest, and I feel something cold and metal settle into my closed fist.

"The walls have eyes. At eleven o'clock tonight, they'll close," she says in a soft, accentless voice I don't recognize. "When you see a light at the window, use this key to get out."

What?

Her fingers curl around my hand, pressing the key inside my palm so hard I think it will fuse with my skin. Then she backs away and gets to her feet.

"It's going to be fun breaking you into little pieces," she sneers, her voice once again sharp and acidic.

Then she turns and leaves.

I stare after her, gasping. But I don't dare look at the new weight resting in my left palm. I'm too scared to.

The walls have eyes. At eleven o'clock tonight, they'll close.

This is a game. It has to be.

She's taunting me with freedom. If I bite, they'll pull me back into this cell and torture me some more. These people—her, Belov—they play mind games. This is a trick. I know it.

But what if it isn't?

I spend the next seven hours veering between wild hope and panicked fear. I pace despite the fact that I have no strength left in my body. When my tray of food appears, I force myself to eat every morsel. If this is an opportunity for freedom, I can't waste it. I have to gather what little energy I have left.

As the little daylight I can see through the bars fades and then disappears entirely, I find myself drawn more and more to the window.

If there's no light like she said there would be, I promise myself I will abandon this futile hope and get into my bed. I'll try to sleep. To prepare myself for another day of torture and mind games.

My cell grows dim, and then full dark. I sit and wait. My eyes go blurry as I search for the light, but my lips keep moving soundlessly as I repeat the words she said to me.

The walls have eyes. At eleven o'clock tonight, they'll close. When you see a light at the window, use this key to get out.

The walls have eyes. At eleven o'clock tonight, they'll close.

The walls have eyes.

The walls—

There.

There it is.

The light.

Trick or not, this is my chance. Maybe my only chance. I turn towards the door and uncurl my hand, stiff from being clenched into a fist for so long. The key is warm against my palm.

When I slide it into the keyhole, it fits beautifully. It doesn't make a sound as I turn it.

I half expect Brit and Belov to be standing on the other side, waiting to dole out their punishment with glee. But there's nothing and no one but darkness.

The thin, pointed windows remind me of an old gothic castle. I follow the tracks of light that spill out onto the floor until I come to a door that appears to be a dead end.

I glance at the key again. Will it open every door I encounter?

But before I can figure out my next move, the door opens. I jump back as a woman walks towards me. For a moment, I assume the feminine figure emerging is Brit, and my heart leaps into my throat.

But then I realize that this woman is much shorter and much plainer. Her eyes land on me.

Come, she mouths.

I follow her silently through the house. When we make it outside, I inhale deeply. I haven't been outside in a week. There's so much air I feel light-headed.

I'm doing my best not to think about how or why this is happening, or what might be coming for me next.

I know in my heart it's Leo. It has to be. There's no other person on earth who has this kind of power, this kind of reach. He's the puppet master, the man pulling all the strings.

He let Belov take me because he knew he would get me back soon. He's always been my savior. Why would this be any different?

The woman opens a tiny door hidden by overgrown patches of shrubs and hanging ivy. "Go," she says softly, her voice deeper than I expected.

"Thank you," I whisper.

"Don't thank me. Run."

So I do.

I rush through the door and towards the blinking light in the near distance. It's an SUV, tinted windows, large and black and well-camouflaged. As I get closer, the lights stop flashing.

The door swings open as I approach. I get into the back seat, chest heaving from my sprint across the lawn, and twist towards the person sitting on the opposite side of the car.

"Le—"

His name is almost out of my mouth when I stop short.

The person sitting next to me is not the savior I've been imagining. It's a petite woman with dark hair and a harsh expression on her face.

"W... who are you?" I ask. "Did Leo send you?"

Her eyes narrow. "No one sent me. I'm here of my own accord. To get you away from that fucking monster."

Her tone is hard as flint, with a regal bearing. Small as she may be, there's something about her that radiates control.

"Who are you?" I ask again.

She looks over, a dark eyebrow arched. "Don't you know me, Viktoria?"

I flinch, rejecting the alien name that I don't want. "Should I?"

"I'm Anya Mikhailov," she says with a smile. "I'm your mother."

2

LEO

"You should have sent me in."

Gaiman's been holding onto this thought the entire time we've been waiting. He's only now decided he's willing to say it and piss me off.

"Fuck that. He should have sent *me* in," Jax offers.

"You're too goddamn loud," Gaiman says. "You'd have fucked up the mission before setting a toe on the property."

The half-smile falls off Jax's face. "Say that again, *mudak*."

"I'll say it as many times as it takes to help you understand," Gaiman says, uncharacteristically harsh today. "I know you're slow."

Jax opens his mouth to respond, but I shut them both down before he can.

"Enough!" I growl. "If sending any of us had been an option, I would have kept you here and fucking gone myself. But all three of us are too recognizable. If one of Belov's guards sounded the alarm, we would have compromised ourselves, Willow, and our spy on the inside."

"Speaking of, what does Agent Thirty-One have to say about this debacle?" Gaiman asks.

"I'll deal with that later," I snap. "For now, I put one man in charge."

Right on cue, there's a knock on the door.

"Enter," I bark.

Pietro opens the door and steps inside. The man is about a head shorter than I am. His short blonde hair is gelled back against his head. His eyes flicker nervously between Jax and Gaiman before they finally land on me.

"Where is my wife?" I ask.

Pietro juts out his chin. "It-it-it wasn't our fault."

Big mistake. There's a difference between holding your own and showing disrespect. I wonder if the man knows what he's done or if he's too stupid to grasp the consequences just yet.

"What happened?"

"We had our sights on the girl," he says. "She came through the door like she was supposed to, but..."

"But *what?*"

"... There was another car." He swallows and continues, "It was dark. The car was camouflaged. We didn't even see it until—sir, the girl ran right for it. It happened too fast."

"Girl?" I repeat. "That *girl* is my wife. Which makes her your boss. And, in this instance, your *one fucking responsibility.*"

"I'm sorry, but she—"

I backhand him suddenly and with so much force that his head snaps to the side. It's an insult more than anything. One that's meant to wound his pride. When he looks back to me, I can see it's worked.

"Don Solovev," he says, lowering his eyes. "Forgive me. I should have done more."

"You should have done fucking everything!" I roar. "Everything it took to get her back! I gave you this job because I thought you were competent. What the hell were you doing while she ran in the wrong fucking direction? Eating fucking popcorn?"

"Boss—"

This time when I hit him, I use my fist.

The moment I connect with his face and feel something break, I feel a surge of satisfaction. It makes me want to land another punch. To break more and more until there's nothing left.

The bloodthirst is harder to squelch once it rises to the surface.

"When I hand down a mission, I expect success," I snarl as Pietro stumbles backwards. "At the bare minimum, I expect competency."

He raises his head to say something. I don't give him the chance. And when I hit him for a third time, he crumples to the ground.

I stand over him as blood pours from his nose. He blinks furiously, trying to get his bearings before more pain descends upon him.

Jax and Gaiman converge around me. They know better than to get involved when I'm meting out punishment, but I can sense their apprehension.

I clench my fist and close my eyes. "Get out, Pietro. Before I end you."

Pietro scrambles to his feet and sprints for the door on unsteady legs. I stay still until the sound of his footsteps has disappeared.

When he's gone, I turn and slam my still clenched fist down on the table. "*FUCK!*"

Then, with the sound of my rage still reverberating around the room, I pick up my phone and dial the number of the person I really want to talk to. I let it ring three times before I hang up.

"Leave," I tell Jax and Gaiman as I sink into my chair. "Both of you."

They don't argue.

The moment they're out of the room, my phone starts ringing. The number is cloaked, so I know who to expect.

"Where?" I growl.

"Corner of River and Third. Forty minutes."

Then the line goes dead.

Cursing, I grab my keys and storm out of the office. Jax and Gaiman are on the other side of the door, but neither one asks where I'm going.

I'm at the corner of River and Third in twenty minutes. It doesn't make sense to have come early, but my adrenaline is pumping. I need fucking answers. What I don't need is to sit and brood in my office. The devil knows I've done plenty of that this week.

I wait on a downslope next to a bridge, hidden from the sight of cars passing overhead. The sound of the river running melts into the traffic sounds. A blur of white noise to blot out my senses and give me a moment's peace from the endless fucking thinking.

Despite all that, I know the minute she's arrived. The expensive whiff of Chanel might as well be a bell.

"Hey, big guy," she says with a confidence that belies her body language.

She stops a few feet away from me. Her long blonde tresses blow softly in the wind. She's always been beautiful, but her beauty has taken on a different quality in recent years. It's sharper. Colder.

Underneath all that, though, she looks deranged.

I always knew there'd be a cost. I said as much to her all those years ago. But she chose to walk into the darkness anyway.

"What the fuck happened?"

"I don't even get a hug?" she asks.

"Cut the shit. We're not here to exchange pleasantries."

She shakes her head, disappointed. "I almost thought you'd be happy to see me. It's been a while, Leo. How long now—a year? Maybe longer."

"You want to catch up? Pretend like shit is normal." I ask. "Fine. But drop the mask."

Her expression falters. "W-what?"

"Drop the mask," I repeat. "You have to play the part with him; I get it. But you don't have to pretend with me."

She stares at me for a long moment, and I can see her wavering. Her lower lip trembles for a second before she manages to regain control.

"If I drop the mask, I won't be able to put it on again," she says softly. "It's been so long."

I take a step towards her. She flinches.

"You're nervous?" I ask in surprise. "Of me?"

"Sometimes, I wonder…"

"Yeah?"

"If I'm playing my part too well," she finishes quietly.

I think back to that day in the warehouse. I still remember the way her nails had dug into Willow's arm. I wanted to take her head off.

The fact that she was working for me didn't even compute. She was *his* creature in that moment. It didn't matter that I'd been the one to place her next to him.

"You're convincing. I'll give you that."

"Are you doubting my loyalties, Leo?" She winces like the words pain her. "I have always been loyal to you. I have always been loyal to the Solovevs."

"I know."

"Do you?" she asks, genuine curiosity in her voice. "Because you're looking at me like I'm a stranger."

"Because right now, you're Brittany," I point out. "You're the persona we created. The monster meant to seduce another monster. The woman I know, the woman I care for, her name is—"

"Don't," she says suddenly. "Please don't. I can't bear to hear it."

"Why?"

"Because it reminds me of everything I lost."

I nod. "Fine. You'll stay Brit then. At least for now."

"Will there ever be a later?"

"There will be," I say firmly. "I swear to you. There will be an end to this nightmare. You'll be back home soon—with me, where you belong."

She looks at me. Then she turns towards the river. For a moment, I see the girl I used to know. The one I'd laughed with in another life.

"I'm sorry about tonight," she says, shifting back to business. "Everything went smoothly until the end."

"What happened?"

"Anya happened."

"Anya fucking Mikhailov," I growl fiercely. "You're sure it was her?"

She nods. "Apparently, she's been casing the joint for days. I only found out after."

"She's got a good team."

"She took the best men with her when she left," Brit explains. "What happened tonight is enough proof: she's not to be underestimated."

"I never underestimated her," I point out. "But I'm counting on her to underestimate me."

Brit smiles. "Already planning something?"

"Always."

She sighs. "He's furious, you know?"

"Good."

"The Silver Star alone would have been hard to lose. But the Manhattan Club as well? You've got some balls on you."

I raise a brow. "You always knew that."

"He's a dangerous man when he's angry, Leo."

"That makes two of us." Her features are ice cold, lifeless. But in her eyes, I see something else. "Has he hurt you?"

She tilts her chin down to hide her face. It's a move I recognize from the old days. Back when our ambitions were born of more than just revenge. It reminds me, deep down, she's still in there. Somewhere.

Whether she can ever come back out is a different story entirely.

"He never stops hurting me, Leo. The pain never leaves." Her voice cracks. "It never will. It doesn't matter how sweetly he talks to me or how gently he touches me in the moments between. It all just hurts."

Her eyes glisten with tears I know she'll never let herself shed.

"Listen to me," I say softly. "If it's getting too much for you, you don't have to keep doing this. I'll get you out."

She's shaking her head before I'm even done talking. "No," she says firmly. "I'm going to see this through. I'm taking the motherfuckers down. I don't care what it costs."

"It might cost your life."

"Is that even worth anything anymore?" she asks.

I should be pulling her out right now. The toll this is taking on her is obvious and devastating. But the call of revenge is too close and too sweet to resist. I still need her on the inside.

"It's worth something to me." I reach out and take her hand.

She stares at our entwined fingers. "What was I like… before all this?"

"You were happy."

"*Happy*," she scoffs. Her mouth contorts as it forms the word, like it tastes strange on her tongue. "It was a fantasy, wasn't it? Right from the beginning. I should have known it couldn't last."

"I may not be able to give you happiness again. But maybe I can give you peace."

She looks down, the mask slipping firmly over her fine features. She shakes her head and steps back.

"Peace died for me a long time ago. There is no peace for me in this world, Leo. I live in the chaos now. I live in the pain." She looks over her shoulder towards the road. "And it's time for me to go back to it."

"You're sure?"

She smiles, but it's not a sincere one. "I appreciate you asking, especially when I know you don't mean it."

"You'll let me know if anything pops up?"

"I always do," she says, turning towards the shadows of the bridge.

Before she can go, I blurt, "She's pregnant."

I don't know why I do that. Mostly because she deserves to know, I guess.

Her body goes rigid for a second. Her expression gives nothing away, but I can read the emotion underneath the mask.

She's jealous.

"You're going to be a father," she says tightly. "Is that why you're so deadset on getting her back?"

"Something like that."

She cocks her head to the side. "We know each other too well for lies, Leo."

I leave that alone. There's no point getting into it with her now. It wouldn't change anything.

"Well, what's your big plan, then?"

"To stop trusting incompetent fuck-ups," I say. "This time, I'm taking care of everything myself."

"I'd have expected nothing less," she says, amused. "It's been nice chatting with you. But, as they say, duty calls."

I nod. "Thank you, Agent Thirty-One."

She gives me a half smile. Then she disappears into the darkness where it's easier to wear her disguise.

3

LEO

ELEVEN MONTHS LATER

The mountain compound is a fortress.

The walls are high, but it's the natural terrain that does most of the work. Rock formations hang precariously over steep falls, jagged edges threatening to impale anyone who tries to scale them.

The only safe entrance is through the main gate. And that's only if you're allowed through by the armed guards.

"Jesus," Jax grimaces. "It's like the pope lives inside."

I focus my high-powered binoculars on the walls. There are lookout towers on each corner of the compound with a pair of guards stationed in each. They're suited up like they're prepared for battle.

In a way, they are.

"She's been waiting for us," I say, mostly to myself.

"I'd say so," Gaiman murmurs. "Seems a little paranoid, if you ask me."

"If she's expecting us, does that mean we can stop skulking around and just walk through the gates?" Jax asks. "I'm bored."

"You want to storm this place?" I prod him. "I'd love to hear how. Maybe we can get in, but then what? Is that a chance you want to take?"

Jax shrugs. "That's not my decision to make, Don."

Jax is lucky he's useful. Even luckier that I like him. I'd throw anyone else off a ledge for that sarcasm.

I roll my eyes and turn away. "Time?" I ask gruffly.

"9:55," Gaiman tells me. "The gates should open in five minutes."

I already know that, of course. I've had a permanent team on Willow's fortress for thirty-three days now.

Every Tuesday at precisely ten in the morning, the gates open and a contingent of two vehicles leave the compound. The first armored jeep carries five men. The second carries five more, plus one additional passenger.

My wife.

Willow visits the town situated seven miles down the treacherous mountain road for an hour, sometimes two. Then she returns back to the compound's walls and stays there until the following Tuesday.

The ritual has been driving me mad. Each Tuesday, I caught a glimpse of her. But I couldn't be seen. I had to stay hidden.

Until now.

Now, I intend to take back what is mine. Not only my wife—but my child, too.

The thought stings. I don't even know if I have a son or a daughter. So far, my men haven't been able to collect any intel on the baby. Willow would have given birth about two months ago, by my estimation. Which means the Solovev heir is living and breathing somewhere behind those walls.

The massive bronze gates start to part, emitting a creak that shakes the mountains. The snow descends from where it's packed around the spikes along the walls.

"There we go," Jax says unnecessarily. "It's game time."

I can sense the excitement rush through the men. They've been preparing for this moment for almost two months, ever since we finally managed to pinpoint Anya's exact location.

The information wasn't easy to come by. It has been a long and bloody process. But I'm nothing if not determined.

To his credit, the man who gave up Anya's position put up a good fight. For that, I gave him a clean death. I can appreciate loyalty, even if it is misplaced.

Like clockwork, the first jeep leaves the compound, blissfully unaware of our position behind the thicket of snow-capped trees. Five seconds later, the second jeep follows the first.

Willow is in that one, but the windows are tinted. All I can make out is the shape of her—smaller, more delicate than the guards around her.

My men have assured me that she is no prisoner. She's been seen in town countless times, her movements free and autonomous.

But brainwashing is a form of imprisonment.

And I plan on freeing Willow from all the shackles that have bound her to her mother for the last eleven months.

The jeeps move towards the cliff path. I grab my phone and make the call.

"Pietro," I say. "It's time to redeem yourself. They're heading your way."

"I won't let you down, boss."

I wait until both jeeps have disappeared down the track before I give the signal to follow. They should meet Pietro and his contingent in six minutes.

Gaiman is behind the wheel. Calm and even-tempered, he's the best driver in situations like this. The vehicle barely makes a sound as we follow at a reasonable distance.

We have to take a more circuitous route than the one Willow is on. It's a necessary measure to avoid being noticed by the guards on the lookout posts. But before long, I can hear the loud purr of the jeep's engines.

I check my time. Only four minutes have passed. The road is narrowing now. We're approaching the far side of the snow-capped hill that will allow for the ambush.

"Not long to go now." Jax is practically bouncing in his seat, giddy as a kid on Christmas morning.

I stave off the excitement. I'll celebrate once I've won. Once Willow is in my grasp.

Not a moment before then.

The screech of tires is barely audible, cushioned by the blanket of snow on the ground.

But the gunshots definitely aren't.

The *pop-pop-pop* of automatic fire echoes through the mountain range, making the trees shiver. Snow shakes into the wind like white rain.

"Speed up," I growl.

Gaiman accelerates. We round another turn and come to a straightaway. Ahead, I can see the ambush unfolding.

Pietro's vehicles have blocked the narrow path down into the village. Anya's black jeeps are halted at an angle. It's clear their intention is to turn around and haul ass back to the secure compound.

But our appearance has just fucked up their escape plan.

Pietro and the rest of my men are already out in the snow, their weapons trained on both jeeps. The shots I heard fired only moments ago have met their targets. Every single tire on the armored jeeps is flat now. Undrivable.

Sitting ducks.

Once the Mikhailov men realize they're trapped, they come out from behind their tinted windows. Like us, their weapons are drawn.

I jump out of the passenger seat and move cautiously towards the scene.

"None of you have to die," I call out. "All I want is what's already mine."

"She is not yours," a husky voice calls back.

The owner of the voice steps forward. He's a huge man, even taller than me. Must be close to seven feet.

"Keep talking and this will end badly for you and your men."

"As long as I am breathing, you will not touch—"

Before he's finished, I pull my gun, aim at his head, and fire. His heavy body hits the ground with a thud. Hot blood melts the snow around his head.

"Anyone else want to test me?" I ask casually. "Or should I keep shooting?"

"Enough!"

The Mikhailov men flinch at the sound of her voice. The back door of the second jeep opens. Thick-heeled black boots hit the snow.

Then she steps out.

But the woman that emerges from the jeep is not who I'm expecting.

She has Willow's coloring. She has Willow's black hair and blue eyes. She has Willow's curves, her scent, her aura.

But this woman is not the same one I married.

Her black hair is shorter than I remember, ending at her shoulders in sharp spikes. Her eyes are harder, colder. Her full mouth is set in a harsh line. The gray turtleneck she's wearing is skintight, as are the black jeans she's paired it with, and there's a new hardness in her body. She's lost weight, gained muscle.

She looks fucking beautiful.

And fucking deadly.

Somehow, in only eleven months, Anya Mikhailov has managed to transform Willow into a mirror image of herself.

Willow takes a step forward. She's unarmed, but she looks perfectly at ease as she approaches me.

"I said that's enough, Leo. Put the gun down."

"It's never enough. You know I'll kill them all."

"I know you'll try. But I won't allow you to hurt them."

Willow has found her dominance. Was this ruthless Bratva queen always lurking under the surface of the mild-mannered woman I snatched from obscurity? Or was she birthed in the last several months by a woman whose ruthlessness has become legend?

I raise my eyebrows. "I'm not really asking."

Her eyes narrow before flitting over my men and then hers. She's taking stock of the situation. Evaluating—not from fear or panic, but from calm certainty. She nods as she makes her decision.

"I'll come with you if you let them go."

"A noble gesture."

"I wouldn't expect you to understand."

I almost smile. "Get in the vehicle, Willow."

She flinches. "My name is Viktoria Mikhailov. Willow no longer exists."

"Is that right?" I ask. "Willow's parents will be disappointed to hear that."

Her eyes go wide. I can see the information piercing through the tough veneer she's painted on. Has she believed they were dead this whole time?

"My parents…"

I turn away from her, unwilling to divulge anything else just yet. "You have five seconds to get your ass in my jeep. You know me, Willow. I keep my promises."

I can see it in her face: she wants to refuse me, to deny me, to fight back like she always has.

But she resists the urge and starts walking towards me.

Even her walk has changed. She moves like a predator, aware of every step and its effect. She knows how to use her new body…

And it's making me very fucking hard.

"Madam Viktoria!" one of the Mikhailov soldiers says, stepping forward helplessly.

Jax has a gun trained on him in seconds, but he ignores that and looks straight at Willow.

"Madam Viktoria," he says again, softer.

"It's okay, Armand," she sighs. "I know what I'm doing."

"Your mother–"

"My mother knew this was a possibility," she interrupts. "She was ready for it."

Then she raises her left leg and gracefully settles herself into the jeep.

Jax and Gaiman are looking right at me. Gaiman's expression is veiled. But Jax's smile isn't subtle at all.

"Hot damn," he mutters.

I resist the urge to roll my eyes as I turn to the Mikhailov men, particularly the one who just spoke. Armand. He's looking after Willow with an expression that speaks to devotion and infatuation.

It's enough to merit a bullet to his leg. But I promised Willow I wouldn't. And like I just told her, I keep my promises.

"Pursuing us is not in your best interests," I inform them. "Unless you want to join the big fucker eating snow."

Armand's expression tapers into hate. "We'll get her back. She belongs here, with us."

I move forward so fast that none of his men have time to draw their weapons. I'm not bothered, anyway. I know my men have my back.

I grab Armand by the throat and pin him against the side of his car, knowing that she's watching.

"There is no 'us,'" I snarl in his face. "There is only me."

I tighten my grip around his neck and choke the air from his lungs. Just when he starts to go blue, I throw him back onto the snow. He gasps for breath as I turn and leave him behind me.

I swing up into the jeep next to Willow, then tap the side. "Let's get the fuck out of here."

Gaiman floors the gas pedal, the engine roars to life, and we rip away down the mountain pass.

The moment we're free and clear of the Mikhailov men, I turn to the beautiful new problem sitting on the seat next to me.

Willow slowly turns to face me. Anger burns in her eyes, but it isn't the firecracker it used to be, burning hot and fast. Looking in her blue eyes now is like looking into the mouth of a volcano. The heat is steady and controlled, but deep. Unending.

"Where is my child?"

"Your child," she smirks. "Funny choice of words."

"You're going to help me get my baby back."

She shakes her head. "I can't do that."

"Why the fuck not?"

Instantly, a switch flips in her. The anger is gone. *Everything* is gone. Looking at her now is like staring at a doll.

She's nearly lifeless as she says, "I can't get the baby because there is no baby to get."

"What the fuck are you talking about?" I ask.

She turns to face me fully. "*Your* child died in my stomach months ago."

Then, slowly, she turns back to the window and refuses to say another word.

4

WILLOW

We drive for fucking ages.

The last half hour has been spent off-roading, bouncing over unpaved terrain. Wherever we're headed, I'm willing to bet it's far more difficult to find than the fortress in which I've ensconced for the last eleven months.

I try and stare out the window for as long as I can, but I can feel his gaze like a physical touch. It's as distracting as I remember.

"Where are you taking me?"

"Oh, are you talking again?" he asks.

Once I do glance over, it's hard to look away again. My memories of him had grown fuzzy. I remembered him in broad swathes, like an abstract painting. The finer details had been blended out.

But now, he is flesh and blood again.

The scar on his neck stands out, as intricate and frightening as ever. I'd forgotten how square his jaw is, how his nose slopes down at a perfect angle. His features are harsh in isolation, but when combined, they form the most handsome man I've ever laid eyes on. Even after everything we've been through, everything he's done to me, I can't deny that.

Sitting next to me in the car, he blocks the window. He seems taller and broader than I remember.

Suddenly, I wonder if I'm strong enough for this. I want to be. It's what I've worked towards for eleven endless months.

But being confronted with the reality of him now, my ambitions seem far-fetched. Hers do, as well.

I have never been more aware of him.

Or of my own body.

A body that betrayed me several times in the early months of life with my birth mother. We were together nearly a year, but there's still a detachment. A wariness I can't shake, a distance I can't cross.

"Where are my parents?" I ask, knowing full well the consequences of asking.

He studies me with a cold, unmoved expression. "If you expect me to answer your questions, you're going to have to answer mine."

I'm actually warm in my layers and boots, but goosebumps dapple my skin. Apparently, dying and being reborn as someone new isn't enough to undo the way my body reacts to his.

"What do you want to know?" I'm proud of the dispassion in my tone. It's a skill I've been practicing. One I intend to master.

"You know exactly what I want to know."

I ignore the twisting pain of the memories and focus on remaining in control, neutral. "It was a boy," I tell him softly.

He doesn't so much as flinch, but I know him well enough to know that information is a blow. His legacy, dead in the womb.

I continue without being prompted. "I started bleeding out in my fourth month. A team of doctors came."

"She didn't take you to a hospital?" he growls.

"I was bleeding out too fast," I speak in the voice Anya uses when she tells me a story from her past. As if it happened to someone else. Mere fact, no emotion. "If they'd moved me, I might have died, too."

He doesn't speak. If he has any feelings about the idea of my death, he doesn't reveal them. I can't say I'm surprised.

"I was bedridden for a month afterwards," I continue. "I was unconscious when they buried him. He's on her compound, if it means anything to you."

"Where?" The single word vibrates with barely contained emotion.

"An unmarked grave," I tell him. "Since I didn't name him, it seemed fitting."

"You should have named him."

The anger surges out, cutting through the distance between us. But I welcome it. Because the truth is that I want him to suffer. I want to make him feel the sting of loss. The same I've had to grapple with.

"What I should have done is not your concern," I snap. "You weren't there."

"Is that an accusation?"

I have to bite down on my tongue to keep my emotions from spilling out. *Show them nothing but indifference, and they won't be able to use your feelings against you.* Her lessons feel timeless, though I've barely scratched the surface of understanding her world, Leo's world.

"I'm just stating a fact," I say. "You weren't there."

He's staring at me, but he says nothing. No explanation or apology. It's foolish to even consider that he might offer me some form of closure.

The man was never in this for me.

He was after my name. Nothing more.

The car finally comes to a stop at the end of a crude gravel path. It seems to lead nowhere.

"Get out," he orders.

I'm ready to argue, to remind him I'm not the same woman he met a year ago. But before I can say anything, he's out of the car. His door slams in my face.

"The whole confident, black widow thing is really working for you," Jax says, twisting around in the front seat with a wide grin. "I'm just not sure it'll work on him."

He chuckles as I climb out of the car and follow down the gravel path after Leo.

The trees get thicker the further we go. Jax and Gaiman linger just close enough to be noticed and just far enough not to eavesdrop. I'd be a fool not to notice they're doing it intentionally.

Clearly, they're blocking me in.

"What's the matter, boys?" I ask them, throwing a glance over my shoulder. "Scared I'll make a run for it?"

"Nah," Jax quips. "I just like the view from back here."

"Jax."

The man flinches at the sound of Leo's voice. It's my turn to laugh as Jax hurries past me to walk with Leo, his shoulders slouched in regret.

Leo says something to him, but they're too far away for me to catch exactly what. Then Jax melts into the trees and disappears completely.

"Where are you taking me?" I call up to Leo.

The moment I ask the question, he turns sharply and walks into the trees. I jog to catch up with him.

The moment I do, the trees open, and I'm looking out on a snowy oasis.

Snow-capped peaks and white valleys flow seamlessly into one another, a single unbroken pane of ice as far as the eye can see.

As beautiful as the view is, I'm distracted by the modern cabin that rises three stories into the clear blue sky.

The façade is mostly glass, framed by logs as thick as a man's waist. Through the windows, I catch glimpses of the interior. A piano soaking in the pale sun. A spiral staircase, a stone fireplace, a shelf of books.

A rock path leads up to the front door. Leo opens it for me as we approach. "Go inside."

When I hesitate, he arches an eyebrow. "Unless you'd prefer to freeze to death?"

I grit my teeth and follow him inside.

I expect Jax and Gaiman to be there, too, but neither one makes an appearance. All the men that accompanied us up here seem to have melted into the snow.

The moment I step into the cabin, warmth covers me like a blanket. I sigh with gratitude—these mountains really are cold.

The living room is beautifully decorated. Rustic furniture, roughly hewn from the trees that carpet the mountainside. Paintings set in thick iron frames depict the landscape in the winter, the spring, the summer, the fall, at sunrise and sunset, in storms and in sunshine. The floor is layered with rugs in every shade of deep burgundy, emerald green, and gold.

I sigh—this time, with irritation. Leave it to Leo Solovev to have a remote mountain getaway that looks like the interior spread of an architectural magazine.

"Your room is on the third floor," Leo tells me as he walks towards the sprawling bar in one corner of the room. "The blue door. It faces the mountains."

I smell the whiskey the moment he opens the bottle and pours himself a drink. My boots click across the wooden floors as I walk to the bar and take a seat two stools away from him.

Truthfully, I'd rather stand on the opposite side of the room from him, my back pressed against the glass so he can't sneak up on me from behind. But I can't show any fear.

Leo feasts on fear.

I don't wait for him to offer me anything. I pluck the bottle from his hand and take a swig right from it.

It burns my throat on the way down, but I don't flinch. When I'm done, I set the bottle back on the counter.

He looks at me with one raised eyebrow. "Trying to prove a point?"

"What point would that be?"

"That you're a tough girl now, I suppose."

Patronizing asshole. Instead of biting back, I take another swig of whiskey. It's safer than getting into it with Leo. This time, it's hard not to wince against the sting.

"You might want to take it easy," he tells me.

"I can hold my own."

Condescension drips from that smile as he reaches for the bottle. Before he can reach it, I slide it away from him, keeping my grip tight around the bottle's neck.

"I'm not done."

"You should be," he says. "But you've never known what's best for yourself."

I answer that with another swig. "Where are my parents? What have you done with them?"

"I've taken care of them," he says.

It does nothing to comfort me. It could mean anything.

"Who is she?"

"Who?"

"You know who," I snap. "The blonde bitch. His creature… or maybe she's yours. I don't even know at this point."

He eyes me carefully, but his expression is completely impassive. "Brit," he says, his lips curling around her name like a caress. "Her name is Brit."

"Brit," I spit. "Right. Who is she to you?"

"She's the woman who freed you from that prison," he says, as though I could ever forget. *The walls have eyes.* That phrase has lived in my head rent-free for eleven long months. I scour every room I walk into now.

"Am I supposed to be grateful to her?"

"If you were smart, you would be. She saved you."

"My mother did save me."

"Your mother intercepted what was meant to be *my* mission," he snaps. "I had a car outside waiting for you. Anya just got to you first."

This is news to me. And it matters more than it should. Not that I let any of that show.

"It doesn't really matter though, does it? She's the one who got me out."

"She wouldn't have been able to if it hadn't been for Brit. If it hadn't been for me."

I'm tempted to take another swig of whiskey, but he was right about the strength. I'm already starting to feel the buzz, and I can't afford to lose sight of my inhibitions where Leo is concerned.

"So she *is* your creature?" I ask, needing to hear the confirmation from his lips.

"One of many." He speaks with a possessiveness that makes my blood boil.

"Is that all she is to you?"

I hate myself for even caring, much less asking the question. But my jealousy is at the wheel, and I can't stop the question from escaping my lips.

He smiles. "You care?"

Fuck it, I say to myself. The only way I'm going to get through this is with a buzz in my veins. I take another swig of whiskey. "I owe that bitch a debt, and I would like to pay it back soon."

"What kind of debt?"

"A debt of blood."

His eyes narrow. "You'll have to get through me first."

I push myself off the seat. If the stools weren't cemented to the floor, mine would have toppled over. "I guess that's my answer."

"Assumptions are a dangerous thing, Willow," he says calmly. "You don't have all the information."

I ignore that. "No wonder she was so cruel to me. I married her man. How silly of me."

"I'm her don," he says. "Not her man."

I walk around the two barstools that separate us and put myself right between his spread legs. "Too bad I don't believe a fucking word out of your lips, Leo."

His eyes burn with a quiet satisfaction that makes my heart feel like it's going to burst into flame. I want to kill him as much as I want to kiss him.

Fuck me.

I jerk away from him before things get out of hand and walk towards the living room. I stop at the edge of the burgundy carpet. The chandelier hanging from the high ceiling gives and refracts light, casting rainbows around the room.

I swing around, aware that the alcohol has set my tongue free but unable to rein myself in.

"Did Brit decorate this place?" I taunt.

"Does it matter?"

"Fuck you."

He smiles. And it unravels me.

I've spent eleven months' worth of nights dreaming of that smile.

And eleven months' worth of days trying to forget it.

Now, it's in front of me, reminding me of everything I've lost. Of everything I'll never get back.

"You're dangerously close to drunk, Willow," Leo says, taking a step towards me. "Go to your room before you do something you'll regret."

I walk right up to him. "You may be able to order that blonde bitch around, but not me. You don't control me."

He lifts his hand to my face. I brace for a slap that never comes. Instead, slowly, he brushes the back of his hand over my cheek.

I freeze, mostly because if I move, I'll reveal everything. My facade will shatter, and he'll know how much this is affecting me.

But in the end, it doesn't matter.

He leans in close, his words a whisper across my skin. "Then why do you tremble when I touch you?"

5

LEO

Willow is a study in contrasts.

Her eyes burn with anger, but her lips have fallen open, softening under my seduction. I can't tell if she wants to kiss me or kill me. I'm not even sure which one I want her to try.

It's thrilling.

Everything about her is thrilling. The last year has ignited a new aspect of her personality. She's changed, inside and out.

The clothes are different—dark, tight-fitting, towering heels—but more important is the confidence she wears. The confidence to wield her looks like the weapon they are.

She's been molded into a version of her mother, but she has something that Anya has never possessed: the perspective of a different life. A normal life.

One that she's realized she's never getting back.

She's a ticking time bomb. And I'm very fucking excited to make her explode.

"Don't flatter yourself," she snaps confidently.

I arch my eyebrows. "So there's another reason you're trembling?"

"Call it preparation."

"For what?"

"A fight," she says.

The next thing I know, her arm is swinging towards me.

She's fast, but I'm faster. Her fist hits my forearm instead of my face. I shove her back, but the fight in her eyes is simmering. She's been waiting for this moment.

She wants to do damage, yes. But it's more than that: she wants to prove herself, too. She wants to show me that the last eleven months has changed her. That she's no longer the woman I married.

She moves again. Her body is lithe, agile. She has a grace that speaks to many hours of intense training.

And whoever trained her trained her well.

Unfortunately, not well enough to matter.

But she hasn't realized that yet. She drops into a crouch, hands up, then makes her move, swinging a leg out in a wide arc designed to knock my feet out from under her.

I step out of the way and let her foot hurtle aimlessly through the air.

More kicks and punches follow. She's a whirlwind of motion. None of it helps her in the slightest. I play with her, side-stepping every blow without breaking a sweat.

Her eyes narrow in frustration as her chest heaves. "You're holding back!" she accuses.

"Did you expect that eleven months would be enough?" I taunt. "I've been training since I was a child. I never learned to play. I learned to *fight*."

She lunges at me, but it's sloppier now. She's emotional and spent by our reunion.

"Fuck you," she growls, trying to land another punch.

This time, I allow her the hit. The punch to the abdomen is more powerful than I expect, but the sting only lasts a few seconds. It hurts her worse than it hurts me.

She shakes her hand out. "Jesus. Are you wearing armor under there or something?"

I smile and lift my shirt to reveal the abs underneath. "I grow my own armor."

She rolls her eyes and pretends to be unimpressed. "Sorry I asked."

"Are you, though?"

Her eyes burn through me as she slides out of her coat and throws it across the sofa next to her.

Now, it's my turn to be impressed. I can't take my eyes off her body.

The coat hid a lot more than I'd assumed. Willow always had an amazing shape, but now she's made of sharp lines and toned limbs.

Her stomach, which was always flat, sports new definition. She's cinched tighter at the waist. She looks strong, capable.

"I've got news for you," she tells me, shaking out her limbs. "I was holding back, too."

She vaults over the sofa effortlessly. Her boots land in perfect synchronicity right in front of me, her black hair flows loose around her shoulders.

I pause and frown. "Why did you cut your hair?"

She shakes her head. "Really?"

I shrug, not bothering to hide my smirk. "Just curious."

The frivolous question seems to irritate her more than anything else I've said in the last half an hour. She throws a punch again, but I dodge it.

"I thought you said you were holding back?" I say. "I couldn't tell."

She moves again, and again, I dodge.

I can tell she's getting frustrated, but I'm not about to give her an easy win. She wants to fight me? Fine. It's all tough love from here, little one.

She's not without skill. Her new body is made for physical combat. But it's more than that. She's got drive and determination. The fire to fuel the engine.

She sends another punch my direction. I pluck it out of the air, spin her around, and pull her into my embrace backwards. Her spine hits my chest with a dull thud.

She doesn't rest, though. She swivels around and tries to knee me in the groin.

I chuckle at her sheer boldness. There is no fight in this little *kiska*.

"Why the hell are you laughing?" she demands.

I side-step another hit to my groin and twist her back around. Once again, her ass rubs against my cock. Instantly, I'm rock hard. Willow notices.

"Is it the fight?" she asks. "Or me?"

I smirk. If she thinks that she can get to me by pointing out my erection, she's got another thing coming.

"It's both," I say. "And those pants you're wearing. Are they painted on?"

"Good luck getting in them to find out."

My cock twitches at the thought.

"Oh, darling…" I back her into a wall. "That attitude is admirable, but misguided. I find out everything, remember?"

"It's not over," she says—even as I pin her against the wall.

"I have to disagree."

"I had the best instructor in the world," she hisses through gritted teeth.

She tries to pry her wrists out of my grip, but it's useless. I press my chest into her and let her hands go. Immediately, she tries to swing at me, and I snatch them back up. I pin them against the wall on either side of her head so she's at my mercy.

"No, you didn't." I lean close, my lips at her ear. "Because you didn't learn from me."

Her tongue runs along her bottom lip, and all I want to do is bite down on it so hard I draw blood. She'd probably bite back, which only makes me more eager to follow through with the carnal instinct.

"This is not over," she whispers, even as her body sags. She's accepting defeat. Maybe not in the bigger war, but in this battle.

"I can teach you a few things," I offer. "For next time."

She glares at me. "I don't need anything from you. You've done enough."

I think of our shared loss. The vile words she spat at me in the car ride over here. I pushed them out of my head the moment she spoke them, but they're still there, burning through the layers of protection I've built.

"Is it true?" I growl, staring her in the eye.

I need this to be a lie. It has to be. If it is, then I'll know. I'll see the truth reflected back at me and I'll know.

She's fully aware of what I'm asking her, but she feigns ignorance anyway. "Which part?"

"The baby."

She stares right back at me. Her eyes don't waver from mine, and I feel the hope shrivel in my chest.

"The baby is gone," she says, in the same detached tone she'd used when she'd told me about her miscarriage. "The doctors said it was stress. I wasn't equipped to deal with everything I went through."

I press my chest into hers, and she gasps. I know I'm making it hard for her to breathe, but in this moment, irrational as it might be, I want her to suffer.

I can see a watery veil form over her eyes. She shakes her head. "It's hard to hear, isn't it?" she asks. "Imagine what it was like to live through. He was such a tiny little thing… an alien creature that felt like mine but didn't at the same time."

If she thinks this tactic is going to give her some breathing space, she's delusional.

I tighten my grip on her wrists until she cries out. "Making me hurt won't bring back your son," she snaps.

"Then we'll make another one."

Her eyes go wide, eyebrows arching with disbelief at first, and then hatred. "Of course," she says. "Of course. Because a child is nothing more than a conduit for your legacy, your power. The child itself doesn't matter at all, does it? It's not a baby to you. Just like I'm not a person to you. We're one and the same: *weapons*."

I don't give her the satisfaction of my reaction. Instead, I pull her hands together, forcing them to connect over her head. Then I pin her wrists down with one hand and use the other to inch down her hard new body.

I'd be lying if I didn't say I enjoy the way she feels. The way she trembles despite herself.

"You've had your fun, haven't you?" she asks when my hand pauses at her collarbone.

"Not even close. Why—have you?" I ask. "Just say the word, and I'll stop."

Her lips press firmly together.

"What was that?" I taunt her with my words as my hand slides over the smooth skin between her breasts. "Did you say something or do you want me to continue?"

"I want you to rot in hell," she spits.

I brush my fingers over her chest, rub my thumb over the hard point of her nipple. "Your body is saying something very different. I think these could cut glass."

"Fuck you," she hisses. "I'm cold."

"Cold?" I repeat. "Let me guess: your pussy also gets wet when you're cold."

Her legs tighten instantly, and I smile.

"You can change your clothes and your personality, Willow. But the one thing you'll never be able to change is your desire for me."

Her eyes blaze. She wants to deny it, but she's scared I'll call out the lie. "Fuck you," she says for the dozenth time since we crossed paths again.

I pinch her nipple between my fingers. "Your wish is my command."

She shivers and says nothing.

With my eyes trained on hers, I unzip her pants and push apart the unforgiving material. "Hmm, not painted on…"

"I heard you took down two Mikhailov buildings," she says.

I smile as I peel the fabric down around her hips. "I did."

Her body is rigid with tension and her breathing is coming in hard. "Was it just a power move? Or revenge?"

I snort. "That wasn't my revenge. It was a promise of what's to come."

"So it'll never end."

"It'll end," I say confidently. "It'll end when that motherfucker is dead."

She trembles as my fingers play at the waistband of her panties. They're black and entirely too sensible, yet somehow she manages to make them sexy.

Or maybe it's just that my cock is charged and ready for her. I've been coming into my hand for eleven fucking months.

No more.

"Which motherfucker?" Willow asks pointedly. "The motherfucker who strapped the bomb to my chest? Or the motherfucker who gave the command? A man who, apparently, is my grandfather."

"You weren't ready for the truth," I tell her, my fingers inching closer and closer to her pussy.

"Bullshit. I wasn't worth the truth in your eyes," she says. "I was just a weapon to you. Not a woman or a wife, but a key. I was just the tool you needed to get your revenge."

I smile. "You are a woman to me, Willow. Want me to prove it?"

Before she can answer or react, I twist two fingers inside her.

She lets her head fall back against the wall. Her lips part in a protracted sigh. I know desire when I see it. More importantly, when

I feel it like I'm feeling it now. Dripping onto my fingers, pulsing around my knuckles.

I lean in and catch her bottom lip with my teeth as I piston my fingers in and out of her.

"There's no point denying it now, Willow." I pull my fingers out of her and back away. She stays plastered to the wall while I slide them into my mouth and lick her sweetness off of me. "I can taste how much you want me."

She blinks at me, mesmerized for a second before she remembers to scowl. "Fuck you."

Then she launches herself at me. But instead of a fist, it's her lips that collide with mine. Her hands rip at the buttons on my shirt.

It's a mess of limbs and heavy breathing while she fiddles with my buttons and I rip her skin-tight gray sweater off her.

She just manages to slide my belt off before I push her against the wall again. She gasps in surprise as I strip her jeans down to her ankles.

But when I do the same with her black panties, she sets to work unclasping her bra and shimmying out of all of it.

The moment she's naked, I step back and admire my work.

She's fucking glorious. There are two defined lines running down her torso, starting just below her peaked breasts and ending just above where I know she's wet for me. I lick my lips.

"There's still time to claim the moral high ground. You can tell me to stop," I say, knowing she won't.

She parts her legs slowly and lets a hand dance down between her thighs. If I were a younger, less experienced man, I would have erupted right here and now. As it is, I'm barely holding it in.

"It's just sex," she murmurs, echoing something I said to her a lifetime ago. "Don't mistake it for anything else."

"She trained the emotion out of you, did she?"

"Don't look so sad," Willow purrs. "Come fuck me, and you'll see my training wasn't all bad."

I approach her like the animal I am. This thing between us is wild and untamed.

I grab her ass with both hands and suck her nipple into my mouth. She gasps and cries out as if she's in pain. I ignore that and continue tasting her, familiarizing myself with this new version of her.

She smells foreign to me, a mixture of leather and spice. It's a new perfume that doesn't suit her. Something dark and controlled.

I grab her wrists again, but she doesn't fight me this time. When I align my cock with her wet slit, she arches into me. But I'm in control now. I press her flat against the wall, hoist one leg over my hip, and thrust into her hard.

She bites down on her bottom lip, fighting a moan, but she won't be able to fight it for long. I slide out and thrust into her again and again, setting a brutal pace. I unleash all the pent-up fury and frustration I've carried over the last several months.

I release her wrists so I can pull her against me with both hands. She clings to my shoulders, fighting for purchase against my onslaught.

But there is none. I never slow.

She cries out with each thrust, her strong thighs quivering around my waist. Faster and faster, a blur of hips—and then she goes rigid. Every inch of her clamps onto me, her muscles contracting against her will.

To drive that point home, she releases a string of frustrated curses. But it doesn't stop what is coming.

Willow comes hard on my cock with her forehead pressed to my shoulder, and it's not a second too soon. I follow after her almost immediately, emptying into her until I'm wrung dry. I stand there five seconds longer, feeling my seed drip out of her slowly.

Then I walk her to the sofa and dump her on it unceremoniously.

"Now that we've got that out of the way, go to your room and wait."

She stands on still-shaking legs. "I don't take orders from anyone. Not even you, Leo Solovev. You don't own me."

I give her a calculated smile. "I think I just proved that I do."

6

WILLOW

I'm going to get out of here.

I don't know how; I don't know when. All I know is that I can't stay under Leo Solovev's roof for a moment longer.

The room isn't as large as the one I had in Anya's mountain mansion, but it's considerably warmer. It probably has something to do with the entire cabin being escape-proof. The windows in my room angle open, allowing a little mountain air through the top and bottom, but not much else. I certainly won't fit.

Aside from a huge bed in the center of the room and a built-in wardrobe that spans the eastern wall, there isn't any other furniture. But with a view like this, there isn't much need for more decoration.

I walk over to the windows and stare at the snow-capped mountains and the pair of hawks flying low in the distance.

It strikes me that they're not low at all. We're just really high up.

I feel trapped. In this cabin, obviously. But also in my clothes. I pulled them back on immediately after sex, but the zipper on my pants is broken and my sweater has a rip down the side. Nothing fits right anymore.

It's all a reminder of what I did. A decision I don't particularly care to be confronted with.

"What the hell are you doing?" I ask myself aloud.

I walk towards the wardrobe and throw the doors open. But apart from a robe, there's nothing inside. Gritting my teeth, I pull off my clothes and discard them in the hamper in the bathroom.

I need to wash him off me. His scent clings to my skin, reminding me of how weak I am.

The shower faces the mountains. Sandblasted glass comes up to my chest before giving way to a single, unbroken clear pane. As soon as I close the door, steam clouds the view.

The water pressure feels amazing against my skin. I tip my head back and let it rinse over me. But the relief only lasts a second.

Because it's Leo's shower.

In Leo's house.

And I can't figure out how I ended up here.

How could I have so severely underestimated him? Or maybe I just overestimated myself.

I worked up to twelve hour days training with Dimitri. I felt strong and capable. I gained in both skill and confidence. But it wasn't enough. Not nearly enough.

Idiot. You were stupid to think that you could best a man who came out of the womb with fight in his veins. Leo Solovev is a Bratva don. You're just a Bratva brat.

I can hear her voice in my head. Hear exactly what she'd say to me if she could have seen my pathetic attempt at fighting Leo.

My mother is not one to mince her words. I hated that about her in the beginning, but as time passed, I grew to feel a begrudging respect for her brutal honesty.

As I turn under the shower spray, I feel tender spots on my thighs and around my wrists. Of course he left bruises. You can't expect to spar with a man like Leo Solovev and walk away without his mark on you.

"Fool," I whisper to the steam clouds circling over my head.

Once the calming effect of the heat begins to fade, I step out of the shower and slip on the white robe. It's made of luxuriously soft cotton, and I squeeze my arms tightly around myself.

But comfort never lasts. I crave it—chase it, even—but the gratification is short-lived.

Kind of like the debacle that occurred downstairs.

My resolve had crumbled within seconds. He pressed himself against me, and all I wanted was to feel him inside me again.

It's just sex, I'd told him. But with Leo, it's never just sex.

It's like that old quote: everything in life is about sex. Except sex—that's about power.

I move around the room, already restless. After months of being continuously active, continuously in motion, being trapped in a room with no escape is suffocating. Correction: being trapped in this *life* is suffocating.

It's the reason I won't have another baby. I can't. No matter what Leo says about making another one.

If I do, that child will be lost to me just as much as the one I miscarried. I'd lose that child to this life, to *him*. To his legacy, his thirst for power and glory.

Anya may be a tough bitch, but at least she gave me the option of which path to walk.

The doorknob turns. I spin around just as Leo steps into the room. He's showered, too. His hair is still wet, and he's wearing different clothes than before. Dark slacks and a light white sweater that hugs every muscle on his body.

I hate that I notice. But more than that, I hate that he looks so good. Who did he have to look good for once I was gone? I wonder if that has something to do with the blonde bitch that still haunts my nightmares from time to time. *Brit.* The name sits on my tongue like poison.

Leo walks into the room without a word. And that's when I realize he's not alone.

Two of his men walk in behind him with large black bags. They place them at the foot of my bed and leave as silently as they came, closing the door behind them on their way out.

Then Leo and I are alone together. My body pings with the awareness of him, but I keep my expression neutral.

"What are those?"

"See for yourself," Leo tells me.

I sigh. "What if I'm not interested?"

"Unless you'd like to spend the next few months walking around in that robe, I suggest you open the bags, Willow."

I frown. "I'm not going to be here for months."

"Of course not. I'm sure you already have an escape plan in place," he says. "But if it's all the same to you, that robe isn't going to keep you warm up here."

Sighing, I grab the first bag and empty its contents onto the bed. There are jeans, sweaters, blouses, and scarves in a rainbow of colors and styles. I'd never admit as much, but they're all exactly my taste.

The second bag is lighter. When I dump it out, the frown freezes on my face. "Dresses?"

Formal dresses, at that.

Leo shrugs. "We're having dinner tonight."

"Is this your way of asking me out on a date?"

He smiles. "Sorry to disappoint you, but no. It's dinner. And a conversation."

I tense immediately. "A conversation about what?"

"The last eleven months."

Fuck. I'm under no illusions about what he wants. He wants my secrets. And if the last hour—not to mention the last two years—has taught me anything, it's that Leo Solovev always gets what he wants.

Especially where I'm concerned.

But not this time. Not my secrets. Those I'm going to fight for.

"Something scaring you, Willow?"

"It's Viktoria, remember?"

"That's a name you have to earn."

"It's a name that was forced on me," I remind him. "By you and all the men who want me to claim it so they can claim me."

"They're too late. I already claimed you," he growls. "I married you before Spartak Belov ever even knew you existed."

I give him a slow clap. "Congrats. You're more of an asshole than he is."

"Smarter, too."

"Is that a fact?"

"I deal only in facts."

"Then let me ask you something," I say, stepping forward. "How long has she been working for you?"

I don't like his smile. It's all confident, all knowing. I'm convinced he can see straight through my skull and read my mind.

"Does she occupy a lot of your thoughts, *kukolka*?"

I feel my knuckles go white as my hands clench into fists. I never used to be a violent person. But I've been transformed in the last year. Into a person whose fists have become hungry for the relief that her soul can't seem to find.

Now, Leo smiles, and as much as I want to launch another attack, I feel the barest hint of hesitation. Because as monstrous as he is, he has a beautiful face. It would be a shame to destroy it. Even if it's deserved.

"Tell me," I demand.

He raises his eyebrows, noting the change in my voice. "That was very good. Commanding. Confident. Almost believable."

"Almost?"

"Your eyes," he says, pointing. "They give you away."

Don't ask. Don't ask. Don't ask.

"How?"

"The tone was pure Viktoria Mikhailov. Self-assured and powerful. But the eyes?" He tips his head to the side like he's studying a piece of art. "The eyes are Willow Powers. Nervous. Filled with doubt."

"You don't know me anymore."

"That implies I ever bothered getting to know you in the first place."

These sparring contests are dangerous, mostly because he's so damn good at them. But my pride is involved now. I don't back down, even though I know I should.

That's another thing that's new. The pride. You can't survive in this world without it. Without pride, what are you? Just a random person with nothing to prove. Nothing to protect.

He smiles. "But I see you, Willow. The girl you once were is still there, hiding behind that tight little body and some slapdash combat training. Little Willow has been forced inward by an exiled queen who respects only brutality and strength."

"You say that like it's a bad thing," I bite back at him. "How can you accuse her of something that you yourself are guilty of?"

"Because I would never use my child as a weapon."

His words lance through me like blades. I fight to hide my reaction. "You used *me*."

"You're not my child. You're not my blood."

"And you hold her to higher standards?" I ask. "Why should that matter? She didn't raise me. She doesn't know me, either."

I regret it the moment I say it. This is why talking to him is never a smart choice. My mouth runs ahead of my caution.

"Life with your mother hasn't been as smooth sailing as you'd have me believe, then?"

I bite my tongue and curse myself for being so easily manipulated. "It's been educational. I needed it."

"Is that right?"

He doesn't believe me, but I'm telling the truth. Anya did teach me a lot. Without her, I'd already be dead.

"Are you going to answer any of my questions?" I ask.

"I might," he says. "But it'll have to wait until dinner."

He eyes the dresses on the bed, and I shake my head. "If you think I'm dressing up for you, you're delusional."

"Do you have something against nice clothes?"

I take a step towards him, summoning up all my strength, all my resolve. "I'm not your doll. I'd rather walk around naked than dress up in anything you choose."

He raises a brow. "If you insist."

I blanche. "I…"

"See?" he laughs. "Stop fighting me, Willow. You can't win."

He heads for the door, but stops at the threshold and looks back over his shoulder. "I'll see you tonight at dinner. Eight o'clock. Don't be late."

Eleven fucking months of training, and standing in front of Leo makes me feel like I'm back at day one.

But I can't give up.

Leo wants me to earn the name Viktoria Mikhailov?

Fine. Challenge accepted.

7

LEO

I follow the smell of cigars to where Jax and Gaiman are sitting on the porch.

"Want one?" Jax offers.

"I'm good."

"Nervous about tonight?" Jax asks.

I glare at him. "It's just business."

He smirks. "Wish I had business like that. Lucky bastard."

He's ignoring his cigar now, drumming his fingers on his legs. Gaiman won't even look at me, but he sighs.

"What's the bet?" I ask.

Jax practically leaps out of his seat. "How the fuck did you know?"

"I know everything, *sobrat*."

"Jesus," Jax groans. "You take the fucking fun out of life."

"Hurry up and tell me what's at stake."

"Gaiman thinks you've already fucked her," he says. "I say no."

I raise a brow. "So little faith in me, Jax?"

"Have you seen her now? She's a fucking spitfire. Even you might have trouble landing that. I mean…" He whistles long and low. "She was always hot, but now she's hot in the same way her mother is."

"You let your dick do too much of the thinking." Gaiman rolls his eyes.

"Sue me for noticing a woman's beauty." Jax turns back to me. "Although Willow looks like she's more likely to bite your dick off now than suck it."

I shrug. "What's fun without a little risk?"

"Took the words right out of my mouth." Jax looks at me eagerly. "So? Which of us won the bet?"

I glance towards Gaiman casually. "Him."

"Are you shitting me?!" Jax yells.

"You're right about one thing," I concede. "She's a spitfire. But it only makes the sex hotter."

"Lucky bastard," Jax mutters again. "Lucky goddamn bastard."

I smirk and then shift into business mode. "Any movement?"

"Anya's men are out looking for Willow," Gaiman tells me. "But we have men arranged at a ten-mile radius from our location. If anyone tries to get up this mountain, we'll know about it."

"And what news of Belov?"

"I kinda thought you'd have better information on that front," Gaiman says. "Any word from Agent Thirty-One?"

"She's been quiet for a while now," I admit.

"Should we be worried?"

"No. She's gone quiet like this before. It's just an abundance of caution. She can't afford to be caught."

Jax and Gaiman exchange a glance. It makes me wonder what bet they have hanging over her life. I decide not to ask.

"So far, our scouts have been reporting activity around two major spots in the city," Gaiman continues. "I think Spartak's trying to rebuild what he lost in the Manhattan Club and The Silver Star."

I snort. "He was a fool to think that loyalty could be rebuilt so easily. He sustained heavy casualties that day."

"Do you really think that a man like Belov cares?" Gaiman asks. "He's not Bratva, not truly. He didn't feel the human cost of his mistake."

"And you think that makes him dangerous?" I ask.

"It makes him reckless. And willing to do anything," Gaiman points out. "We don't know what he's planning."

"We never did. I've got as far as I have because my guesses have been right."

"And you have a spy on the inside," Jax points out.

"That helps."

"Does the ball and chain know?" Jax asks.

"She doesn't need to know," I say. "I'll keep my secrets so long as she insists on keeping hers."

"Is that what tonight is all about?" He turns and peers through the window into the dining room, where a small contingent of staff is preparing the room for our dinner.

"No. Tonight is about reminding Willow of the way things work in this world."

"How romantic. No candles?" Jax asks with a teasing smile.

"I'll save that for my dinner with you," I drawl. I push out of my seat and wave them off. "Now get out, the both of you."

"Off to the servants' quarters we go," Jax groans.

"Shut up and walk," retorts Gaiman, shoving the larger man in the back.

Before they disappear down the path that will take them to the staff cabins ringing the main house, Jax stops and gives me a wink. "Don't break any of the furniture, boss man."

I ignore him and head inside.

I remove my coat and hang it behind the door. It's much warmer inside than out, but it's hard to completely keep out the chill when you're situated this high up. It sits in your bones in a way I can't shake.

The maids finish in a hurry and disappear. I settle into my seat at the table, thoughts churning.

Moments later, I hear Willow's door open.

I notice her bare feet descending the staircase first, but I think nothing of it. At least not until I realize that her legs seem to be going on forever. I didn't give her a dress *that* short.

Then the juicy curve of her ass appears, and shock radiates through me.

At the base of the spiral staircase, she swings around to face me. Her dark hair hangs loose, but given that it rests just above her shoulders these days, it doesn't offer much in the way of coverage. Her breasts are bared, her nipples pointing right at me. Along with the V between her legs.

"Eight o'clock," she says lightly, stepping off the last step. "I'm right on time."

I bite back a smirk. She's a bold one. Always has been, really. But now she has the fire inside of her to let it all burn.

"The waiters will be out in a minute," I say casually.

She cocks her head to the side and smiles. "Great, I'm starving."

She walks over to the table and places her hand on the chair, but she makes no move to sit down. She stares at me, her self-satisfied smirk a challenge.

"Sir, can we serve—"

The waiter, whose name has already slipped my mind, comes to an abrupt stop the moment he enters the room and catches sight of Willow.

He's carrying a bottle of sparkling water that nearly topples from his hands. Willow lets out a little giggle that's entirely unlike her.

"Oops," she says. "I'm sorry. I didn't mean to startle you."

"I… I… you… you didn't… ma'am."

His cheeks are flushed with color. Even though he's trying not to look at her, his eyes can't help drinking her in.

And all I can think is, *Stop looking at what is fucking* mine.

"Get out," I growl in a low voice that echoes across the room. "And stay out until I call for you. Tell the others."

The waiter trips in his haste to get out of the room and disappears into the kitchen. I get to my feet slowly and glare at Willow.

"What?" she asks, with a shrug of her shoulders. "This is what you wanted, isn't it?"

"I offered you clothes."

"And I said I'd rather go naked than wear what you'd picked for me. You gave me your blessing. Thus, here we are."

"Is that what I gave you?" I ask, rounding the table so that I'm standing right in front of her. "My blessing?"

"That's what I took it to mean."

"Then you were mistaken."

She smiles and I can see her confidence grow by the second. "Well, I'm here now. And like I said, I'm hungry. Are you going to feed me?"

"Not like that."

My eyes rake down her body, but she seems unconcerned. She gives a deep sigh and sits down. "Well, don't make me wait too long. Whatever that is smells delicious. You can tell the cute waiter to bring out dinner."

I clench my fists. She's really going for it.

"Go get your robe," I tell her.

She looks up at me with a sweet smile. "I'd rather not. I kind of like walking around naked. It's very… freeing."

She's feeling triumphant, but the night has only just begun. Snarling, I spin away and leave her sitting there at the dining table by herself.

When I return, it's with two plates of food from the kitchen. Her expression sours. I plunk one plate in front of her and take my seat.

"Bon appetit."

"Where are the waiters?" she asks.

"In their rooms down in the lower cabins for the rest of the night," I tell her. "Probably jacking off to you."

She shrugs. "Glad to have given them a show."

I swallow my anger and regard her with new interest. If she's willing to go this far just to piss me off, I'm curious about what else she'll do.

"That's true. Not every man can claim to have seen his boss's wife naked. That'll make you giving them orders so much more interesting."

She wrinkles her nose. "Why would I need to give them orders?"

"You're the mistress of the house."

She snorts derisively. "Don't patronize me."

"I wouldn't dream of it."

She leans back in her chair, and I can't help but be distracted by the sway of her breasts. She's flawless. Truly and completely flawless.

"I'm your prisoner, Leo. Nothing more."

"What you are is stubborn. That's the only reason you've been confined to your room."

"Meaning what? If I comply, I can walk around naked anywhere I like?"

"I don't see why not."

She regards me coolly, but I can see the wheels in her head spinning. "I don't trust you," she says at last.

She crosses her legs, shielding her pussy from view. But the knowledge that it's there, bald and brazen, is very tempting.

"The feeling is mutual."

She narrows her eyes. "Oh, that's rich. What have *I* done to merit distrust?"

"You spent eleven months with the enemy."

"Is she an enemy, then?"

"Anyone who is not Solovev is an enemy."

She considers that for a moment. "She's also your mother-in-law."

"Is that supposed to mean something?"

"What happened to blood being thicker than water?"

"She isn't blood."

"Right," she says with a clipped nod. "And as you so astutely reminded me earlier, neither am I."

I can tell she wants to cover herself, but she's resisting the urge. She's backed herself into a corner with this one, and now that the waiters have been exiled from the cabin, the purpose of her mission is moot.

"Would you like to go put some clothes on now?" I ask.

Her eyes spark. "Am I making you uncomfortable?" she challenges.

"Not at all," I reply. "I'm just thinking of you."

"Ha! That's a first."

"Who else would I be thinking of?"

"Your blonde whore, probably," she mutters. Her cheeks redden instantly like she hadn't meant to say that out loud.

I raise my eyebrows. "Does Brit really bother you that much?"

"Has it ever crossed your mind that she might be a double agent?" she demands.

It's a perfectly legitimate question. But only to an outsider. Only to someone who doesn't know the history.

"No."

"How can you be so sure?"

"Because I'm sure of Brit. I trust her implicitly. And that's not something I say about many people."

She lets that statement sink in. "Who is she to you?" she asks at last, bested by her own curiosity.

"Someone very important."

I know that in her mind, I'm confirming the suspicion that's been festering. But I don't mind assumptions being made, not in this case. In fact, I'm pretty sure it can work in my favor.

Her face is a battleground. Emotions warring for control. Jealousy, anger, lust. I watch her for a long few breaths, curious which one will win out. The eventual victor makes me smirk.

"Don't be jealous, little one," I say softly.

"I'm not jealous of her."

"That spark in your eye says otherwise."

"You're a fucking bastard," she spits.

"You're hardly the first woman to call me that."

"Yeah?" she snaps. "Is that what Brit called you, too?"

"No," I tell her. "But then, I'm not done with her yet."

Her chest heaves, and it's difficult not to stare at her breasts. But I also don't mind being caught. She wants to prance around naked? Then I get to fucking stare.

"She's probably not going to be too happy about this," Willow says in a measured tone.

I shrug. "You are my wife."

"Sure, yeah, whatever the hell that means."

"In your mind, maybe nothing. In the Bratva? It means everything."

I can sense the question on the tip of her tongue: *But what does it mean to you?*

But she stops short of asking. Instead, she runs her hand down her chest, between her breasts. She does it slowly, teasing me.

I stand up and walk around, enjoying how she tenses as I lean on the table's edge in front of her.

"How about some wine?" I ask.

She eyes the bottle on the table. "Fine."

I pop the cork with my teeth. But I don't reach for a glass. Willow watches with curiosity as I bring the bottle towards her. But she doesn't move. She's trying to play at control, ease.

It works—until it doesn't.

Suddenly, I turn the bottle over, allowing a stream of burgundy wine to flow onto her naked body.

"Jesus!" she gasps as she scrambles in her seat, trying to escape the waterfall of wine.

I put my hand on her shoulder and force her back into her chair. Pinned in place, the wine coats her chest and runs down her flat stomach before pooling between her legs.

"I didn't think your pussy could get any sweeter," I murmur, setting the bottle back on the table.

"What the hell are you doing?"

"You walked down to dinner stark fucking naked," I rasp. "What did you think was going to happen?"

"You can't just have me anytime you please."

"I think you'll find I can have anything I want."

I shove my knee between her legs, resting it against the chair, and lower my mouth to her breasts. When I lick the wine off her, she trembles.

I run my tongue up her stomach, following the trail of sweetness, and then suck her nipple into my mouth. My cock strains impatiently while I feast on her.

Gradually, I move downward. I shove her legs apart and pull her ass to the edge of the chair. I take a moment to admire her tight little pussy before I shove my tongue inside her.

"Fuck," she gasps. "Fuck…"

Her fingers snake into my hair as I go down on her. Her taut limbs turn to putty. Her juices flow out of her, coating my tongue with a rich, sweet taste.

Apparently, her body has missed me even if she claims she hasn't.

As much as I want to give up on my mission and just enjoy the moment without agenda, it's not in my nature to let desire overpower ambition. I can't lose sight of my goal just because her pussy sings for me.

With my tongue deep inside her, I reach up and grab her nipple. I twist it between two fingers as I circle her clit, flicking it lightly with the tip of my tongue.

"Fuck… st… stop," she moans, weakly pulling on my hair to try and steer me away.

The attempt is almost laughable. She's literally soaking my chin with her desire.

I pull out for a moment, just so I can enjoy the needy expression on her flushed face. "If you really want me to stop, you're going to have to be a lot more convincing."

She glares at me. "Fuck you."

I grin. "In a moment, *kukolka*."

She bristles, but doesn't say a word. Instead, her legs inch further apart, practically begging for me.

I thought taking down two Mikhailov buildings was the adrenaline rush of a lifetime.

Turns out taking down one Mikhailov princess is even better.

I grab a hold of her hips and pull her down on top of me. I position her perfectly so that she's sitting on my face. Then I slap her ass, encouraging her to ride my mouth.

She wastes no time. Her hips jerk back and forth while my tongue laps inside her. Her moans grow louder, echoing off the high ceilings. I know she's moments away from coming, though she's fighting it with every ounce of her willpower.

Then she can't hold off anymore. She comes undone. She lets go. The tension in her face and body melts, and she is euphoric.

For a few moments, she is relaxed. At ease.

I intend to make full use of that.

8

WILLOW

I'm weak for doing this. Weak for letting it happen.

Most of all, I'm weak for wanting it.

But I can't stop now. I'm too close.

For a fleeting moment, I was able to look out into the world and see myself differently. I could visualize who I would have been if Anya had raised me. If I'd been brought up in this life the way Leo was.

But now I know it doesn't matter how hard I train. When it comes to him, I'm just *weak*.

He slaps my ass and I buck into his tongue. It rolls around my clit, and I suck in air like my life depends on it.

The orgasm unfurls over me, softly at first before the rest of it drops like a hammer. I writhe wildly, my limbs completely beyond my control. But Leo has me. He holds me up and I sag into his embrace until all I can feel is the gentle buzzing of the pleasure working its way through me.

He peels me off his face and lays me out on the floor. I'm dizzy. My legs feel like jelly. I go where he puts me as easily as moving a doll.

He hovers over me for a moment, and I see his beautiful face. Then he descends. His lips glide down my neck, across my collarbone, over my breasts. His tongue laps at the juices—both my own and the wine—dripping down my legs, and my eyes roll back in my head at the light, fluttering touches.

"You missed this, didn't you?"

His words reach me from miles away. They're soft, gentle. It reminds me of a simpler time, when I believed loving him was my future. My child's future, too.

"You should have fought harder," I whisper, the words slipping from my lips. "For me. And him. You should have fought harder for us."

As soon as the words are out of my mouth, I realize I don't regret them. Not yet, anyway.

"I'll fight for the two of you now," Leo snarls. His voice is still quiet, but there's no mistaking the undertone of steel there.

For some reason, that reassures me. Hot and cold, soft and hard, no one does that like he does. It makes me want to reach for him. To wrap myself in his arms and let him heal me.

"It's not safe for him here," I say. "It's not safe for either of us."

Suddenly, his warmth disappears.

I have a second of confusion before horror slices through the high of my orgasm. *What did I just say?*

The answer comes to me a moment later: *the truth.*

I sit up, the fog clearing, panic replacing the pleasure. Leo is already on his feet, fully clothed, staring down at me with murder in his eyes. I'm keenly aware of how naked and vulnerable I am right now. I get to my feet and put distance between us.

"He's alive," Leo menaces.

"You tricked me."

"I asked you a question," he says. "And you gave me your first honest answer."

There's no way out of this. No denial I can make to fix this. I've taken it too far. But that won't stop me from fighting back. "I did what I had to do to keep him safe."

"Does the she-devil have him?" he sneers.

"Yes."

He takes a step closer, and I back up against the fireplace. "We're going to get him back."

"No."

"No?" he repeats incredulously. "Why the fuck not?"

"He's safe with her."

"Safer than he would be with his own father?"

"Yes."

Before I can avoid it, he has my arm in a vice-like grip. "Let me fucking go!" I cry out.

He doesn't listen, of course. He just pulls me forward, and I smash into his chest. My nakedness is no longer the distraction it was at the beginning of the night. He's consumed with anger now, with rage. I can see it in his eyes: he wants to punish me.

"You made me believe he was dead," he snarls. "You lied through your fucking teeth."

"I did what I had to do," I repeat.

"Why?"

"Do you really have to ask that question?" I ask. "I don't want my son to be a pawn in a war. You want revenge for your brother, I get it. But I don't want my baby involved. He deserves better."

"He was born into it," Leo snaps. "There's no escaping the blood in his veins."

"I don't believe that," I say. "I can escape, and I can take my boy with me."

He twists my arm, and I cry out in pain. "Let's make one thing clear, Willow. He's not your son. He's fucking *mine.*"

I can feel tears pinch at the back of my eyes. *Tears are just proof of your weakness,* Anya said again and again those first few months. *There's no use for them.*

I had spent so many endless days training the tears out of me. But look how easily he can undo all my hard work.

This is my fault. I allowed him into my life to begin with. I let him play the knight to my damsel in distress. In doing so, I ensured I would never be anything else.

But I have to try, don't I? If not for myself, then for my son. He's the only thing I've done right in my life. I'll do whatever it takes to protect him.

I shake my head. "He's not yours, Leo. You're nothing more than my sperm donor. That child… I carried him in my stomach for nine months. I fed him at my breasts. I slept by his side and soothed his nightmares until the moment you plucked me from the mountains and caged me here. I am his whole world and he is mine. And I will die before I let you or anyone else use him as some political prop in your schemes."

"And you think your mother is different from me?" he barks. "From Belov? From Semyon?"

"She made me a promise."

"What promise is that?"

"That my son would have the life I choose for him."

He snorts. "And you believed her?"

I consider lying, but I decide not to in the end. "No. I don't trust anyone. But I needed her protection at the time, and I needed her resources. I will take what I can until I can find a way for us to disappear."

He brings his face to mine and speaks through his teeth. "It won't matter where you go or how completely you disappear, Willow. I will always find you."

"You can't have him!"

He twists my hand again. As painful as it is, I refuse to cry out. "Hurt me all you want," I hiss, blinking the tears out of my eyes. "I won't let you hurt him."

"What makes you think that's my intention?"

"Intention doesn't matter. All that matters is the outcome. As long as he remains part of your world, he will get hurt."

"Scars will make him strong. Pain will make him sharp. It is how men of the Bratva learn."

I shake my head and pull away from his grip. Surprisingly, he lets me go. "Don't you understand? I don't care if he's strong, I don't care if he's powerful, I don't care if he's the king of the fucking world or a janitor in the middle of nowhere. I want him to be *safe*! I want him to be *happy*! He deserves that much."

"Wake up, princess," he growls. "This is the Bratva. No one gets what they deserve. They get only what they fight for."

"Yeah? Well, I plan to fight for my son."

"I guess that puts us in each other's way," he says darkly. "And guess what I do to anyone who's in my way?"

I can feel the tremble inside me, working its way to the surface. But I bite down so hard on my tongue that I taste blood.

Leo has always been larger than life to me. He still is.

But I have to believe in myself now. If I claim defeat before the fight has even started, then there's no hope for me or my son.

So I walk forward, putting myself right in Leo's path.

"Would you kill me, Leo?" I whisper. "If it comes down to it, would you really kill me?"

He doesn't hesitate. "I will do whatever I have to."

I nod. "Okay," I say, calling his bluff. "Then do it."

He raises his eyebrows. I reach back towards the table, pluck one of the steak knives from beside an untouched plate of food, and offer it to him blade-first.

"Go ahead," I say. "I'm sure you can do some damage with this. You probably know where to aim. So do it. Get me out of the way."

He stares down at the knife in my hand. When he raises his eyes to me, there's a small smile on his face. It makes my stomach roil with unease. But I hold my ground.

"Is this your idea of a challenge?" he asks. "If I refuse to kill you, that somehow proves that you mean more to me than I'm currently admitting?"

He moves closer, taking over control of the knife from my hand but leaving it right where it is between us. The handle of the blade is pointed right at my chest and the point is digging into his.

He presses closer. I see the tiny pinprick of his own blood appear on his shirt. "If I keep you alive, it's because of your name," he snarls.

Closer. More blood. A thin trickle now.

"Viktoria Mikhailov is worth more to me alive than dead. Your name is the one thing your mother gave you…"

Closer still. The stream thickens. The knife is buried a quarter of an inch into the muscle of his chest and he hasn't so much as blinked.

"… and I won't waste it."

He flings the knife across the room. It stabs deep into a wooden beam with a *thunk* and wobbles in place.

"You overestimate our connection, Willow. You always did," he continues. The knife may be gone, but his words are stabbing me just as painfully. "You were a vessel, one that carried the child that will help bring the Mikhailov fucks to their knees. You're alive right now because I still need your name. And you will stay alive for as long as I need it."

"What if I refuse?"

"Your parents will suffer."

Cold horror washes over me as the threat sinks in. My parents… my *real* parents. The ones that raised me and loved me and supported me. The ones that forgave me without missing a beat the moment I ran back to them.

"You… you were the one that sent that bitch after them?" I gasp.

"No, Belov did," he says casually. "But like you said before, Brit is my creature. She stands by his side and sings his praises, but she works for *me*. As far as Belov is concerned, Brit killed them. He didn't ask to see bodies because they're not important enough to merit proof. But I knew their deaths would serve me no purpose. I knew I would need them alive to keep you in line."

I shake my head, anger and resentment grappling with the burgeoning fear inside me. "You'd really hurt them?"

"I think you already know the answer to that."

I stare at his face, trying to search for the lie in his eyes. But I can't see anything but grim determination. In any case, I can't afford not to believe him.

"They've done nothing."

"You're right. They've done nothing. But that won't save them if you decide not to cooperate with me."

I shake my head. "How did I not see you for the monster you are?"

"You were too busy seeing the back of your skull every time I made you come."

I back away from him, trying to muster up the right amount of hate for the man standing in front of me. I need to hate him; I have to.

I wait for the black emotion to fester and cement itself in my soul.

But it never comes.

Even after everything he just said, I can't make my feelings for him disappear. Instead, I keep looking for a way in, a window into the man I thought I'd glimpsed back when I'd believed falling in love wasn't the black hole that it is.

"Don't hurt them," I say in a small voice.

"You're the one who holds that power," he says simply. Almost sadly.

Then he grabs me and throws me roughly over his shoulder. I scream and rail at his back, but he ignores me as he carries me up the staircase and towards my room.

He swings me off his shoulder and throws me on the bed. I flop around gracelessly. By the time I manage to straighten up, he's already gone.

I hear the turn of the lock and then… silence.

Broken only by the sound of my rising heartbeat as guilt and regret take hold.

9

LEO

I bury the axe in the trunk, sending shards of bark flying. Before the dust even settles, I yank the blade free and hack at the stump all over again.

"Jesus Christ, Leo!" Gaiman approaches me cautiously from the left.

He keeps his distance. Probably because I'm swinging an ax around. But it's not going anywhere. My grip is strong, even if anger has made my technique sloppy.

"Leo, for fuck's sake, just stop!" Gaiman says, when I don't halt my hacking at the sight of him. "Fuck, man."

I keep going until I've split the stump in two. Once it's completely destroyed, I throw the axe onto a fresh bed of snow. It sinks beneath the powder.

"I take it dinner didn't go well," he says wryly.

"I got the truth she was hiding."

The moon is perched high above us, radiating silver light over the entire mountain range. It's bright up here, and somehow even that is pissing me off.

Gaiman approaches slowly and leans against a tree. "Tell me."

"The baby… the boy." I'm still panting from trying and failing to burn off the anger inside of me. "He's alive."

His jaw drops. "*What?*"

"She lied to me about the miscarriage. She had my baby," I growl. "And then she told me he fucking died."

"Jesus," Gaiman whispers, looking up towards the moon.

"I knew it," I continue. "I *knew* that my son was out there. I just didn't think she could lie so goddamn convincingly."

In that way, I underestimated her. I won't make that mistake again.

"She's had a crash course in deception," Gaiman points out. "We always knew that Anya Mikhailov was no sleeping dog."

"I was going to keep the bitch out of it," I snarl. "But now she's placed herself right in the middle of my war."

Gaiman tenses noticeably.

I'm not in the mood for tact tonight. "What?" I snap. "Spit it out.

"Do we have the resources to go after both Anya Mikhailov and Belov?"

"I don't give a shit if we do or not. She has my fucking *son!*"

I yell the last word. It echoes across the mountains. Birds caw and flock out of the trees. Gaiman isn't perturbed. His expression is calm and measured, unshakeable as the mountains around us.

I'm glad he's the one who found me here. Jax is useless in moments like these. All he knows how to do is make stupid jokes that make me want to rip his head off with my bare hands.

"Leo, I know. We have to get the boy back," Gaiman says quietly. "But we also need to be smart about this. We have to ask ourselves: is he in danger with her?"

"She's a Mikhailov. The answer is self-evident."

"She's also his grandmother."

The knowledge is a little bitter now that I'm confronted with it, but it's the bargain I entered into. "That doesn't mean I trust her."

"Neither do I. But that's not the point," Gaiman argues. "We don't need to trust her. We just need to trust her with him. At least for now. At least until we can deal with Belov."

"He's still weak. It can wait."

"He is for now," Gaiman agrees. "But he's rebuilding fast. He's going to hit us back for taking those two buildings down. You know that as well as I do. We didn't cripple him with a second blow while he was at his weakest, so we lost some time."

Gaiman is right. I know he is. Instead of hitting Belov again, I put all my resources into finding Willow.

I shake my head. "This is my fucking son, Gaiman. Everything else can wait while I get him back."

Gaiman looks down for a moment. I can tell he's biting back his words. But I'm too lost in my sorrow and anger to give a shit.

"I don't even know his name," I whisper, mostly to myself.

Gaiman looks up at me. "His name is Solovev. That's the only name that matters."

I nod curtly. He's right.

"Do you think she'll help you get him back?" Gaiman asks.

"I'm not really giving her a choice."

"The woman in that bedroom is not the same one that Belov stole, Leo," he says. "She's more Anya than anything now."

"She's pretending. That hard mask she's wearing? It's a façade. And it's slipping more and more every day. But if she needs motivation, I can give her that."

"With what?"

"I have her parents."

Gaiman raises his eyebrows. "Benjamin and Natalie are sitting pretty in a cozy little house you bought for them."

"She doesn't know that."

He smirks. "How long do you think it'll be before she figures you out?"

"There's no figuring me out, Gaiman," I say. "You should know that better than anyone."

He smiles, and I feel some of the tension in my chest release. I sit down on a broken hunk of the stump I just split. Gaiman leans on a tree a few paces away.

"I've been having a lot of dreams lately," Gaiman says unexpectedly.

"Yeah?"

"About… when it happened."

I know exactly what he's talking about. I know it from his broken tone and the look in his eyes. Hollow, desperate, filled with unresolved anger.

"It's been eight fucking years, Leo," he says. "Can you believe that?"

"I stopped counting a long time ago."

"I used to watch Pavel with Petyr and Logan. I wanted to be like them."

I smirk. "You got more than you bargained for, huh?"

He shakes his head and looks off into the distance. "I never imagined the three of us would end up in their shoes. It was so simple back then. They had the responsibility; we had the fun."

I remember all too well. But I don't comb through the memories much. Mourning is a waste of time. Purpose—action—revenge—that's all that matters.

"It was right that they died together," Gaiman says. "Petyr and Logan… there was no one closer to Pavel than the two of them."

I thought about their wasted lives and the people they'd left behind. Sometimes, opportunities can be born of grief. I have weapons now because of what Petyr, Logan and Pavel left in their wake.

"What happened to their families?" Gaiman asks. "I never followed through like I probably should have."

"It wasn't your job to follow through. It was mine."

"And did you?"

"Logan had no one. He was an orphan who found his home in the Bratva. Pavel and Petyr were the brothers he never had. Petyr was an only child raised by a single mother. Luda Yolkin was her name."

He nods and strokes his chin. "Where is she now?"

"Trying to survive. Like the rest of us."

I'm sick of talking. It's not doing anything to clear the demons in my head. If anything, it's only stirring them up more.

I turn and head back towards the house, but stop before I step into the trees. "I'm getting my son back, Gaiman. Belov will have to wait."

"That's what I'm worried about," Gaiman sighs. "What if he doesn't? What if he attacks us before we're ready?"

"Don't you know me at all?" I ask. "I'm always ready."

∼

In the cabin, I go up to her room and crack open the door. When I peek through, I see her in a fighting stance, shadow-boxing with thin air. She's so absorbed in it that she doesn't notice me slip through the entrance and lean against the wall to observe.

She's wearing tight black leggings and a black tank top. Her hair is twisted back in a high ponytail that's just begging to be grabbed.

Her movements are lithe and efficient, obviously well-coached. The foundations are there, but there's much more she needs to learn.

"You jump when you throw a punch," I say. "Keep your feet planted."

She whirls around, eyes wide, both fists raised. "Get out of my room."

"*My* room, remember?" I remind her. "My house. My mountain."

"Right—because everything's fucking yours. Me most of all."

"Glad you've finally accepted that."

She moves forward as though she's about to continue her punching exercise, but she stops a foot away and lowers her hands.

"What do you want?"

"Answers."

She crosses her arms. "Then you might as well leave. You're wasting your time."

"You don't think I have a right to know about my son's birth? His name?"

"You're not going to have a chance to know him, so it would be cruel to give you details."

I smile darkly. "Anya really did a number on you, didn't she?"

"This is not about her."

"You're not like her, Willow. Stop pretending."

"The name is Viktoria," she corrects, but even I can sense the half-heartedness of those words. "And I am not the powerless little girl you deigned to save from a bad marriage. As you so rightly pointed out, I do have a name of my own. And that name carries weight."

I raise my eyebrows, impressed yet again. "And you're planning on using that name, is that right?"

"Why not?" she asks. "If I can't escape this life, then maybe my only other option is embracing it."

"That was quite the change of heart."

"I guess I can thank you for that," she snaps. "You're the one who made me realize that power is the only way to be heard in this world. And I'm done shouting into the abyss while everyone ignores me."

"You've developed a penchant for hyperbole. Is that also courtesy of Anya?"

She narrows her eyes. "You have no idea how much I want to kick you in the balls right now."

"She may be your mother, but that doesn't make her any less of a monster."

"How the fuck would you know?" she explodes. "You don't know her!"

"Do *you*?"

She bites down on her bottom lip. I feel my cock come to life despite the fact that I still want to wring her neck.

Fighting or fucking—it's always one or the other with us. Both options seem tempting right now. Especially with the way the tank top cups her breasts and highlights how hard her nipples are.

"She was a woman who made her own way in a world dominated by men," she says. "She may not be the warmest person, but that's what the Bratva does. It hardens you."

I roll my eyes. "You think I give two shits about the fact that she's a cold bitch? I don't. In fact, I respect it. But Anya Mikhailov is a woman without loyalty. Just like Spartak Belov."

She shakes her head, and I can tell that nothing I'm saying is getting through to her. "And you have loyalty, do you?"

"Fuck yes, I have loyalty. Loyalty to my men and my Bratva. Anya and Belov? They work only for themselves."

"She'll protect him," she snaps. "He's her *grandson*!"

"He's nothing more to her than a trump card."

"Like I was to you?"

"I made you my *wife*," I say, moving forward. "I gave you my fucking last name. Don't you understand? You have power as a Mikhailov and you have protection as a Solovev."

"Don't pretend that you did this for me."

"I didn't do any of it for you," I admit. "But it's funny how everything worked in your favor anyway, isn't it?"

"Don't. Don't. You're trying to get in my head, and I won't let you."

I grab her by the neck and pin her against the wall. She barely reacts.

"You can't intimidate me, Leo," she whispers. "You've made the mistake of telling me that I'm too important to kill."

I almost smile. "You're forgetting one thing."

"What's that?"

"I get whatever the fuck I want," I growl. "And I *will* get my son back. With or without your help. But if you help, I might let you see him again."

I can see the naked fear in her eyes, but she lifts her chin in defiance, apparently forgetting my hand is still around her neck. "My mother will never surrender him to you."

I shake my head. "You're putting too much trust in a woman you barely know."

"She's my mother."

"Which means fuck all." I sigh. "I thought you were smarter than this."

Her hand curls around my wrist. She doesn't try to pull my hand away; she just rests hers there and looks in my eyes. "I wasn't smart enough to see you for who you really are. You had me fooled from the moment we met."

"Don't blame yourself for that," I say, leaning in close. "I'm good at what I do."

My breath tickles her nose. And then I release her. She inhales sharply and stays pasted against the wall as I turn away.

I want to look back over my shoulder before I leave, but I swallow the instinct.

This game is all about appearances.

And Willow still isn't ready to see all of me.

10

WILLOW

There is no time.

Now that Leo knows about our son, things are only going to get worse. I have to get out and warn Anya before anything can happen to my baby boy.

The door to my room is locked from the outside, but Anya didn't just get me a personal trainer—she also taught me plenty of tricks Leo doesn't know a thing about.

I steal two springs from the soft-close drawers beneath the wardrobe and uncoil them. It's possible Leo has some advanced type of super lock on the door, but I have nothing left to lose at this point. Might as well try.

I can't roll over and play the subservient wife. I can't give up. If the last eleven months have taught me anything, it's that fighting is the only way to survive in the Bratva.

The black bags my clothes were delivered in are too big to be useful, but it's fine. I don't need to take much with me. Just a good coat and a solid pair of boots. I'll figure everything else out on the way.

Once I'm dressed, I kneel in front of the door and start on the lock. Seconds later, I hear a click.

"No fucking way," I breathe.

Can it really be this easy?

I decide not to look a gift horse in the mouth. I open the door as quietly as I can and step out into the corridor. Only one of the hallway lights is on, making the shadows beyond cluster close and thick.

It strikes me that I'm walking through the cabin without a weapon. Maybe I can pick one up when I pass through the kitchen.

I make it all the way downstairs before I hear movement. Unfortunately, it's coming from the kitchen. No weapon for me, then. I change direction and move towards the front door as silently as possible.

"Ma'am?"

I stop short and turn towards the voice. It's one of the maids. She takes a tentative step towards me.

"You should be in your room, ma'am," she says. "It's late."

It doesn't take a genius to understand she's giving me an order.

Fuck 'lady of the house.' All I am to these people is a prisoner.

I plaster a fake smile onto my face and act casual. "I'm just gonna go for a little walk," I say, knowing there's zero chance that excuse is going to work. "I'll be back in, like, fifteen minutes. I need some fresh air."

Her smile tells me that she's not buying what I'm selling. "I can open a window for you, ma'am," she says, edging closer still. "It's too cold out there for a walk."

"Oh, I don't mind. I like the cold."

"You know there are wild animals in these parts. I'd be careful about going out there at this time of night."

I wave away her concern. "I can handle it. I was always an outdoorsy kinda gal."

Her smile is as fake as mine is. "I'm afraid I can't let you out, ma'am."

I manage to keep the smile on my face, but just barely. "I don't see why not."

"I have my orders, ma'am."

The smile drops and I narrow my eyes at her. "And what were your orders?"

"To make sure you stayed in your room," she says pleasantly.

"You do realize that aiding and abetting abduction is a crime, right?"

She doesn't seem in the least bit concerned as she takes a step toward me. "I'm not worried."

"Is that because you're stupid or just delusional?"

She doesn't seem at all bothered by the insult. "I know Don Solovev will protect me."

"You're putting way too much faith in a man you don't really know."

"But I do know him," she says. "I've worked for his family since I was eighteen years old. And before I worked for the Solovevs, my mother did. The Solovev brothers protect their own."

"Do you have a name?" I ask, inching closer to her.

"Nicole."

"Nicole," I repeat. "I'm going to give you one chance to do the smart thing and let me walk out of here."

She sighs. "Like I said, I'm afraid I can't do that, ma'am."

I suppress a sigh of my own. "Very well then. Hard way it is."

I lunge forward and land a punch right on her nose.

I hear a crunch. She stumbles back, and I see the blood oozing between her fingers.

I don't bother hanging around to find out exactly how much damage my strike did. Instead, I launch myself out of the front door. The moment I'm out, cold air wraps around me like a cloak I can't remove. The coat I grabbed is doing next to nothing to keep me warm. My teeth are chattering by the time I've taken half a dozen steps.

"Fuck me," I groan. I head towards the thickest line of trees, hoping it will lead me to the route we used to get up here in the first place.

The trees offer protection from the wind and provide a relatively easy path to follow. I can still see our footprints in the snow from when we arrived. I do my best to step in the tracks so as to hide my own.

The moment I step through the other side of the trees, however, the wind slaps me in the face with its frigid hand. My teeth start chattering. I wrap the coat a little tighter around me, but that does fuck all.

This might kill me. But I don't give a shit. Better to die in the attempt than to wither in captivity.

I keep going. Away from the protection of the trees, fresh snow has fallen. My boots sink with each step, making the journey doubly hard. The jeep tracks from when we arrived are barely visible now, but I can make them out just enough to stick close.

I follow them down in the dark. I probably should have taken a flashlight or something, but that would have involved wasting more time in the cabin. Time I couldn't afford to spare.

I walk so long that I start to lose feeling in my extremities. It's too fucking late and too fucking cold to be out like this. I don't stop or slow down, though. Doing either only makes the cold worse.

Then, off in the distance, I spy rooflines peeking out over the snow.

"The village," I breathe.

It's not the main village I'm familiar with. This is a much smaller one, probably miles away from the rest of civilization. But it'll do. I just need to find a phone and make a call. My mother's men will be here as fast as possible.

Then I can get back to my son.

Some women talk about childbirth weakening their bodies. In my experience, having my boy made me stronger. It made me realize what I was capable of. It's how I know I'm capable of this.

It takes me another half an hour, at least, to get down to the edge of the village. But there's a well-marked path to follow and it's downhill. I'm grateful.

It's late, but there is a little convenience store with lights on. I walk up to it and knock.

There's a clunking noise from within. A few seconds later, an older woman pokes her head up from behind the counter. She's obviously doing some kind of inventory, and her expression is scrunched up with annoyance.

She squints at me through the clear glass doors, but she doesn't step out from around the counter.

"We're closed," she calls out.

"I'm sorry, but all I need is a phone," I yell through to her. "I just need to make a call."

She gives me a suspicious once-over. "You shouldn't be out in this cold. You'll get frostbite." I'm hoping that an invitation to enter is coming, but she remains stubbornly behind her counter.

"I just need to make a quick phone call, that's all."

"Try the motel down the road," she says, unswayed. "They have a phone."

Gritting my teeth, I stalk back down to the sidewalk and follow her directions down the road. The motel sign screams "VACANCY" in neon, bathing the snow beneath it in pink and blue.

The building itself is dark and quiet, but there's a foyer entrance off to the side that's lit up. I head inside the lobby and take a moment to appreciate the warmth that washes over me the moment the door closes. It feels like the best hug of my life.

The little lobby is set up with a front desk in front of a wall full of keys to each of the rooms. It's old-school, almost charming. As is the man behind the desk. He's in his fifties at least, with a thick woolen sweater and the mustache to match. His eyes go wide when he looks up and sees me standing there.

"Hi," I say, offering a friendly smile. "I'm sorry to bother you, but I was hoping there was a phone nearby that I could use?"

He blinks and stumbles over his words. "Um, well, I suppose… yeah… hold on a second…"

He goes into the back room, and I turn towards the glass doors that I just walked through. I expect to see Leo standing on the other side of the glass, hot on my trail.

But there's no one.

Instead, I see the building of motel rooms. The siding is a deep, saturated green and the doors are light wood with golden door knockers. As far as motels go, this one's pretty nice. From the outside, at least.

I hear footsteps, and a moment later, the man re-emerges. He seems to have gained a little more composure. But I'm not above disarming him with my charm if it comes to that.

"I'm sorry, ma'am," he says. My heart sinks. "Our phone lines are currently disconnected. The whole area is down from the last snow. It should be fixed first thing in the morning."

It's a struggle to keep the smile on my face. "Do you have a cell phone I can borrow, then?"

"No cell reception for the last few hours." He notices the disappointment on my face. "It happens up here," he says. "I can offer you a room, though. Even give you a discount."

"Can I pay when I leave in the morning?" I ask, deciding not to tell him that I have zero cash on me.

"Of course, ma'am."

I breathe a sigh of relief for old-school trust and accept the key to a room on the second floor. He offers to walk me up, but I decline politely and set off to my room.

I hate the idea of being stuck here so close to Leo and his men, but I don't have a choice. I won't make it much longer out there in the dark and the cold.

The room is spacious and cozy with two twin beds. I don't have a change of clothes, so I stay in the ones I'm wearing and settle on the bed furthest from the door. The warmth is comforting. It's almost enough to distract from the fact that my stomach is rumbling.

One more night, I tell myself. One more night and then I'll be able to call Anya. She'll send a team out to get me.

Morning will solve everything.

But for now, I'm so tired…

∽

I don't know how long I've been sleeping when I hear something from outside. At least, I think I hear it. My mind is groggy and my eyelids are heavy, though. I can barely muster the strength to open them.

"Hello?" I croak into the darkness of the room. "Is someone there?"

I frown and blink away the sleepiness. Is that…?

The next thing I know, I'm struggling for breath. I try to scream, but there's a bag over my head, cutting off my oxygen. Hands grab me on either side, strong and rough.

"No! No!" I rasp.

Is this a dream? It has to be. *It has to be.*

But it's too vivid, too real. Even through the bag on my head, I can smell the scent of perfume. It's familiar. I'll remember that smell until the day I die.

I'm torn from the bed and tossed into a chair. There are at least two sets of hands on me. As I breathe and my training begins to kick in, I can pick out scents, voices.

"Tie her up."

That voice—so confident and clipped. Filled with the kind of control I've tried to embody the last several months.

Oh God.

The bag is pulled from my head, and I squint at her blurry silhouette. When my eyes finally adjust to the light, they confirm what I already know.

Brit.

"Hi, Willow. Long time, no see."

"You fucking bitch," I hiss.

She pretends to be offended. "Is that how you greet me? After all I did to set you free?"

"I don't imagine you did it for me."

"True enough," she says with a shrug. "But I did it all the same."

My hands are tied behind the chair. I struggle against the bindings. "Let me fucking go."

"Sorry, dear. Afraid I can't do that."

"What was the point of setting me free if you were just going to re-capture me?" I demand.

Her blonde hair spills over her right shoulder in a messy braid. She's dressed in all black again. Dark trousers, tight black sweater. She looks like a supermodel on a spy mission.

"Just following orders," she says.

"*Whose* orders?"

The door opens and closes again. "Mine."

11

WILLOW

Leo stops next to Brit, his eyes dark and annoyed.

They're both dressed in black. He is broad and muscled; she is lean and lithe. Of all the thoughts I should be having right now, the only one I can focus on is: *They make a beautiful couple.* Looking at them together feels like staring into the sun.

My eyes burn. All I want to do is squeeze them closed. I try to focus my gaze on just Leo instead.

"What the hell is this?" I demand. Stupid question, but I can't help asking.

"What do you think?" he asks. "I warned you about crossing me."

"Sue me for not accepting my own imprisonment."

"It's for your own good."

I groan. "I'm getting really sick of that phrase. That's all you've been saying since you first ruined my life."

"You mean the life where you were getting beaten up by your deadbeat ex?" he asks without missing a beat.

My eyes flit to Brit's no matter how hard I try to stop myself from looking at her. I feel an acidic burning in my chest. It takes me a moment to realize what it is.

Hatred.

I hate that she's so beautiful.

I hate that she stands next to Leo like she belongs by his side.

I hate that they clearly trust each other—"implicitly," as he said.

More than anything, I hate the way he talks about me in front of *her*.

"It was a better life than this," I say, doubling down. "At least I wasn't a prisoner in my own home."

"You were a prisoner in someone else's home," Brit scoffs. "I'd say that's worse."

"Seriously?" I ask, gaping at her. "Who asked you for your opinion, you psychotic bitch?"

"Hmm, I think she might still be holding onto a little unresolved anger," she says in an aside to Leo, punctuating it with a sardonic giggle.

"Untie me right now, and I'll resolve it," I growl.

Brit's eyes flare. She smiles at Leo. "Well, I'll be damned: the kitten grew claws."

"Fuck you!"

"I like the new look," she remarks as though we're old girlfriends catching up. "Really, it suits you. Very femme fatale without being too obvious. Were you trying to copy me?"

I glare at Leo. "What the hell is she even doing here? Shouldn't she be sucking Belov's cock somewhere?"

He doesn't answer. Instead, he throws Brit a look. I have no clue what it means, but she does. Because they've known each other for years. Because they care about each other.

And here I am, tied to a chair in some godforsaken backwater mountain shithole, forced to look up at both of them.

"Temper, temper," she chides as she sits down on the bed, crossing her legs with flare. We're at eye level now, but it still feels like she's looking down on me.

I revert back to ignoring her. "Let me go," I tell Leo.

"I don't see why I should," he says. "I warned you. You ran anyway."

"Because you gave me no choice!"

He moves forward quickly and puts his hands on the arms of the chair. "I gave you the best choice of them all," he snarls. "And somehow, you still think you're safer with them."

"Not *them*," I snap. "Anya."

"She saved you from Belov, so now you worship the ground she walks on. Is that it? She can do no wrong now?" He rolls his eyes. "Would be nice if you'd consider giving me that kind of trust."

"Maybe you should have thought of that in the warehouse," I shout. "Maybe if you'd tried to save me, I'd trust you, too."

He narrows his eyes. "Would you have preferred to have your head blown off? You had a bomb strapped to your chest. One wrong move on my part and you would have been nothing but a bloodstain on the concrete."

"I'm starting to feel like that would have been preferable."

"Oh, stop being so fucking dramatic," Brit hisses, inserting herself into the conversation.

She pushes herself off the bed and leans in, resting her elbows on her knees. Her eyes are bright and filled with a resentment I don't understand.

"You have air in your lungs, a husband who can protect you, and a child," she hisses. "So why are you complaining?"

I stare at her. "You do remember that you're the woman who woke me up with a knife against my throat, right?"

She shrugs, but doesn't bother denying it. "I was following orders."

"Whose?"

"Belov's, of course," she says. "Do you really think I go around pulling knives on sleeping women just for kicks?"

"You seemed to be enjoying yourself."

She gives me a chilling smile. "I know how to play a part."

"Is that what you're doing now? Playing a part?"

"Always."

I look at Leo to gauge his reaction, but he seems to be perfectly at ease with anything and everything this bitch says or does. I feel like I'm going insane. Does he not see what I see?

"Leo, you have to let me go."

"*Have to?*" he repeats, raising his eyebrows. "No, I don't have to do anything."

"My son needs me."

"Actually, he needs me. *His father.*"

I shake my head. "You'll only use him like you used me. And anyway, I don't see why you need me at all. You obviously have your whore."

A smile splits through Brit's face instantly. "Oh, honey, don't feel threatened. I can share."

"Brit…" Leo says gently. Then he sighs. "I have to go. I have things to discuss with Jax and Gaiman."

She nods. "Of course. Don't worry. I can handle things from here."

She sidles up to him, hips swishing, and presses her hips to his. Leo stands there and allows it. The acid in my chest flares painfully.

"Have you changed your mind?" she murmurs, just loud enough for me to hear.

His answer is immediate. "No."

She raises her hand to his chest and runs her fingers along his pecs. "Then be careful out there, big boy."

His expression is flat, impatient, but he doesn't push her away like I want him to.

"Come with me," he tells her.

They head out of the room, leaving the door slightly ajar. Enough that I can see them talking, their bodies close, voices lowered. Brit's eyes flicker to me for a moment, but she doesn't hold my gaze. Her expression suggests that I'm nothing more than a minor inconvenience that needs to be dealt with.

She reaches up and squeezes Leo's arm. He says something; she smiles. He looks pissed, but she seems to be enjoying herself.

Especially when she leans in and kisses him softly on the cheek.

As chaste a kiss as it might seem, I can sense the threat she poses, the message she's trying to give me.

If Leo senses that, he doesn't show it. He turns and leaves without so much as glance towards me.

Brit walks back into the room and clicks the door shut. I know there are men posted outside the room, but that doesn't make me feel any better about the fact that Brit's the only one in here with me.

I've been alone with her before.

It wasn't fun.

"So… how've you been?" she asks nonchalantly.

"He seems to trust you."

She raises her eyebrows, and the smile on her face gets a little wider. "I'd say so."

"Is he right to?"

"Is that concern in your voice?"

"I know what you've done…"

She sighs and rubs her temples. "You've met Spartak Belov. Tell me, do you think a man like him likes being argued with? Do you think he likes being defied?"

"So you were just doing his bidding?"

"Now, you're starting to understand."

"I don't remember him being there any of the times you tortured me."

"Tortured you?" she repeats incredulously. "Oh, honey, you think that was torture?"

She waves her perfectly slender hand in my face. Even her nails look manicured and fresh. How does this woman pull off such flawless beauty and still manage to be terrifying?

"I've tortured people before. What you experienced was nothing of the sort. A spa day in comparison."

"I should be grateful, then? Is that what you're saying?"

"I'm saying you need to stop thinking of yourself as a victim," she retorts firmly. "People who see themselves as a victim end up as one. You want more than that, don't you?"

"Is this the part where you give me your whole backstory?" I ask. "Justify every bad choice you've made and paint yourself out to be the unlikely, misunderstood heroine?"

She snorts. "Fuck no. I'm no heroine, nor do I pretend to be. I'm just trying to survive."

"By hurting other people."

"How many times must I remind you that I saved you? It isn't my fault you got into the wrong car."

"Did you get in trouble for that?" I ask, hoping she did. "I bet Leo was pissed."

Her eyes narrow for a moment, and I know I'm right. Leo must've been livid when he realized the mix-up. "He was… not pleased."

I'm surprised. I hadn't expected her to cop to it.

"But then, Leo always runs a little hot," she continues, a soft smile washing across her face. "I know how to cool him down."

She gives me a wink, and I'm back to being furious.

"You realize who I am, right?" I ask.

"That is an excellent question. Who *are* you?" she asks. "Viktoria Mikhailov or Willow Powers?"

The way she asks it gives me pause. Like she's genuinely curious. Her eyes are bright and cunning, her lips pursed in quiet expectation.

When I don't answer right away, she gives me a sympathetic nod. "I thought so. You don't know who you are anymore."

And just like that, the woman who haunts my nightmares just held a mirror up to my worst fears.

I don't know who I am. Not really.

Am I Viktoria Mikhailov?

Or am I Willow?

And if it's the latter, which Willow am I? Willow Powers? Willow Reeves?

Willow Solovev?

I look at Brit. The lines of her face are hard. There's something worn about her. She's been through something, but that's no surprise given who she works for and with.

"Who are you?" I ask, turning the question back on her.

"Me?" she asks. "I'm an enigma. A contradiction. I am everything and nothing."

"Am I supposed to decipher that riddle? Because I'm not sure I care about the answer enough to put in the work."

"Darling, you can lie to everyone else, but not to me. I can spot a lie a mile away. Do you think I would've survived so long if I couldn't?" She smiles. "You care entirely too much. About me. About Leo. About me and Leo… together."

I tense, hating that she's right. But I stubbornly cling to denial. Denial is comforting and easy. It's the best way to combat the raging fear in my gut.

"You're wrong," I say. "I don't care. In fact, I think the two of you are made for each other."

She smiles. "You're right about that. More right than you know. We've suffered the same losses and battled our demons together. We've comforted each other through the worst times."

Her words are sharp and painful. I want to run from them, but I'm the one who's invited them in.

"I love Leo Solovev," she announces, standing up slowly and approaching me like a protective lioness. "He is and will always be my family. Now and forever."

She leans down so we are eye to eye again. "You want to know who I am?" she asks, her smile slipping away. "*That's* who I am."

My heart feels like it's going to burst out of my chest, but I force myself to speak up again anyway. "Let me go, then. Let me go, and I'll be out of your way for good."

She cocks her head to the side and regards me with curiosity. "Do you imagine he'll forgive me for that?"

"What does it matter?" I ask frustratedly. "He doesn't want me. He doesn't love me. You're the woman for him."

"But *you're* the woman that'll deliver him the Mikhailov Bratva on a silver platter," she hisses. "And I'm not fool enough to stand in his way."

I shake my head. "Is this your whole purpose, then? Running around trying to please the men who pull the strings?"

"There's only one man I want to please. The rest, I couldn't give two fucks about."

So many half answers, so many glimpses at a bigger, darker truth. *Who are you?* I want to scream at her again and again until she paints the whole picture. But I know better than to ask. She'd never spill it so easily.

She's a mystery, like she said. An enigma.

"Borek!" she calls.

The door opens and a hefty guard enters the room. "Yes, ma'am?"

"Prepare the jeep," she says. "We're leaving in five."

"Where are we going?" I ask in a panic.

"Where do you think?" she asks impatiently. "Back to the cabin. Did you really think that escaping Leo would be so easy?"

I frown. "What do you mean?"

Her mouth turns up in a cruel smile. "Did you know you jump a little when you punch? You should work on that. But it was still a mean jab. It broke Nikki's nose."

I stare at her in shock. "You were watching?"

She nods. "Riveting stuff. Couldn't look away."

"Then you could have stopped me. Why let me get this far?"

"Isn't it obvious?" she asks, like I'm stupid. "To help you realize that no matter how far you run, no matter where you go… we will always find you."

The fear that sparks inside me has nothing at all to do with the threat. It has everything to do with one simple word. A word that acts as the line in the sand, ensuring I'm firmly on the outside looking in.

We.

12

LEO

"What the hell were you doing back there?"

She gives me an innocent smile which, on Brit, is lethal. "What ever are you talking about?"

"You were flirting with me. Did you think I wouldn't notice?"

She smiles and drapes herself on the arm of the recliner I'm sitting in, positioning herself so my arm is wrapped around her ass. Which of course is exactly the moment Jax and Gaiman choose to walk in.

Great. Just fucking great.

"Pardon, boss," Jax says with a wicked smile. "Are we interrupting something?"

"Jaxson Harper," Brit says, with a smile that matches his, "have you been working out? You're filling out."

"I was going to say the same thing about your—"

"Any news about Anya's movements?" I ask, cutting off any potential sparring match between the two. When they get going, they're insufferable.

Jax pouts, but Gaiman cuts right to the chase. "She's searching, but so far no luck. Our guys have succeeded in throwing her off the scent."

I pull my hand out from around Brit and get out of the armchair. "Good. But I doubt it'll stay that way for long. She's closing in."

"Does that mean we need to get out of here?" Gaiman asks.

"That bitch isn't going to chase me off," I say. "I'll leave when I'm good and ready. And if she gets wind of the fact that we're here, all the better. She's got something of mine."

"I never did say congratulations," Brit says. This smile that doesn't quite reach her eyes. "You'll make a good father. If you get the kid back, that is."

I glare at her. "*If?*"

"You know what I mean," she says with a wave of the hand. "I never speak in absolutes anymore."

"That's because you've spent too long with Belov," I snap. "I'm different."

"I can see that," she says appreciatively, her eyes running down my body.

I glare at her, trying to figure out why she's embarrassing herself.

"Jax. Gaiman," I say gruffly. "Get out."

Jax gives me a wink before he leaves the room. "We'll make sure the wife doesn't hear anything she's not meant to."

I head for the door, push the dumbass out, and slam it right on his smirking face. Then I turn to the blonde siren who's got her innocent smile back in place.

"What?" she protests mischievously. "A girl can't have a little fun?"

"I'm serious: what the fuck are you playing at?"

"You seem really tense, Leo," she says with a shrug of her shoulders. "I'm just trying to loosen you up a little."

"And piss Willow off in the process?"

"That's just a delightful bonus."

"What is it with you two?" I ask. "I get what you were trying to do. You had a part to play and Belov was watching. But I know you, Brit. A tiny part of you was enjoying hurting her."

She looks off to the side, and I can see her struggling for control. She's become a master at concealing her true feelings. But that's easier to do when no one knows who you really are.

I know, though.

I know everything.

"You're reading too much into it," she says finally.

I put myself in her line of sight, forcing her to look at me. "Who do you think you're talking to?"

"Okay, so maybe I'm jealous," she snaps. "Is that what you wanted to hear? Well, there you go. Sadistic bastard."

"You're jealous of Willow?"

She purses her lips and looks away. I take the moment to study her.

Her beauty has changed over the years. The softness that I used to admire is all gone. It's been washed away by blood and tears. I used to think she was the most beautiful woman I'd ever laid eyes on.

But that was before.

Before grief cleaved her into two separate people.

"You realize the only reason you get away with that shit is because of our shared past, right?"

"Meaning what?"

"Meaning, if any other person had touched Willow the way you did, I would have killed them myself."

She raises her eyebrows and stares at me for a long while, trying to gauge how serious I am. "Fuck. You mean it."

"Of course I mean it."

"I'm afraid you're just making me more jealous."

"I get it, Brit. You're bitter and angry. Join the fucking club. But when it comes to Willow, there's a line. Even someone as broken as you can understand that."

I can see the twitch in her jaw. I can see the losses she's suffered over the years. Not just her happily ever after, but the person she used to be along with it.

"I got it, boss," she says, sharp and professional.

She's affected. It's obvious in the way she straightens her spine and lifts her chin. I hate going don on her. But there are some things I can't let slide.

"I wonder if you do."

She glances over at me. "You may not realize this, but I do understand."

"I know."

She nods. "He was the same way with me. Fiercely protective. Possessive, sometimes. But I loved it. I was happy to belong to him."

"You didn't just belong to him," I correct. "You belonged *with* him. You were his partner."

Her mask drops for a moment. And in that moment, I see the loss. All these years later and it's still there just as fresh as the day it happened.

"I couldn't have done this without you, you know?" I say.

She smirks, but it doesn't reach her eyes. She's losing her touch. "That's very charitable of you, but we both know it's bullshit. You've always been determined, and you always have a bulletproof plan."

"You know as well as I do that plans don't always pan out. There are too many moving targets. Too many changing circumstances."

"All true," she says. "But if anyone can do it, you can. If I hadn't been in the picture, you would have found another way in."

She's right. I would have. But I don't think it'd be helpful to agree to that now. Things feel fragile.

"I'm glad you were in the picture," I say instead.

She doesn't say anything, but her fingers start to tremble.

I move forward. "Ariel."

She snaps her gaze to me. Her eyes are bright with unshed tears, her face twisted into anger. "Don't. That is not my name. Not anymore."

I ignore her and walk forward. "Brit is who you are with him. Brit is a persona, a character we invented to get close to Belov. She is not who you are."

"Isn't she?" Ariel asks. "Because I've done horrible things, Leo. I've killed men and tortured women. I've hurt so many, many people."

"And you've done it all under his orders. That's not on you."

"Is it on me if I enjoyed it?" she whispers. "Giving other people pain made me feel less of it myself."

I stare at her, unblinking. Then I reach out and take her hand. "You did what you had to do to survive and cope. And to infiltrate Belov's circle. Don't think I don't understand how much you had to sacrifice along the way."

She blinks away her tears and pulls her hand from mine. "Sometimes, I think I might be going insane," she says softly. "Sometimes, I think it would have been easier if I'd died that day. With him. Like Petyr and Logan did."

"Ariel…"

She flinches again. Then, with a sharp exhale, she straightens her posture and puts her game face back on. Tucking away years of pain behind a mask that has, bit by bit, become fused to her face. "We're getting off track. I came here to give you sensitive information. I didn't want to risk using a phone."

There's no point trying to press the issue.

"How much time do you have?" I ask.

"Spartak is in Russia right now. He'll stay there for at least another week. Which is why I'm here."

"And if he checks in on you?"

"My alibi will hold up."

I nod. Ariel's not a stupid woman. If she says she's covered her tracks, then I'm not going to question her. "Why's he in Russia at all?"

"Mercenaries," she says simply.

My gaze snaps to hers. "Surely he wouldn't be so desperate already."

"Then you're overestimating him," she says. "You know Spartak. He doesn't care about Bratva rules. He doesn't care about honor or loyalty. It doesn't matter to him where his men come from, so long as he has the numbers. So long as they fight for him."

"He needs money for the kind of mercenaries it would take to go against a Bratva."

"He's got money," she says. "He's got access to all Semyon's bank accounts. The old man is getting bled dry."

"All of them?"

"All of them," she confirms.

"Speaking of Semyon, where is he?"

"Out of commission. Most days he stays locked inside his room with no one but his nurse."

"Just the nurse?" I ask.

"Just the nurse," Ariel confirms. "Most days, I think she's the only one who sees or speaks to him."

I nod. "That's just as well."

"Leo, after both buildings went down…" She shakes her head. "Spartak lost his shit. No one saw it but me. He likes to give the illusion of calm, but I've never seen him more furious. It's the reason he sent me into Willow's room. He watched from cameras he had installed. He wanted me to hurt her."

I clench my jaw. Ariel notices and hurries to explain.

"I couldn't get away with not hurting her at all, but I hurt her as little as possible. The only reason I got away with it is because Belov never entered the room. If he had, he'd have known just how much I was pretending."

"How much could you be pretending?" I grit out. "She looks at you like you're the devil himself."

"She's lucky it was me," she says softly. "When Spartak tortures his victims, it gets a lot worse. The only thing that spared her was her name."

The thought of Spartak laying a single finger on Willow makes me want to tear this room apart. Just so I can wrap my hands around something. Burn off some of the rage I've been holding onto for far too long.

But I'm not about to lose it in front of Ariel. Especially since I know it's not her fault.

It's mine.

She's been undercover for too long. She's in way too deep. If I could save her, I would. But pulling her out now will change the course of my mission. And I can't afford to change plans now. We've come too goddamn far.

"After she disappeared that night, his anger only multiplied. The sole reason he managed to retain control over the Bratva is because there was literally no one left to lead," she says. "Semyon was locked away in his room, Anya had disappeared, and Willow… she wasn't a player yet. Men left the Mikhailovs after that night."

"How many?"

"Not many, only a dozen or so," she says. "Enough that Spartak's ego took a hit. He hunted down the men who ran. He murdered all of them."

"Ariel—"

"And I helped," she says, nearly choking over the words.

"Ariel…"

She looks back up at me. Her eyes are shining with tears she's struggling to hold back.

"You can let it out. You don't have to lie with me."

She shakes her head slowly. "No. No, I can't. If I let it out, I'll never stop. And you still need me in there."

"We're close, Ariel," I tell her, putting my hand on her shoulder. "We're so fucking close. And after it's done, you'll be free."

"Will I?" she asks, searching my face. "I'm not sure freedom exists anymore, Leo. Not for me. Not the way I once had it. These ghosts will haunt me forever. Pavel. Petyr. Logan. And if we succeed, Belov will haunt me, too."

"I won't let him," I say fiercely.

She looks at me and a smile flits over her lips. She's managed to stave off the tears. But just barely.

She reaches up and cups the side of my face. "You remind me a lot of him, you know."

"Do I?" I ask. "I didn't think I was anything like him."

"When you started this, no. But now… I can see it."

"Is that a good thing?"

She nods. "Pavel was the best man I knew. He restored my faith in people."

I take a step back. As much as I've missed Ariel, being around her is hard, too. The weight of our shared loss is too much to bear sometimes. And being with her reminds me of it constantly.

In many ways, I've moved on from that day. I've learned to cope.

But I'm not sure Ariel has.

"Once I've avenged his death—*their* deaths," she corrects softly. "I won't have a purpose anymore."

"You can start again. Fresh. Free from all this."

"Start *what* again? I don't know if I even want to."

"You don't have a choice, Ariel," I tell her. "It's death or survival."

"Death doesn't seem so bad," she whispers. "At least I'll see him again."

I shake my head. "Don't say that."

"You have something to live for, Leo," she tells me. "A wife, a child. You have a future. But I don't."

"But you could if you wanted it. Do you think Pavel would begrudge you meeting someone else and moving on?" I ask. "I know that's what my brother would want for you. It's what I want for you."

She just shakes her head. There's no arguing with that kind of solemnity, that certain. "I can't be happy without him. I realized that a long time ago."

She turns towards the window and stares at the dark clouds overhead. It's started snowing. I can see the tumbling flakes reflected in Ariel's eyes like ash falling from a fire in the sky.

"She loves you, you know?" she says suddenly.

I snort. "She doesn't know how she feels."

"I've looked into that woman's soul," she says. "She is in love with you. Even if she doesn't want to be."

I almost smile at that.

13

WILLOW

All my fears seem to culminate in the darkness.

I try to fall asleep, but the room is so dark I can't tell when my eyes are opened or closed. It feels like I'm tumbling heels over head into a black hole, being swallowed alive by empty space.

But somewhere between anger and hopelessness, I manage to drift off.

And when I do, I see so many things.

My son.

My parents.

I see all the people that used to inspire fear in me: Casey, Brit, Belov. They're all moving images, rolling around inside my head, reminding me how far off-track I've gotten.

Accept it.

Her voice is as commanding and impatient in my dreams as it was in real life.

I twist in the bed. As comfortable as it is, I feel like I'm being pricked by needles from every angle. When I manage to find a bearable spot, it doesn't stay that way for long.

Accept it.

I hear his crying between flashes of nightmares.

It's been days since I held him, touched him, talked to him. What if he forgets me? What if he only remembers that I abandoned him to a woman whose body can't bend into a hug?

Children *need* to be hugged.

Children *need* to be kissed and loved.

"Accept it."

"I don't fucking want to!" I yell, turning to her as she stands there, invading my space.

My hand trembles over my burgeoning belly and all I can think, irrational as it may be, is: I wish that Leo was here. I wish I were with him now.

"Your name is the only reason you're alive right now," Anya says.

"Everyone keeps fucking telling me that. I'm sick of hearing it. I'm so, so sick of hearing it."

I remember thinking she was beautiful when I first stepped into that car and encountered her. Her hair was raven-dark like mine. Her eyes had the same blues and grays as mine. The same sadness. The same distance.

"Don't be a fool. That baby will inherit your name," she replies. "You need to do more than just accept your name; you need to embrace it."

"I am not a Mikhailov," I snap. "And I'm not a Solovev, either. I am a Powers. Willow Powers."

A flicker of irritation flashes across her eyes. "I chose those idiots because I knew they'd be good to you," she says. "But now, I think they may have been too *good* to you."

I try to suppress my desire to recoil. What kind of woman says something like that to the daughter she gave up? She doesn't seem to even realize how hurtful those words are. How they slice me open along the same scars that have been building on my heart for years.

"What does that even mean?" I ask.

"It means you're weak. Soft. You're a victim."

I stare at her in disbelief.

Anya strokes her chin. "Maybe it was a mistake. I thought giving you a normal life was my gift to you. But I see now how naïve I was. They would have found you in the end."

"They?"

"My enemies."

I don't say anything, and she moves closer.

"Like Leo," *she says harshly.*

My hand falls protectively against my belly. She notices; of course she does. Nothing gets past this woman.

"He's your enemy, too, Viktoria."

"I'm carrying his baby," *I remind her.*

Her eyes fall on the bump. It's only just popped, still easy to conceal from anyone who isn't as observant as she is.

"You're not that far along. One simple procedure and the child won't be a problem anymore."

I go cold. This woman can't be my mother. I'm not even sure she's human.

"Tell me you're joking," *I rasp.*

"He won't have a hold on you then. It's for your own good."

I take a step forward, my face hardening. My jaw twitches as I stop only inches from her face.

Had I really thought she was beautiful when I first laid eyes on her? All I can see now is a monster.

"If you try and hurt my child, I will fucking kill you," I promise her. And it is a promise. "I don't care that you're my birth mother. I don't care about your name, either. I will fucking kill you."

Her eyes go wide for a second. And then... she smiles.

"There might be hope for you yet," she murmurs.

Then she turns and leaves.

I go to the window after she's gone. I cradle my stomach and stare at the high walls that separate me from the rest of the world.

I don't want to be here.

But where else can I go?

The answer is obvious, as much as I hate it.

Leo...

Leo...

Leo.

Heat grazes across my left arm and I wake with a gasp. My eyes fly open, but there's still only darkness. Endless, churning darkness.

I feel the weight pulling me to the left, sinking the mattress. Someone's here with me.

As soon as the thought solidifies, I know who it is.

His natural scent is thick and rich, no different than the ancient trees that surround this cabin. There's a hint of cigar smoke on him.

There's something else too. Another smell, floral but darker. Like rich cherries and poison ivy. I can't quite place it, but it feels familiar.

Suddenly, a light flicks on.

I blink against it, the room coming into focus for the first time in God-knows-how-long. I've lost track of how long I've been here.

Then I realize the light is coming from outside. A porch light shining through the blinds just enough to let me see.

When I look to the left side of the bed now, I can make out his sleeping form.

Leo is on his side with his back turned to me. The sheet is pulled over his waist, but his chest is bare, rippling with muscles that somehow manage to look flexed even in sleep.

Christ, he's beautiful.

I hate it, and I hate myself for thinking it. But I still give myself several more seconds to admire him. Because for a second, I'm okay. Everything is okay.

But fantasies can't last forever.

I look around, searching for something—a heavy object or weapon I can use to force him to listen. I see something glint on the bedside table over his shoulder.

A gun? No. It's far too bright for the dull dark metal of a gun.

It's the blade of a knife. Which will work just as well.

I'm about to steel myself to tip-toe out of the bed so I can reach it… when he moves. He twists around and his eyes are open.

"I wouldn't," he says calmly.

I sit up. The sheets pool around my waist. I'm wearing a thin t-shirt that's too big for me, but Leo still studies my shape. He can't help himself.

"Where am I?"

"I would have thought it was obvious," he says, gesturing around to what I can see is a very large bedroom. "My room."

"Why?"

"Because you lost the privilege of having your own space. You need to be watched, and I don't trust anyone else to do the job anymore."

I pull back the sheets and attempt to get out of bed, but he grabs my arm and pulls me down. I sink into the mattress. The moment I'm down, he swings his leg over and gets on top of me.

"Get off of me," I grunt.

"Let's get one thing straight, Willow. You may have called the shots in the Mikhailov compound. But here, I'm the one who's in charge."

I laugh right in his face. "If you think I called any shots there, you're out of your damn mind."

He looks down at me with a smile. "I thought so."

"Excuse me?"

"Anya is a controlling bitch. I just wanted to hear you say it."

"Get. Off. Of. Me."

"Stop struggling. You're only going to hurt yourself."

"And that's your job, isn't it?" I bite back at him.

"I never intended to hurt you," he says quietly. "You were simply collateral damage."

It's a fact for Leo. He doesn't have regret. He isn't apologizing. He's telling me the way it is. He wouldn't change anything that's happened in the last year and a half.

"Well, then, that makes it all better," I hiss sarcastically.

He sinks into me, pressing his hard chest against mine. I can feel every single one of his muscles taut and flexed.

He stares down at me, and I find myself holding my breath. His eyelashes are long, framing bright eyes. It feels like he's trying to break into my soul and steal the few secrets I have left.

"What's he like?" Leo murmurs. "Our son."

Our son. That word is far more comforting than it should be. I've felt so alone for so long that the thought of someone wanting the same things I want is… well, it's something. I bite my tongue and turn my head to the side so that I'm not looking into his hypnotic eyes anymore.

"He's safe."

"You're insane if you truly believe that."

"Anya will protect him. She owes me."

"You need to stop thinking like Willow," he hisses into my ear. "You need to start thinking as if you were Bratva. You need to think like Viktoria."

"I *am* Bratva," I remind him.

"No, you're not. You're trying to be, but you're not. Because if you were, you'd know you can't trust Anya for shit."

I push at his chest, but it's like trying to break through solid steel. "Tell me what you did to my parents," I snap.

"If you're not going to answer my questions, why should I answer yours?"

"Because you owe me, too."

He smirks. "You really don't get it, do you?"

He releases me all at once. Instead of moving, I lay there, cold from the lack of him. He's on his side of the bed, leaning against a pillow with his hands behind his head and his eyes staring beyond the ceiling above.

When I think I can make it, I spring out of bed and run straight for the door. It doesn't even strike me that it might be locked. Not until I twist the handle and find myself well and truly trapped.

"Are you serious?" I growl, twisting around to face him.

"What did you expect? You would have had freedom of the cabin if you'd just stayed put."

"Open the door."

"I could," he says. "But Brit's downstairs."

"I can handle that bitch."

He raises his eyebrows. "That's your pride talking. You're no match for her."

I can't deny it—that stings. No matter how true it is. All at once, I remember the scent I picked up on earlier: cherries and ivy.

He was with her before he came up here. It's her scent that's all over him.

"Who is she to you?"

I know I've asked the question before. But I need an answer before I go insane. An answer that'll help me stop obsessing over their strange and mysterious relationship.

"She's family," he says.

We stare at each other, and I feel the chasm between us grow wider. I try and bury my love for him somewhere in that chasm, but it refuses to submerge.

"You're really not letting me out of here, are you?"

"No, I'm not."

"Fine," I say. "Then the least you can do is give me the damn bed."

He smiles. "Why? Having trouble keeping your hands off me?"

I narrow my eyes at him. "Don't flatter yourself."

"I'm not. You're just easy to read."

He sits up a little and my eyes fall instantly to the mountain range of his abs. He chuckles a little, letting me know that he knows exactly what's caught my attention.

I move to the bed, grab the corner of the sheet, and rip it off him.

Leo doesn't move. Doesn't flinch. He doesn't seem bothered in the least that I stole his blanket, despite the fact that he's lying there naked.

And hard. Completely fucking hard.

"Jesus," I gasp.

"Something wrong?"

"You're sick," I say, pointing at him. "Fighting with me really does turn you on."

"Hm," he remarks, as though he hasn't noticed. "Apparently it does."

"Put some pants on."

"I like sleeping naked."

I roll my eyes and grit my teeth. He's impossible.

Changing course, I drag the sheet over to the sofa in the corner of the room and settle myself on the cushions. I've just gotten nestled in when he looks over at me. The gleam in his eyes is impossible to mistake.

"You think it's gonna be that easy to seduce me?" I snap.

"Yes."

"You don't affect me as much as you think you do."

He smiles. "I'm in your head, Willow. You can't deny that."

"I don't waste my time thinking about you," I lie.

"Somehow, I don't believe it."

"Because it's not what *you* want to believe."

"No," he says easily. "Because just before you woke up… you were crying out my name."

14

LEO

The steady rapping on the door wakes me up. I roll out of bed and answer the door.

Ariel's waiting on the other side. She raises her eyebrows as her gaze flickers down to my erection.

"Had a good morning, boss?" she asks. "Or was it a really good night?"

She tries to peek into the room, but I pull the door closed.

Willow is still sleeping. She tossed and turned for hours before she finally settled down in the early pre-dawn. I'm certain I'm partially to blame.

Ariel sighs, disappointed. "So protective. It's cute."

"You're talking a lot," I snap. "But you're not really saying anything."

"Right down to business, huh? I don't even get a good morning?"

She's managed to get a hold of herself since last night. She needed to get some things off her chest, and I needed to remind her of who she really is.

But that can't last forever. She has a job to do. And being Brit and Ariel at the same time just takes too much out of her.

She can only choose one.

When I snap my fingers at her, she sighs and gives her report. "Anya's getting closer to finding our location," she explains. "Some of her men almost caught sight of me when I was heading into the village this morning."

"Why were you in the village to begin with?" I demand.

"Because I had to make a call," she says. "Belov may be in Russia, but he still keeps tabs on me."

That annoys me, but I have no choice but to let it go. "You spoke to him?"

"Yes."

"Why didn't you tell me?"

"I'm telling you now."

"I meant *before* the fucking call, Ariel," I snap. "Why didn't you tell me before?"

"Because I didn't really think about it."

"Jesus. What's the point of you being my spy?"

"I'll tell you everything he told me," she says. "He's cutting his trip short by two days, which means I'll have to leave a little earlier than planned."

Now, I understand why her alter ego is back. She's preparing herself, getting back into character for the asshole whose days are numbered.

"Okay. What else?"

"He got the mercenaries he wanted."

I shake my head. "He actually went through with it. Crazy son of a bitch."

"There was never any doubt."

"How many?" I ask.

"A thousand."

"Seriously?"

She shrugs. "He likes to be prepared."

"A thousand men," I repeat. "Do you have company names?"

"Nope. He wasn't interested in giving me details."

"Does he ever?"

"Sometimes," she says, a little defensively. "He trusts me."

I give her a pointed look. "You're too smart to believe that, Ariel."

"I've been at his side for six years."

"And he still checks up on you," I remind her.

A flicker of doubt crosses her face, but she lifts her chin. "You may know Belov. But I know Spartak, okay?"

"Just be careful."

"I always am."

I nod. "How big was the contingent of Anya's men that you saw earlier?"

"Just one jeep. Five men, tops."

That's good news. "So she's still just feeling the territory out."

"Yeah, but it's only a matter of time."

"I'm not waiting on her to make my move."

Ariel raises her eyebrows. "You're not?"

"I want my son back," I say harshly. "Go inform Jax and Gaiman of everything you just told me."

"No need. Jax was with me this morning. I'm sure he's already filled Gaiman in."

"Since when do you and Jax hang out?" I ask, unsure about how I feel about that.

She smiles. "A girl's gotta keep herself entertained. And Jax is nothing if not entertaining. Especially since your head has been turned by the wannabe Bratva princess."

"Careful what you say."

She raises her hands in defeat and backs off. "I'll leave you to it."

I head back into the room and walk over to the couch where Willow is sleeping. She's still wrapped in the throes of her dreams, one arm thrown over her head, the other tucked under her chin. She looks peaceful.

I ought to let her stay that way. Reality can be cruel; hers in particular. Dreams can be an oasis for the haunted and the damned.

Unfortunately for Willow, I've never been one for running from your reality.

I head into the bathroom and fill a glass up with cold water. Then I walk right back to the sofa and dump it over her head.

She wakes with a gasp. "What the fuck?!"

"Morning," I say pleasantly. "Have a good sleep?"

"You bastard!" she hisses as she wipes the water from her eyes.

I sit down on the arm of the sofa. "It's time you start pulling your weight around here."

She narrows her eyes. "Oh, I can't wait to hear this."

"I'm going to make contact with Anya."

She goes still for a moment, her muscles tensing. "Why?"

I don't bother answering. She knows why.

She sighs. "What do you want from me?"

"You're the one who's going to write the letter for me," I tell her.

She gets to her feet. "Unless you plan on forging my handwriting, Anya will not get a letter from me."

"Don't make this harder than it needs to be."

"As far as I'm concerned, you're the only one making this harder."

Water is still dripping from the ends of her hair, soaking through the thin t-shirt she's wearing. The cold water certainly woke her up. She looks fit to pounce.

"I will get him back, Willow. With or without your help."

"Then you'll have to do it without my help," she says determinedly. "Because I'm not about to lift a damn finger to make your life easier. God knows you haven't done that for me."

"You're saying you think he's better off with her?"

A shadow passes across her face, and I know that her relationship with Anya is not quite as warm and fuzzy she would have me believe.

"I'm saying I want to control this narrative," she says at last. "And I won't be able to do that so long as you're at the reins."

"You're compromising our son's safety because you want to feel like you're the captain? For fuck's sake, I thought you were smarter than that."

She presses her lips closed and crosses her arms. The move only accentuates the swell of her breasts, and the water slowly soaking into the cotton doesn't help.

"Don't make me do anything I'm going to regret, Willow," I say in a low voice, stalking towards her.

Her eyelashes flutter, and she backs away. But I don't stop advancing. I keep moving, matching her step for step, until her back hits the wall.

"You're not going to intimidate me, Leo. You may be a big strong Bratva don, but that means nothing to me."

"No?"

"I'm not her."

For a moment, I genuinely don't know who the fuck she's talking about. Then it clicks.

"No, you're definitely not Brit," I agree.

Her eyes flash with anger, but she doesn't say anything else. Ariel was right—Willow is jealous. She hates herself for it, but every time she looks at Brit, she doesn't just see her torturer—she sees a threat to whatever she has with me.

I can use that to my advantage.

So I keep going. "Brit may not have been born into the Bratva, but she was made for it."

Willow tenses. "That's quite the pedestal you have her on."

I nod. "She's an amazing woman."

Nothing about that statement is a lie. I do have her on a pedestal, and I do think she's an amazing woman.

Not many others would have survived so long in an enemy camp without suspicions being raised. She played her part to perfection.

She was one of my two most useful assets on the ground, and I wasn't about to say anything different to soothe Willow's ego.

"I'm sure she's *amazing*," Willow snaps sarcastically. "So why don't you share a bed with her?"

I try very hard not to smile, but I know she can see the corners of my mouth twitch up. I have to admit, I'm enjoying this a lot more than I thought I would.

"What makes you think I don't?"

Her eyes flare for a moment before she manages to get her expression under control. "She doesn't strike me as the type to share."

"Oh, she can play nice when I ask her sweetly."

Finally, Willow breaks. She slams her hands against my chest. "Move."

"I don't think so."

Her fist flashes through the air, but I'm ready. I block her once. Same with the second punch.

But she's prepared, too. She spins around and knees me in the stomach. It's a surprising blow, but I take it in stride. I straighten up and shove her back against the wall.

She realizes she is losing the upper hand, and her movements become more forceful, more frantic.

She's good. I can't deny that. There's some talent there, but it's still rough. It needs to be properly honed before she can be truly dangerous.

She sends a roundhouse kick my way, but I grab her leg and swing her around in the opposite direction. She nearly stumbles onto the bed, but she catches herself just in time.

Her eyes are wild as she charges at me again. And it's already got my cock hard.

Time for what was always meant to happen next.

I push her down onto the bed. Her t-shirt rides up, revealing the fact that she's not wearing panties underneath.

I grab her ankles and drag her forward so that her thighs are parted around my legs.

"You should never fight without the proper gear," I say.

"You can't just fuck me whenever you like!" she yells. "You want sex? Go downstairs to your whore."

I lean in and press my body against hers. "All I'm hearing is that you're very concerned with where I stick my cock."

"I don't give a shit about where you stick your cock. As long as it's not inside me."

I snake my hand down between her legs and probe them open. "Then why are you wet?"

She pushes me again, and I let her up, chuckling.

She puts distance between us, shooting daggers at me with her eyes, but I'm too busy admiring the slim lines of her thighs that lead up to her sweet, tight little pussy.

"Stop it," she snaps.

"Stop what?"

"Stop using me like I'm your plaything. I'm a person, Leo. Not a tool or a weapon or… or a name."

"I'm aware of that."

"Are you?" she asks. "Because as far as I can tell, you brought me into your life so that I could deliver you the Mikhailov Bratva. You married me because you wanted my name. And you made sure to get me pregnant so that you'd have a child that would unite the two Bratvas."

She releases a quivering breath. "I don't know who I am anymore, Leo. I belong nowhere. The only thing I have anymore is my son. When I'm with him, I feel… like myself. Even though I don't really know who that is. At least I'm his mother. But you want to take that from me as well. You'll make him to be your son. And then I'll have nothing left."

"You're being ridiculous, Willow—"

"Am I?" she asks, as her walls start to break down. "Because you took everything about me and destroyed it. Including my love for you."

I raise my eyebrows, wondering if I just heard her right.

"What?" she asks, defensively. "You didn't know that I loved you? Well, I *did*. At some point in this whole ridiculous fucking charade you've concocted, I fell in love with you. And I was stupid enough to believe that when you married me, you loved me, too. In your own way. I convinced myself that we could be happy, that we could build a life together."

She shakes her head. "And then I learned that it was never about love at all. You never wanted me. You wanted my name. You wanted power. You wanted a key."

The emotion pours out of her, leaving her looking pale and shaken.

"I loved you, Leo. Wholly and completely," she says. "But not anymore. You took that from me, too."

15

WILLOW

You'd think rage and hurt and sadness would crowd out the hunger, but apparently not. Even after storming into the bathroom and locking the door behind me, I keep waiting for it to burst open as if I'd never locked it. For a maid to walk in with a tray of food and Leo's orders that I eat something.

But no one comes.

The message is clear: if I want food, I'll have to come downstairs and get it.

At some point, I hear the clunk of someone unlocking the outer door of the bedroom. I can get up, go down—if I choose to. But I sit for a while longer, unsure of how and what I'm feeling and unwilling to go downstairs and face him.

But hunger is winning this war. I'd rather face Leo than sit in here and starve.

I slip on a pair of tight blue jeans and a black cropped sweater, then comb my hair out and stare at my reflection in the mirror. My stomach still has a good amount of definition, even though I haven't been keeping up with my training or my exercises.

I was surprised to find that I actually enjoyed training in the mornings. It was a small relief from the stuffiness of Anya's house. Sometimes, it felt colder inside the castle than it did outside in the snow.

Satisfied with my appearance, I head downstairs. Before I even reach the ground floor, I hear voices. Leo's and a woman's. A flash of her blonde hair confirms who it is.

"Well, look who decided to join us for dinner," Brit remarks with a snake-like smile.

One look at her and my confidence dries up like an old husk. The woman looks like she's ten feet tall, especially in her black stiletto heels. The dress she's wearing is off-white, strapless, molded to her figure. It makes the gold in her hair pop. Gold hoops in her ears and a simple gold chain hanging around her slender neck finish the look.

"Aw," she says, making no effort to hide the condescension in her tone. "You dressed up for us. How sweet."

The table is set beautifully. But there are only two seats. Given the fact that my door was unlocked, I know I'm supposed to be down here. Which means this is just another game Leo is playing with me.

I look at him in the corner of my eye. He says nothing.

"Why don't you sit down, Willow?" she suggests, rubbing salt into the wound.

I force my face to stay neutral. "There doesn't seem to be a seat for me," I say. "So I'll just make a plate and take it up to my—"

"Nonsense," Brit says, cutting me off. "You *must* join us. Right, Leo?"

He still doesn't answer.

He's wearing jeans and a shirt that's rolled up at the sleeves. He's left the first three buttons open, revealing the sculpted perfection of his pecs. His hair looks like it's been freshly washed, drops of water still clinging to the curls.

But his eyes don't land on me.

"Where do you propose I sit?" I snap. "On the floor?"

Brit smiles. I loathe how beautiful she is.

"Take my chair." She gets up and gestures towards her empty seat. "All yours."

I know there's a catch. The moment I sit down, I realize what it is. Brit walks around the table and puts her hand on Leo's shoulder.

"Make room for me, handsome," she coos.

He doesn't move, but she doesn't seem to care; she just settles herself down on his lap. The two of them seem to look at me at the same time, waiting for me to react.

My jaw twitches, but I choose to focus on the breadbasket sitting in the center of the table.

"This is much better, isn't it?" Brit asks.

"This cabin is massive. There have got to be more chairs around somewhere."

Or a mountain she could throw herself off. Whichever.

"But I so prefer being on Leo's lap." She runs a slender finger across his jawline. "Such a handsome man."

My eyes flicker to the butter knives on the table. If I aim properly, I can blind her in one eye. Or maybe leave a scar on her flawless face. That might make this dinner a lot more interesting.

When I raise my eyes, I find that she's staring straight at me.

"Thinking of all the ways you can hurt me right now?" she asks pleasantly, wrapping an arm around Leo's neck.

"Among other things."

She laughs and rests her back against the front of his chest. He's stiff, mute. He doesn't look like he's particularly enjoying her presence on his lap. More like he's tolerating it.

So I have to believe that he's just trying to piss me off. The unfortunate part is… it's working.

The waiters bring soup and salad out, and I realize that my appetite has all but disappeared. Brit, on the other hand, looks like she's having a blast. She reaches for a grape on the cheese board and pops it into her mouth.

She chews slowly, sensually, her eyes never leaving mine. *Imagine this is Leo in my mouth*, she's saying.

The moment the thought crystallizes, I see it unfold in my mind's eye. I picture Brit getting on her knees in front of Leo. I see her unzipping his pants and pulling out his dick. I see his head tilt back as she takes him between those perfectly plump lips and sucks him off with all the confidence and power that I can never seem to muster.

I only snap out of the waking nightmare when Brit cranes her neck towards Leo and bends her lips to his ear. She whispers something to him.

There's an ease in their body language that makes me feel queasy. Maybe it's a good thing I haven't eaten since yesterday.

Leo's eyes snap to Brit's. He looks… annoyed? At least, I think he does. But that may just be wishful thinking on my part.

He says something to her. I don't catch the words, but his tone is harsh and commanding. Brit just laughs, though, and turns back to me.

"Something you probably don't know about Leo," she says. "He's funny. He just doesn't mean to be."

I bite down on my tongue and choose to stare at the cheese plate in front of me. I'm desperately craving alcohol. There's wine on the table, but I already know I'm going to need something stronger.

"Can I feed you something, Mr. Solovev?" Brit murmurs.

She doesn't wait for him to answer. Instead, she plucks a strawberry from the cheeseboard, takes a bite, and then offers the rest to Leo.

That feeling in my chest is growing. It's cold at first, but it's the kind of cold that burns, makes it harder and harder for me to breathe.

A phrase comes floating up from the recesses of my memory.

If someone is in your way, remove them. Anya's words, spoken to me in the midst of an endless training session, when my muscles burned and all I wanted was to quit.

If someone is in your way, remove them. Anya's philosophy, shown to me in every single thing she's done since the day I was born to her. I was in her way back then, so I was removed. That should have given me a new lease on life. But it didn't. It just meant that one day, she'd come back and claim me. And she's done exactly that.

If someone is in your way, remove them. Brit is in my way now, and I want her the fuck out of here. I can imagine it so perfectly. The sight of my fist, burying itself in her face. All that red blood on all that blonde hair.

"I'm not hungry," I mutter, pushing my chair back. "Excuse me."

"What's wrong, honey?" Brit asks innocently. "Something the matter?"

"*Don't* call me honey," I say, my tone dripping poison.

She smirks and glances at Leo. "It would seem your precious little wife is jealous."

Leo looks right at me, his eyes sharp and filled with fire. "No. Not possible. She can't be jealous. She'd have to care to be jealous. Isn't that right, Willow?"

This is his payback for what I said in the room this morning. For claiming I don't love him. For throwing my hatred of him in his face. This is punishment for that.

"Fuck you," I hiss. "Fuck you both."

I twist around and head towards the stairs.

"Wait."

I hate myself for stopping, but his voice sends a current straight through my body. I glance at him—at them, rather.

"My room. Not yours."

I narrow my eyes and shake my head. The moment I do, I realize my mistake. He snaps his fingers and two guards materialize out of nowhere.

They drag me up the stairs to Leo's room.

I struggle, but I don't scream. This is humiliating enough without me adding fuel to the flames. I can feel her eyes on me the entire time.

She's laughing at me.

And as she does, the thought runs through my head one more time. With all the violence and fire that my mother infused in it.

If someone is in your way…

Remove them.

16

LEO

"Get off."

With a laugh, Ariel gets off my lap and retakes the chair opposite me. She crosses her legs and reaches for the wine. "You have to admit, that was fun." She swirls the wine in the deep glass and takes a long sip, then swallows, sighs, and smacks her lips as though she's finally found the relief she was craving.

"Since when do you drink red?" I ask. "That was always his preference."

"Exactly."

"Do you even like the taste?"

She shrugs. Her smile falters for an instant before she regains control of it. "It transports me," she says quietly. "I can almost imagine kissing him if I drink enough of the stuff."

"Not sure you need any more alcohol right now."

She narrows her eyes at me. "Alcohol is the only thing that's kept me going these past eight years."

"I was hoping you'd say it was me."

The smile comes back, but it's darker now. Half-hearted. "She's kinda perfect for you, you know," Ariel observes grudgingly. "I might actually like her if she didn't look at me like she wanted to take my head off."

"Can you blame her?"

"I tortured her a little so that he wouldn't torture her a lot," she says defensively. "I had a role to play."

"You don't have to lecture me."

"That's not why she hates me. You do realize that, don't you?"

I grab a beer and take a swig. "Who knows what's going on in that head of hers? Anya's definitely fucked with her."

"It's not like you to play coy," she says pointedly. "It's charming—but out of character."

"Ariel…"

"She hates me because of what she thinks is between us. I think that's your strongest point of entry right there."

"You're underestimating how stubborn she is."

"And you're underestimating how hot you are."

"Ariel…"

"I only do it because it makes you uncomfortable," she quips. "A girl's gotta have some fun, you know?"

Her smile deepens and transforms. It becomes warmer. For a moment, I see a flash of the girl she used to be before circumstance turned her hard and cunning. Before life broke her in ways that cannot be fixed.

I head upstairs to my room. Patrik and Moritz are standing guard outside. I dismiss them with a nod and go in.

Willow is standing in front of the window, her back to me. The moment she hears the click of the door shutting, she turns around slowly. Her eyes are shining but she's not crying. She just looks… broken.

I know I'm pushing her. I know I'm not being kind.

But I never promised to be fucking kind. I can only be what I am: the man who always gets what he wants.

"Are you fucking her?"

Willow's question is direct and certain, unwavering in a way she wasn't always capable of. She wants a clear answer. An end to the torment of not knowing.

A kind man would put her out of her misery. Unfortunately for her, I'm the farthest thing from it.

"Why do you care?"

She glares and crosses her arms over her chest. She's still in her tight blue jeans and black crop top. I can see the toned abs of her stomach, and her strength is fucking sexy. She's not wearing makeup, but she doesn't need any.

It would probably only get smudged anyway.

"Cut the shit, Leo," she snaps. "What's your deal with her?"

"I already told you."

"No, you haven't. All your answers are vague and evasive. I'm missing part of this story, and I want to know what it is."

"I've told you before: everything in the Bratva has to be earned."

She rolls her eyes. She's hurt, but she's trying to project confidence. She's trying to carry herself with the same self-assurance that Anya does. That Brit does.

But I know her well enough to read past the facade.

"I know why you married me," she says. "I know why you want me here. But why am I in this room with you, Leo? Because let's face it: if you wanted me locked up, you could do that anywhere. I don't need to be in *your* room."

If she's expecting some honest, straightforward, and vulnerable answer, she's talking to the wrong person.

"You're right," I say with a nod. "You don't need to be here. This way is just more fun."

"So that's it, then?" she asks. "This is just a game to you?"

"None of it is a game, Willow. That's what I'm trying to make you understand. Our son should be here with his parents."

"You say that like I'm going to be a part of his life if you have your way."

"Why would I keep you from him?" I ask.

"Because I disagree with you about how he should be raised."

"He's Bratva, Willow. There's no escaping that fact."

She shakes her head. "I want him to be more than just Bratva."

"It's an all-encompassing life, an all-consuming world. There won't be time for anything else."

"That's exactly what I'm afraid of."

"You realize that this child is Bratva on both sides, right?" I ask. "He's a Solovev, but he's also a Mikhailov. Just because you decide something different doesn't mean everyone else will. It won't save him. It hasn't saved you."

She stares at me, and for the first time, I see understanding bloom in her eyes. "Belov will never stop coming after him, will he?"

"That's right," I agree. "He will never stop. Would you rather I have him? Or Belov?"

She takes a step forward, fear and desperation dripping from each word as she says, "Are you sure you can trust that woman?"

I suppress a sigh. "Yes."

"She knows about him. She knows I have a son."

"Brit wouldn't say a word to Belov."

"How do you know?" she growls. "How can you be *sure*?"

I move closer. We're inches from each other now. So close that I could bend down and our lips would be pressed together.

"Do you think I'm stupid, Willow? Do you think I'm a fool?"

Her eyebrows knit together. "No. But smarter men have been duped by a pretty face."

I snort with derisive laughter. "There's so much you refuse to understand."

She flinches, then straightens up to her full height and says, "You clearly care about Brit very much. How can you trust that she's not a double agent?"

"Because I do."

"Well, I don't."

"That's because you don't want to. You're letting your jealousy cloud your judgment."

Her eyes go wide with betrayal. "You don't know the first thing about what I'm feeling, Leo."

"Then why did you choose to storm out of dinner just now?"

She grapples with an excuse, but I've caught her off-guard. She's struggling to find a lie that she can half-believe enough. "I wasn't hungry."

I smirk. "Then you wouldn't have even left your room."

"You don't know me, Leo."

"Denial again? Don't make that a habit, Willow. People who live in denial never have a handle on reality. In the Bratva, that can get you killed."

"And wouldn't that make things easier for you?"

I raise my eyebrows. "Is this the part where I'm meant to reassure you that I would be lost without you if you died?"

"You're a complete fucking asshole." She stomps over to the window, staring out for a moment before she looks back at me. The moonlight streaming in turns her blue eyes silvery. Her skin glows.

With her blue eyes and dark hair, Willow is a match for Ariel any day. Problem is, she just doesn't know it.

"Brit is loyal to me," I say, doubling down on her anger. "And as you know, I value that above all else."

"I was loyal to you once, too," Willow whispers. "Then I found out that the only reason you wanted me at all is because you were using me in some macho power play."

"It was necessary."

She rolls her eyes. "You and Brit deserve each other."

"If you believe that, then why are you so affected by her presence?"

"That has nothing to do with you," she snaps. "The woman tortured me in that cell they kept me in for days."

"She was being watched. She had to—"

"Don't!" she practically screams. "Don't do that. Don't make excuses for her."

"They're not excuses if they're true."

"Do you love her?" she demands.

"Would it matter to you if I did?"

She shakes her head. "No. I told you before: I stopped loving you a long time ago."

"Then what, Willow?" I ask calmly. "What's got you so riled up? Is it the thought that I'm fucking her?"

Her eyes narrow dangerously, and I know that she's reached her limit. One more little push and she'll go tumbling right over the edge…

"Because if you need to get off, all you have to do is ask," I tell her.

Oops. How clumsy of me.

Her lips turn up in a twisted, furious smile. "If I want to get off," she says slowly, "I can handle that myself."

Then her fingers curl around the edges of her shirt and she pulls it up and over her head. The bra she's wearing underneath is red and lacy. She discards it unceremoniously. Her breasts spill out, and I admire the soft swells.

She unzips her pants and pulls them down her legs. Once they're off, she kicks them to the side. The panties she's wearing aren't modest like I'm expecting. They match her bra. Red, lacy, and just sheer enough that I can see the milkiness of her skin through the fabric. She pulls them off too and flings them onto the window seat behind her.

I stay where I am. How far is she willing to take this?

She walks to the bed and sits down on the edge of the mattress. She leans back, affording me an uninterrupted view of her tight little pussy.

Jesus...

Willow parts her legs slowly. And with her eyes trained on me, she raises her fingers to her mouth and starts sucking them off. My cock hardens to rock. I know she can see my erection straining against my pants.

She sucks her fingers, then trails them down between her breasts until she reaches her clit. A soft moan escapes her lips as she parts her legs a little wider and runs her wet fingertips up and down her slit.

I stand still. I'm entranced, completely taken up by the confidence in her gaze. The thought of watching her make herself come is too tempting to miss.

So I stand there and watch.

She plays with herself for a few moments, her eyelashes fluttering deliberately. Then she slips her fingers inside of herself.

"Ahh…"

The moan is soft, but it travels through me, giving my dick another reason to strain against my pants. She pushes two fingers inside to the knuckle.

Her breasts tremble with every movement, and I run my tongue over my lips, imagining myself sucking them while she bucks against her own hand.

She picks up speed. Her whole body trembles with it, faster and harder, until she falls back onto the soft mattress and arches her back and cries out a whimper that makes my cock throb.

She isn't a good enough actor to fake this. It's real.

As her eyes lock on mine, I realize that she isn't just getting off on the power play here. She's getting off on *me*. Her eyes never waver from mine as the orgasm rocks through her body. I'm as much a tool in her pleasure as her fingers were.

Then it's over. She rocks back and falls limp on the bed. Her breasts rise and fall with her breathing, and I resist the urge to touch them. To touch her.

Everything about that was sexy. Even her desire to make me suffer.

Maybe there's more Bratva in the little *kukolka* than anyone realized.

Including me.

When she's caught her breath, she sits up and licks the juices off her fingers. Her eyes find mine.

"See?" she says, releasing her fingers from her mouth with a pop. "I don't need you to get off."

Then she saunters over to the sofa. She slinks onto it, still naked, pulls a sheet over her body and pretends like she's no longer aware of my presence.

But this time, I know she's faking.

17

WILLOW

MONTHS AGO—ANYA'S MOUNTAIN RETREAT

"Tell me about my father."

"What do you want to know?" She has this way of looking at me where I swear she isn't blinking. Paired with the piercing blue of her irises, it's unsettling.

"What's his name?"

She looks out towards her garden, if you can even call it that. The trees are brittle and covered in snow and the pathways are naked on both sides. It makes the place feel sterile, but I feel like that was an intentional choice. It reflects the woman who made it.

"Mattias Coltrane," she says.

"Mattias," I repeat, trying to let his name sit on my tongue for a few moments. I expect to feel something. But nothing comes. "Did you love him?"

She frowns, as though she's disappointed I even asked. "Love? I was so fucking young. Who knows what I really felt? But at the time, I suppose I thought I loved him."

My hands are resting on my belly. I've gotten so big that I can barely see my feet, even though I'm lying down. I really want to be able to change position, but I doubt Anya will be of any real help. It's either wait for the nurse or fend for myself.

"Who was he?"

"He was one of your grandfather's Vors," she explains. "Although maybe calling him a Vor is overstating things a little. He didn't have the mark yet. But he was on his way to getting one. A rising star within the Bratva; that was what I heard. That's what made me pay attention."

"What happened to him?"

Her eyes snap to mine, and again, the way she looks at me is unnerving. I wish she'd just blink a little more. Maybe I just want her to because it would remind me that she is, in fact, human.

"He was murdered. By your grandfather, actually."

Again, I wait to feel something. Shouldn't the tragic story of the death of the father you never knew make you feel something?

Maybe I'm just too pregnant to feel anything at all. Maybe all I'm capable of being is tired.

Or maybe it's the way Anya says it. She delivers the fact without any sense of delicacy. No warning, no disclaimer. Just bang in my face. I stare at her for a long time, but she never offers me anything else. Not even comfort.

"Why?"

"My father had other plans for me," Anya explains. "He wanted me married off to another man. It was already arranged and I ruined things by sleeping with one of his men. My father was furious. And, if I'm being honest, that was the whole point."

"Did you know he'd kill him?"

She frowns and for the first time, I wonder if maybe there's a heart buried in there after all. "I was young and naïve enough to believe that it would be a fight that I could win. I usually won my fights, anyway. I didn't think this would be so different."

"Losing him must have been hard for you."

"I was angry for a long time. In fact, I don't think I've ever stopped being angry."

That's the first vulnerable thing she's said to me in months. It doesn't really make me feel close to her, but it does give me some hope for the future.

"Is that why you have such a bad relationship with your father?"

She shakes her head. "That happened long before Mattias, but it certainly drove in the wedge that broke our relationship. He expected me to just dust myself off and move on. Be the good Bratva princess he expected me to be."

"But you stayed with him afterwards."

"After I gave you up, I came back," she confirms.

The fact that she glosses over the part where she gave me up and just returned to her life doesn't affect me as much as I would have thought. I've come to manage expectations where Anya is concerned.

"Why?"

"Because I knew I would leave one day," she says. "And I needed resources. I needed money. I needed men. The Bratva is built on loyalty, so I needed to build a group of men who would follow me one day instead of my father. And I knew that would take time."

"But your father didn't suspect anything?"

"He was too busy trying to marry me off to a suitable man who would expand his business interests and make his Bratva stronger."

I frown. "You've been married, haven't you?" Leo told me about it, but I want to hear the story from her.

"Twice," she says. "Both to men my father picked for me."

I already know what she's about to tell me. Even though my chest tightens a little, I don't feel the horror I probably should. More than anything else, that's what alarms me. Am I already getting used to the brutality of this world? Does that mean I'm becoming a part of it?

"I killed them both as soon as I could," Anya tells me. "I don't think I made it to a year with either one."

The way she says it makes me shiver. There's pride in her voice. And even if I doubted that, the pride in her eyes is hard to ignore. "How could you have done it?"

"Well, with Oleg I drugged him first and—"

"No!" I say, horrified that she assumed that was what I meant. "I'm not asking you how you murdered your husbands. I'm asking… how could you?"

She raises her eyebrows. Pride gives way to disappointment.

"You think I should feel guilt? Remorse?"

"Either," I say. "Both."

"Why?" she asks coldly. "He probably never felt it when he killed or stole or raped. So why should I?"

"Because it's the sign of a decent human being," I snap.

Her eyes flash for a moment. Then they drop to my belly and she swallows her indignation. "This is the Bratva. None of us are decent human beings."

"I'm not Bratva."

Her eyes are cold even when she smiles. "Does that sense of superiority keep you warm at night?"

"My conscience is clear."

"You'll raise a son who will command a Bratva, kill men, hurt women, commit God knows what other unspeakable sins. Enjoy that clear conscience while it lasts, daughter."

I stare at her in disbelief, wondering how I came from this woman. But it makes things clearer for me. It makes my choices easier.

I have to get out.

Present Day

My eyes dart open, scared awake by a nightmare… or a memory. It's hard to keep track of which is which anymore.

Light sneaks through the half-open blinds. In the distance, fog rolls between the mountain peaks.

I glance to the bed. The top half of Leo's body is exposed, the sheet wrapped around his waist. The dawn light catches his muscles in all the right places. He looks like a sculpture. A masterpiece.

I could walk over there and kill him while he sleeps. I could… but I won't.

Not simply because I'm starting to believe it would be impossible to go through with it. But also because, underneath all the bitterness and anger, I know I couldn't take a life. Much less *his* life.

He rolls onto his back, and my heart rate picks up. My body's reaction to him is maddening. Even now, I imagine walking over to him, letting him pin me to the bed. Writhing in delicious agony as he steals another little piece of my soul.

But I can't afford to lose any more of me. I need to be strong.

For my son.

For myself.

I twist on the sofa and turn my back on him, then shut my eyes and try to find solace in the unreal.

～

When I wake again, several hours have passed. The bed is empty and Leo is gone. A breakfast tray waits for me by the window seat. I didn't even notice the maid come and go.

I eat and then spend the morning doing push-ups, pull-ups, crunches, and burpees. I do whatever I can to stay fit, but also burn off the agitation that tickles under my skin.

I find myself looking forward to dinner, to the simple act of leaving this room behind and walking downstairs. I try to tell myself it has nothing to do with Leo, but I'm past the point of lying to myself.

As soon as my door is unlocked, I get dressed. I opt for ripped jeans and a white sweater. Nothing sexy this time. I'm done participating in the games.

I head for the dining room, but I stop short when I notice that there's only one person sitting at the table tonight. Just my luck.

She's dressed in dark trousers and a cashmere halter in powder blue. Her blonde hair has been piled in a messy bun at the top of her head. As usual, she looks stunning.

"Where's Leo?"

She smiles without looking at me. "Working. You'll have to make do with me tonight."

"Are you supposed to be my babysitter?"

She shrugs. "I'm just hungry."

I hesitate, but I'm not backing down in front of her. I walk carefully around the table and sink into the open seat.

"Wine?" she asks, raising the bottle.

"No."

"Really? It's excellent."

"I'm not much of a drinker."

"Right," she says, with a nod. "I get that."

"What exactly do you get?"

"Well, you saw your husband act like a drunk fool all the time," she says. "That must have turned you off of the stuff."

I glare at her. "First of all, he's my ex-husband. And secondly, I'll thank you not to make assumptions about me or my life. Just because you know a few random facts about me doesn't mean you know *me*."

"Oh dear. Touched a nerve, have I?"

She knows damn well she has, but she's getting off on goading me. Another thing that she and Leo have in common. They really are made for each other.

"We may be having dinner together, but that doesn't mean we have to talk."

"I don't do well with silence," she says.

"Why is that?"

She looks up at me. "It's easier to hear the voices in my head when it's quiet."

I raise my eyebrows. For the first time, she isn't smiling. Isn't smirking or putting on a show. I think she's serious.

But I don't care.

"Well, I have nothing to say to you."

"Are you sure?" Brit asks. "Because the look on your face tells me you have a few things you'd like to get off your chest."

"I'm fine. This isn't a therapy session."

She laughs. "Pity. I would've made a great therapist."

"I think you've got that backwards. You're the ideal patient."

"We've all got our issues."

I shake my head. "No. No. We're not doing this."

"Doing what?"

"Having a conversation like we're… like we're friends or something."

"Trust me, darling: I'm under no illusions about what we are."

"Great. Then silence it is."

I grab a piece of bread and bite into it savagely, tearing it the way I wish I could tear into her. But it melts on my tongue, and I can't help but give a little sigh of relief. I didn't realize how hungry I was.

I help myself to some pasta from the bowl in the center of the table. Brit already has some on her plate, but she's barely touched anything.

If things were different, I might have asked her why she isn't eating. As it stands, I don't care if she starves to death right in front of me.

A door opens and closes in the kitchen, and I instinctively turn towards it, expecting Leo.

But it's just a server refreshing our waters.

"I told you he's not going to be coming for dinner," Brit tells me with a spark in her eye. "He's got important things that require his… undivided attention."

"I don't give a shit what he does." I stab my pasta with unnecessary force.

She gives a snort, and I drop the fork before I get the urge to stab her in the eye next.

"I *don't* care what Leo does," I repeat.

Brit leans in, her blue eyes brighter in the light from the chandelier above us. "Honey, you may be able to get away with those half-assed lies in the outside world. But not here. Not with me."

"I think you're projecting, *honey*," I say, trying to muster up the same level of condescension she seems to be able to manufacture so effortlessly.

"I never project. I've always been good at feeling my own feelings. And I'm an expert at reading other people's."

"If you know how I feel, then you know exactly how I feel about you."

"I do," she answers immediately. "And even though I understand, your feelings towards me are misplaced."

"Misplaced?"

She nods. "This is the Bratva, Willow. If you want Leo, you need to take him. Regardless of who's in your way."

There are so many things I want to counter in that one sentence that I don't know where to begin. "I don't—that's… Jesus!"

I run a hand through my hair, trying to get my thoughts in order and my outrage in check.

"I don't want Leo," I snap at last. "And if you're implying that I'm jealous of you because of that then… then… well, then fuck you."

She raises her eyebrows. "So you're saying you don't care about Leo? You have no feelings for him whatsoever?"

"None," I say, proud of the way the word snaps out of my mouth with conviction.

She pushes her chair back and gets slowly to her feet. "Then I guess you wouldn't care if I head into his office right now and fuck his brains out?" she asks.

My heart jumps into my throat at once. Why didn't I just stay silent? There was no danger in silence.

She nods. "Brava to you, then. I'll be back." She sashays away, through a door I didn't notice, and disappears.

I sit there, staring off after her, wondering what the fuck I've done. If I follow her now, it'll only prove her point. It'll confirm everything she's just accused me of.

But if I go back up to my room like I should, I'll just imagine it happening. I'll imagine her stripping naked, climbing on top of him...

I get to my feet and stare at the threshold she just walked through.

"Fuck," I mutter out loud. "Fuck!"

"Something wrong, ma'am?"

My head snaps to the side as one of the waiters enters from the kitchen. He's looking at me, waiting for some sort of request or order. He's not the waiter who walked in on me naked. I haven't seen that man since that night. And I'm pretty sure I know why.

"Ma'am?" he asks. "Is something wrong?"

"Yes," I say with a grimace. "Everything."

18

LEO

I look up from my files and see Ariel closing the door behind her.

"I'm working, Ariel."

She walks around my desk and stands in front of me. A seductive smile tugs on her lips. "A handsome man like you shouldn't need to slave away so often."

She pushes my legs apart with her knee and climbs onto my lap. She's playing one of her games; I just don't have the patience for it tonight.

"Get off me," I grunt. "I've got shit to do."

She leans in, voice low. "This'll be worth it. Just hang in there."

"You're supposed to be getting information out of Willow."

"I got something better."

"What?"

"Proof of her feelings for you."

"Jesus Christ." I roll my eyes. "Get the fuck out of here, Ariel."

She pouts, but refuses to budge.

Instead, she wraps her hands around my neck and grips me tightly. "The easiest way to make her cooperate with you is by forcing her to accept her feelings for you. I'm just helping to speed that process along."

"You realize she's not in here, right?" I ask impatiently.

"No," she purrs, a glint in her eye. "But she will be."

She's getting off on the high of playing puppet master. A trait that Belov has obviously encouraged over the years.

It's a trait I'm going to have to rein in if she persists.

"I don't have time for—"

The sound of incoming footsteps cuts me off.

Ariel fixes me with an 'I told you so' look and leans in. Her lips are almost touching mine. "Come on," she wheedles. "Play along with—"

My door flies open.

Willow is standing on the threshold looking furious. She's dressed simply tonight in jeans and a white sweater. It's the look that suits her best.

Her eyes narrow in on Ariel straddling me. I wait, wondering what she's going to do next. But she just stands there, watching the two of us like she's waiting for something to happen.

"Um, something wrong, Willow?" Ariel asks pointedly. "Because if there's nothing, we were kinda in the middle of something."

Willow's jaw twitches dangerously. Her eyes spark with fire. But nothing escapes her lips. Not even an insult or a curse. Ariel turns to me and shrugs.

"Guess she wants to watch."

She leans in and starts kissing my neck. I feel nothing at all. The sensation is pleasant, but there's no desire. I'm just detached.

And then, suddenly, Ariel is yanked off me with a scream.

Willow has Ariel by the hair for a moment before she drops her to the floor. Her eyes rise slowly to mine. I wait for the eruption that will inevitably follow.

But she does nothing.

Her gaze flits from me to Ariel and back again. Then she turns around and runs out of the room. The door slams shut. Silence takes over once again.

Down on the floor, Ariel has a hand on the back of her head. She's wincing. "I wasn't sure she had it in her. But at least you have your answer."

I don't even spare her a glance as I walk around her and follow Willow out of my office.

"You're welcome!" Ariel calls after me as I go.

In the living room, I realize the front door is open. I stride over and see Willow arguing with two of the guards stationed outside. They've clearly blocked her path.

"… Fuck you! Let me pass," she's growling. "I'm not trying to escape, you dipshits. I just want some air. Let me fucking pass!"

One of the guards catches my eye. I give him a small nod, and just like that, the two of them part, allowing her to move past them. She goes silent for a moment, but doesn't question their change of heart.

Maybe that's because she's already aware of my presence.

If so, she doesn't show it. She doesn't so much as glance backward before she plunges into the dark forest.

I follow behind her at a leisurely pace. I know that Jax and Gaiman are down below, ready to intercept if I lose sight of her. For now, I keep my eyes on her silhouette flitting between the snow-cloaked tree trunks.

She keeps a steady pace on her way down, but she veers right suddenly, walking away from the path.

"I wouldn't if I were you," I call after her.

She doesn't turn around or slow down. "Stop following me."

"Can't do that. It would be a shame to have you die of frostbite after all the effort I've expended."

"Oh, right," she yells. "You're not done using me yet, am I right? Still need me for something else?"

"Your son is the one that needs you."

We play this game of follow-the-leader for several more minutes before her pace finally starts to slow. When I catch up to her, we're surrounded by a thick wall of trees now, all of which have been stripped of their leaves and their life.

"You done with your tantrum yet?" I ask her.

She whips around. "Why are you following me?"

"Among other things, I'm trying to make sure you don't get eaten by a bear," I tell her.

She freezes. "There are bears out here?"

I nod. "Wolves, too. Which is why all this stomping around isn't exactly a good thing."

"Fuck." She eyes the surrounding forest suspiciously.

"You lived in these mountains for almost a year," I tell her. "You weren't told there were wild animals roaming the forest?"

"I didn't get out much."

She tries to pull away and resume her wandering, but I grab her by the elbow. "You're going to be dead on your feet soon."

Eyes flashing, she shoves at my chest hard enough to break my grip on her. "Get out of my—"

The effect is lost when she stumbles back and lands ass-first in the snow.

I give her a moment, then squat down so I can look her in the eyes. "Satisfied now?" I ask. "This is no time for a night stroll. It's below zero and you don't even have a jacket on."

She sets her jaw. "Just leave me here."

"So you can freeze to death?"

"That actually sounds pretty damn good from where I'm sitting."

A shiver runs through her body. Her lips are starting to look a little blue. I've had enough.

"Come on. It's time to get back to the cabin."

"No."

I glare at her for a moment. Then, seeing she is set on not budging, I grab her arm, yank her up, and fling her over my shoulder. She gives a little cry of protest, but she goes limp against my body just a few steps into the return journey.

I'm guessing she's more relieved than she's willing to admit.

The walk back to the cabin feels twice as long, but I never slow or waver. The guards hold open the door as I approach and enter without breaking stride.

Willow doesn't say a word as I carry her upstairs and into my room. I bypass the bed and head straight for the bathroom. There, I set her down on the edge of the tub and start running warm bathwater.

Steam rises from the tub. Willow watches it like it's a smoke signal. Like she's trying to decipher a message.

"Remove your clothes," I tell her.

She raises her eyes. "I'm not removing anything for you."

"Don't flatter yourself. You need to get warm."

"Then leave so I can get warm without you."

"You're so stubborn you'd sit here and shiver to death before you'd get in a bath I ran for you."

Her eyes narrow. "I should slap you."

"That would be hard to do with no circulation in your fingers."

She glances down at her hands. They're white and stiff. "Still not stripping," she says.

"Fine."

I grab her sweater and pull it none too gently over her head. She struggles, but the effort is weak. She underestimated how much energy it takes to tromp through knee-high snow in Arctic temperatures.

I move to her jeans next.

"Leo… stop," she says quietly.

"We can do this the easy way or the hard way, Willow," I warn her. "Which is it going to be?"

She tangles her fingers with mine, but they're freezing cold and her attempts are half-hearted at best, so when she sees it's an unwinnable fight, she sighs and lets her hands drop by her sides.

Satisfied, I stand her up and pull her pants and underwear down. She steps out of them without a fuss. Her eyes are swimming with unreadable emotion.

"Get in," I instruct. "Or do you want me to do that for you, too?"

She shakes her head, leans over to check the temperature, and lets out a hiss that quickly cools into an audible sigh. She steps into it and sinks below the surface.

She steps in and slowly slips into the water up to her neck. A second later, a deep and content sigh rings from her body as her fingers thread the water.

"Better?" I ask, joining her at the edge of the tub.

"This doesn't make you a hero."

I laugh. "The ship sailed on that a long time ago." I pause, then ask, "Why did you run out there tonight?"

She freezes and her fingers disappear beneath the water. "Because I needed space. Don't flatter yourself: my reaction had nothing to do with you."

"Then what did it have to do with?"

"Her," she snaps. "She just knows how to push my buttons."

"Apparently, I'm your button."

Her eyes snap to my face. She opens her mouth, but then decides against whatever it is she was about to say. Instead, she takes a deep breath and submerges her entire body under the water.

She stays down for nearly twenty seconds. Long enough that I start to wonder if she intends on staying submerged forever.

But when she comes up again, she doesn't look any more relaxed.

"She's not who you think she is, Willow," I say, once she's wiped the water out of her eyes.

"What's the story now?" Willow scoffs. "Is she some undercover superhero? She's saved the world a million times, but she protects her real identity by being a first-class bitch?"

I almost smile. "I told you she was family."

"Yeah, yeah… because the Bratva is a family. Spare me."

"You're not listening," I say. "She's *family*. She's my sister-in-law."

19

WILLOW

"Your brother's wife?" I ask.

He nods. "Well, technically, they never made it down the aisle. Pavel was killed before that happened. But they were engaged."

I stare at him, but all I can see is Brit.

Wait.

"Brit's not her name, is it?"

Leo chuckles. "No."

"You told me her name a while ago," I say. It doesn't take long to remember the moment. "The boat. You said it belonged to your brother and he named it for the love of his life."

He nods.

"*Ariel*," I whisper softly.

I think about Brit. I see her long supermodel legs, her blonde hair, her porcelain skin. She's not Brit at all. Her name is Ariel and she loved Leo's brother once upon a time.

I let that sink in. To Leo's credit, he stays quiet. The silence gets heavier and heavier as I absorb the truth of what her identity truly means.

"Spartak Belov killed your brother," I point out.

"Yes, he did."

I shake my head, unable or unwilling to fully comprehend just yet. "She… she's with him now. Stuck with Belov. *Belov.*"

"She's with him because she has to be," he tells me. "For now. It was a necessary part of our plan."

I frown. "She's had to fuck the man that murdered the love of her life for the last eight years?"

"Not quite eight years," Leo tells me. "But yes, that is part of what she's been doing."

"That's… that's insane."

"No. That's Ariel. I told you, she's one of the strongest women I've ever known in my life."

The jealousy is still there, but it's fading. Morphing to fit this new understanding.

"But… how? How could she be with a man who did *that*?"

"That's a question you'll have to ask her. But I think it has something to do with purpose."

"Purpose?" I repeat dumbly.

"Losing Pavel nearly broke her," he explains. "She became a shell of the person she was. There was a moment there when we thought we were going to lose her."

He doesn't elaborate on what he means, and I don't ask. I still feel like I'm running to keep up with this insane revelation.

"I set up a plan to get back at Belov. I wanted to destroy the Mikhailovs and avenge Pavel's death and the deaths of his Vors. Then Ariel made a suggestion. It took years of preparation and training," Leo says. "It took strength beyond anything I've ever seen. But she was determined. Right from the start, her only goal was avenging Pavel's death. She lived for nothing else. It's what gave her the strength to keep going."

I look down at the way the bathwater ripples with my every movement. "Well, fuck," I breathe. "How am I supposed to hate her now?"

He smiles. "You're stubborn. I'm sure you'll find a way."

I sink into the water, head whirling. Above me, Leo looks out of the window to the craggy mountains beyond. His expression goes distant with old memory.

"You have no idea how powerful the Mikhailovs were at the time," he murmurs, almost to himself more than to me. "Pavel didn't believe in finding trouble where there was none. He was okay with dividing up territory so long as Semyon and Spartak respected the boundaries. He was young. Naive, maybe."

"What about you?"

"What about me?"

I raise my eyebrows. "Where were you during all this? Weren't you his right-hand man?"

His eyes turn inward, cloudy with regret. "I was not interested in the responsibility of running the Bratva. Besides, Pavel had his own men. Petyr and Logan. The two of them were—"

"His Jax and Gaiman?" I offer.

His lips twitch. "More or less. The three of them grew up together. They were a team. I didn't think it was necessary for me to be involved in the inner workings of the Solovev Bratva. It was enough for me to follow orders."

I almost smile. "I can't imagine you following anyone."

"I was different back then," Leo tells me. "And he was my brother. I would have followed him into hell."

He doesn't look sad—not outwardly, at least—but it's not hard to sense the chasm of grief that lives at the core of him to this day. Enough to spend ten years fighting a war from the shadows.

The silence grows wary, filled with ghosts that I'm still too unfamiliar with to truly mourn. But I do feel empathy. For Leo. For Pavel. For Brit—or rather, Ariel.

"Were you close?" I ask abruptly, breaking the heavy quiet.

"Close with whom?"

"Her. Ariel."

"Not particularly," he says with a shrug. "But we grew closer after Pavel's death. She was the only one who felt his loss as keenly as I did. Maybe more so."

"You told me she disappeared. That she moved on."

"I said she did what she could to survive," he corrects. "And she did. She became a weapon."

"How does she separate it in her head?" I ask. "The woman she really is from the woman she pretends to be?"

It's a question I've been grappling with for a long time, too. Since the moment I learned my real name, my real identity. Who knew I would find myself sympathizing with the woman who had made my life hell?

"That's a question you'd have to ask her," Leo says. "There are many things you might understand better if you bothered to listen."

Rage and jealousy I've been holding onto for so long ebbs away with the water lapping gently against me. In its place is a tender sadness. I want to summon up that anger again—God knows it's the only thing that's been driving me forward for a long time now—but I can't. It's gone down the drain.

Even when I look at Leo, I can't manage to hate him.

"Come on," he says quietly. "Get out of there before you go pruny."

I lift my fingers out of the water. "Too late."

But I get to my feet regardless. He brings a thick, white towel over and holds it out for me to step into. I stand there suspiciously for a moment, waiting for the other shoe to drop. It always does with him.

Not this time, though. He just tucks it around me and gently caresses me through the fabric to whisk the water away.

Then he sighs, turns, and leaves me standing on the bathmat, wondering what else I don't yet know.

I follow him into the room. He's seated on the edge of the bed, taking off his shoes and unbuckling his pants. There's still a noticeable bulge beneath his boxer shorts that I can't take my eyes off of.

"My eyes are up here," he jokes.

I blush. "I wasn't staring."

"Liar, liar," he says. He shimmies out of his pants, gets under the duvet, and closes his eyes. "Turn off the lights when you're going to sleep. I'm exhausted."

"The mighty Leo Solovev is admitting to being tired?"

He cracks open one eye to glare at me teasingly. "I had to lug around a hundred and fifty pound woman at least two miles because she thought she could out-stubborn the cold. Do you know anything about that?"

"Hm. Nope. Doesn't sound familiar."

He smiles, lets his eyes close again, and settles against the pillows. I watch him. The bed looks appealing. The man beneath the covers looks appealing, too.

But climbing in with him would be admitting… something. Defeat, maybe?

"What's wrong?" he asks.

"Nothing."

"If you want to get into bed, you can," he offers.

I stand in place, gnawing at my lip and debating. In the end, there's no point denying it's what I want. Groaning, I walk around the bed and exchange my towel for one of the oversized t-shirts in the wardrobe.

Leo chuckles lightly beside me as I get into the bed. I grab a pillow immediately and smack him with it. That doesn't exactly stop the chuckling, but it gives me some small amount of satisfaction.

I lie back against the soft mattress and before I can stop myself, a contented moan slips between my lips. I bite it off as soon as I can, but when I look towards Leo, he's watching me.

"Are you trying to tell me something?"

"No," I retort. "I just… it's been a while since I slept on an actual bed. The couch isn't very comfortable."

"And whose fault is that?"

"Shut up."

He flips onto his back, looking up at the ceiling, so I take the opportunity to admire him. Everything about him is perfectly proportioned.

"Okay," I say softly. "I'll admit it."

"Admit what?"

Tonight, something has shifted between us. His revelation about Ariel has softened something inside me. It's made me remember what we could have been if we'd stayed in our little bubble.

Maybe I'll regret opening up to him in the morning. Maybe I'll regret it in five minutes.

But I do know that some secrets can turn to poison if you hold on to them for too long.

So I take a deep breath, and I let it out. He already knows, but it's hard to say all the same.

"I was jealous."

20

LEO

"You don't say," I drawl sarcastically. "You? Jealous? I don't believe it."

"Shut up," she grumbles again. "This is… hard for me."

Willow won't meet my eye. Her cheeks are flaming scarlet and her fingers twist and churn in her lap.

I twist onto my side and support myself on my elbow so that I can look down at her. "Well, you were a convincing liar."

"Really?"

"No," I say with a snort of laughter.

She's annoyed enough that she shoots me a glare and I catch her eyes. She looks away almost immediately, her body tense once again.

"What was your childhood like?" she asks suddenly.

It's an obvious ploy to change the topic, but I decide to humor her. "It was very different than yours."

"Yeah, thanks for that," she says, rolling my eyes. "I can see it all so clearly now."

"It's not something you want to see. There's no childhood when it comes to the Bratva, Willow."

She sighs. "That's what I'm afraid of."

She's only inches from me. The covers puddle around her waist. I can see the peaks of her breasts. Her nipples poke through the fabric.

I reach out on instinct and run my fingers over them. She shudders at my feather light touch but doesn't move.

"You're focused on the wrong thing," I tell her. "True, I didn't have a childhood. But now, I have everything."

"And you think it was a worthy trade?"

"I was prepared for my life," I explain. "I was ready. And when shit blows up in my face, I know how to handle it."

"Unlike me."

I shrug. "You weren't prepared."

"I doubt it would have made a difference," she says, sounding mildly disappointed. "I'm not like you, Leo. I'm not like Ariel, either, for that matter."

"Ariel wasn't always the weapon she is today, you know."

"Is that supposed to be inspiring? Is that supposed to encourage me to keep going?"

"No. Fear of death should be encouragement enough."

She shoots me an annoyed look. "Is this your way of comforting me? Because it's not working."

I smile sadly. "I hate to break it to you, but I'm not the comforting type. You'll get hard truths from me and nothing else."

She pops up on her elbow and turns to face me. It's the first time in a while she doesn't seem skittish in my presence. Her eyes graze over my body and then they dip down for a moment.

"That's the only hard thing I'll get from you, huh?" she asks cheekily.

As if in answer, my erection pushes against the sheet.

Her eyes widen. When they work their way slowly up my body back to mine, I know what she wants.

No more pretending. No more fighting.

I push the sheet off her and slide her t-shirt up over her hips. When I reach her panties, her legs part instinctively. I push my fingers inside the fabric and find her slit.

I knew she was turned on, but I didn't expect her to be as wet as she is. My fingers slide around in her juices, making it easier for me to touch her, play with her lips, and coax her open.

She sinks into the pillow, and I slide on top of her. I want to see her face as I touch her. It's been too long. I can't remember the last time I touched her like this—like we had all the time in the world. Like our enemies would wait.

When I sink two fingers into her, she shudders. Her eyes close, and her legs open even wider.

"Kiss me," she whispers.

I lean in and press my lips to her neck first. I kiss a line up her throat and around her jaw. When I finally reach her lips, she clings to my face and holds me there.

I slide my tongue into her mouth, exploring her while my thumb rubs her clit. She breaks the kiss and moans into my mouth when I find the perfect spot. Her body is practically humming, the orgasm revving up already.

When she's right on the edge of coming, I pull back. "Not like that," I say to her shocked expression. "You're only going to come with my cock inside you."

I strip off my boxers as she wriggles out of her panties and shirt. When we're both naked, she reaches for me and wraps her hand around the base of my dick.

"This is going to be a long fucking night," I warn her.

Her answer is to lean forward and slide her tongue from my balls all the way up to the head of my cock.

I tip my head back and breathe deeply, giving myself over to the moment. Willow starts at the head, taking me in shallow thrusts before she swallows me whole. I curl my fingers in her hair and press her against me. Until I feel my cock hit the back of her throat.

I pull out to allow her a moment's breath and then I guide myself in again. I'm warming her up, easing her into it. Once she's ready, I gather her hair into one hand and start fucking her pretty little mouth.

She's got one hand on my hip, but the other one is working between her legs.

When I pull out, she collapses on the bed. She's breathing hard, her chest rising and falling wildly. But her eyes never leave mine.

Finally, she's admitting what she wants. I'm not going to let her get off easy.

I crawl over her and take her nipple in my mouth. She throws her arms over her head and arches her back, giving herself to me.

But it isn't enough.

I need *all* of her.

I press a knee to knock her thighs apart, then line up and bury myself inside of her. Her heels lock around my back as I sink all the way into her until our hips are flush.

"Yes," she gasps.

I pull out just far enough to slam into her again. Her body shakes with the force of it.

We're both already teetering on the edge, desperate for release. The road has been paved, so all that's left is to drive into her and hold on for the ride.

I roll my thumbs over her nipples and nibble at the soft flesh of her breasts as she writhes beneath me, begging to come.

Then her moans turn to screams as her body clenches around my cock. And not a minute too soon, because I empty inside her seconds later.

We roll to opposite sides of the bed, both spent and exhausted. Drops of perspiration cling to her chest. It's impossible to know if it's hers or mine. I lean in and kiss them away anyway.

She strums her fingers through my hair lazily.

When I'm done, I lie back, knowing I'm going to sleep well tonight. At least as well as it's possible for me to sleep.

"Pasha." She says it so softly I almost don't hear her.

"Huh?"

"His name. Our son's name," she offers awkwardly. "It's Pasha."

I turn to her but don't say anything. Pasha is a Russian derivative of Pavel. Which means…

"I named him after your brother," she confirms. "Pasha Leonardo Solovev."

"Leonardo?" I repeat.

A faint blush creeps up her cheeks. "After you."

I nod. The tightness in my chest is strange and inexplicable. I don't know what to call it or what to do with it. But it's not a bad feeling. Not entirely, at least.

Willow takes a deep breath as though a load has been lifted off her mind. But I sense a new worry clinging to her. Or maybe it's not new at all. Maybe it's always been there, hiding behind bravado.

"It feels nice to say his name out loud," she whispers. "I've avoided it for so long."

"Why?"

"Because it hurts to say. It hurts to be separated from him."

"You know you have the power to change that, right?" I remind her.

She looks me in the eye. "I'm scared."

"Of me?"

"Of this life. Of what it will do to him."

"This life will find him either way," I tell her. "The same way it found you. And you weren't prepared. Do you want the same for Pasha?"

She sighs. "Stop talking sense—it's confusing me."

I relent. This battle between us will not be solved tonight. She still needs time to accept. To understand.

"What does he look like?" I ask instead.

She smiles. It's the first genuine smile I've seen on her in weeks. Maybe the first one I've seen since I met her in that club almost two years ago.

"He looks like you, Leo," she says softly. "Just like you."

I chuckle. "I bet that pissed you off."

"You would think so, but no. It comforted me, actually. I felt like I had a part of you with me."

She goes quiet. She's said more than she wanted to. Revealed more than she should have.

But it just confirms it: tonight was progress, far more than I expected. In time, she'll write that letter to Anya just like I want her to. This will resolve and then we can decide what comes next.

"Leo," she says softly.

"Hmm?"

"My parents, are they—are they alright?"

I look at her and nod. "As far as Belov is concerned, they're dead. Ariel's orders were to kill them and wait for you. But she faked their deaths and transferred them to me."

"So they know?"

"I told them only what they needed to know," I admit. "And yes, that includes your true identity."

"How did they react?"

"Like any parents would. They were scared. But I assured them that I would find you. That I'd get you back."

"Where are they now?" she asks with wide eyes.

"I've set them up in an apartment by the city. In time, I'll move them to a house of their choosing. They're not apartment people."

She smiles. "You noticed?"

"They've never complained about anything, but a couple of visits and I could tell."

She sits up a little and looks at me with an awed expression.

"What?" I ask.

"You… you visit them?"

"When I can spare the time."

Her expression softens. "That… I… I don't know what to say."

"You don't have to say anything," I say.

She twists around and straddles me. Her hands rest on my chest as she leans in. "Thank you, Leo," she says, pressing a kiss to my cheek.

The motion brings her ass into contact with my cock, which is starting to come back to life. "Careful now," I warn her, gesturing down.

"You promised me a long night, didn't you?" She rolls her hips again playfully, a light dancing in her eyes.

I slap her ass and roll her over, pressing my length against her thigh.

"I did," I growl. "And I always keep my promises."

21

WILLOW

I wake up before Leo. I stretch out, relishing in the soreness. It's a reminder of every beautiful thing we did last night.

The sex is the easy part. Always has been. It's everything else between us that makes me want to scream or cry or both.

Sighing, I swing my legs off the side of the bed and pad into the bathroom. I fill the tub with hot water, already aching to slip beneath the steaming surface. I'm leaning over to check the temperature when hands come down around my hips.

"Jesus!" I gasp. "I didn't even hear you come in."

I try to turn, but Leo grips me tight and forces me to stay where I am, my back pressed against his chest. It takes me only a second to register that he's hard. His erection is pressed between my ass cheeks.

"After last night, that thing still works?"

"No rest for the weary." His voice is raspy from sleep.

"Leo, I can barely walk straight this morning."

I don't need to see his face to know he's smiling. Cocky bastard.

"A little more won't hurt," he murmurs. He smooths his fingers up the back of my neck and pushes me forward so my stomach hits the edge of the bathtub.

"I beg to diff—"

But the words die on my lips when he presses the head of his dick against my pussy. Already, my muscles are protesting. I need to stretch and hydrate and eat something.

Yet… heat pools low in my stomach with every touch.

"If you really can't take it, I'll stop," he promises. But that's a lie and he knows it. My body wouldn't let him stop if the world were ending.

"Just get it over with," I snap as bitterly as I can, even though I don't mean a word of it.

He slaps my ass so hard that I cry out. Heat blooms across my backside, but the sting is countered by Leo's teasing.

He pushes his cock into me just a little and then pulls out. He does this again and again, until my legs shake with anticipation.

Then suddenly, the warm press of his body is gone. I'm about to glance over my shoulder to see what's happening when I feel his tongue on my pussy.

"F-fuck!" I splutter. He starts eating me out, moving with slow and gentle determination.

Water is still running in the bath, and the room is filling with steam, but all I can concentrate on is not collapsing beneath the onslaught of Leo's tongue. My knees are going wobbly.

When my juices start dripping down my thighs, he stands up and fills me with one hard thrust. I cry out.

How could I have thought for even a second I'd had enough of this? Enough of him? How could I ever go back to a life without it?

He moves in slow thrusts at first, but I'm greedy for the animalistic way he took me last night.

"Harder, Leo," I breathe. "Harder…"

"Say my name again, baby," he growls, increasing the pace of his thrusts.

"Leo," I breathe. "Leo, Leo, Leo."

He fucks me right into yet another orgasm. I've lost count at this point, but we've long since crossed into double figures. I'm still coming down when he slides out of me.

"Turn around," he growls.

I drop to my knees in front of him. He pumps his cock three times and then bathes my chest with his seed. There's a lot of it for a man who came multiple times last night.

When he finishes, I sit back on my heels and stare up at him, exhausted and amazed.

"Now, get in the tub," he orders again. "You're going to need to soak a while before you feel human again."

I frown. "You're not getting in with me?"

He shakes his head. "I've got work to do. A quick shower is all I need."

I watch him get into the shower, still too weak to get up just yet. He's halfway done by the time I manage to peel myself off the floor and climb into the bath.

But the moment the water hits my body, I moan. "Oh God, this feels good."

Leo steps out of the shower and grabs his towel. I openly stare at his body while I sink below the surface of the water. His muscles are as craggy and hard as the mountains outside the window. Peaks and valleys, with veins winding through everywhere I look.

"You keep staring at me like that, and I'm going to come over there and fuck you so hard you won't be able to walk for a week."

"For *another* week, you mean. I'm already down for the count."

"I have a feeling you'll be hungry for more in no time. God knows I am."

"I'm surprised you have anything left."

"Always, *kukolka*," he says with a wink. "Oh, by the way—you have freedom of the house. Don't waste it."

He presses a kiss to the top of my head and disappears into the bedroom.

I close my eyes and soak away my soreness. When I emerge from the tub almost forty minutes later, the water is cooling to room temperature and I feel invigorated.

I dress quickly and head downstairs just because I can. I haven't been able to explore the cabin like I want to.

The interior is a combination of modern and rustic. I end up in a sitting room at the back of the cabin with huge paned windows that overlook the mountain vista. Floor-to-ceiling bookshelves flank the view on either side.

I approach the window and admire the view. The sun is rising over the mountains in the east and drenching them in pure golden light. It's the first time I've had the time or energy to really take it all in. I've been a little preoccupied grappling with an identity crisis, the reappearance of the mother who gave me up as a newborn, nearly miscarrying my son, and then fending off—well, failing at fending off, to be more accurate—the man who swore to track me to the ends of the earth. Gazing at the scenery hasn't been high on my priority list.

"Nice, isn't it?"

I whirl around and find Ariel sitting in one of the armchairs by the window. The furniture is so deep and cozy that she is almost hidden from view. I stare at her, trying to decide how I should feel. What I should say.

"I like to read in here," she says by way of explanation, snapping a book shut.

I glance at the title. *Anna Karenina.*

"Have you read it?" she asks.

"No."

"It's a classic."

"I'm aware." It's hard not to be short with her. It's all I've known.

"Anyway," she says, putting the book on the table beside the armchair. "I was just on my way out—"

"Leo told me everything," I say quickly.

She leans back into the armchair and nods slowly, like she'd always known this day was coming. "Did he now?"

I take a deep breath and sit down in the chair opposite hers. I look at her, and I can't make heads or tails of what is her mask and what is *her*.

"Do you still hate me?" she asks.

"A little."

She laughs. "I don't blame you. I bet you still have a few souvenirs of our time together."

"You don't sound particularly remorseful."

"Oh, honey," she says. "If I felt remorse for every bad thing I've done, I'd never get out of bed in the morning."

"Why even do it then?" I ask, blurting out the same question I'd asked Leo last night.

Her wry smile dims. "I didn't really have a choice."

"You could have chosen to leave. Go someplace new, meet someone new. Live a life away from all this."

She cocks her head to the side. "That would have involved loving Pavel a lot less than I did. Less than I still do."

"Moving on doesn't mean you don't still love him," I say. "He would want you to find someone—"

"There will never be anyone else for me. Ever," she says with finality. "The best I can hope for is to make it right."

"But how do you…"

"What?" she asks patiently.

"How do you stay sane?" I finish quietly.

"Sanity is a fickle thing. Honestly, during that first year with Belov, I wasn't sure I could do it," she admits. "I had to play this character. A femme fatale—no conscience, no remorse. I had to seduce the man who'd murdered my fiancé while I was still in the depths of grieving. The first time he touched me, I had to physically stop myself from crushing his throat."

This is the first real conversation we've ever had. I feel like I'm speaking to the real person beneath all the beauty and bravado. Not some distorted, nightmare version of her that's meant to intimidate and terrify.

"The first time he took me to bed, it felt like a small piece of my soul was breaking off, splintering away from the rest of me."

"And yet you've done this for years now."

"Yes… because it is the only way," she says. "I want more than justice for Pavel. I want revenge. I want that fucking bastard to suffer before he dies."

I nod, drinking it all in but not sure how to process it just yet. "Can I ask you a personal question?"

"You've asked me a few already," she points out. Then she sighs and gestures. "Go on, out with it."

"You've probably been alone with him countless times over the years, right?"

"You're wondering why I didn't just take one of those opportunities and kill him."

"Well… yeah."

"Because it's not as simple as that," Ariel explains. "The man is paranoid. He never lets his guard down. It's one of the reasons he's risen through the ranks the way he has."

"But surely you could just—"

"If it was as simple as slashing his throat, I would," Ariel interrupts. "But you want to hear something honest? A part of me is truly terrified of him. If I make one wrong move, I don't just die. I die in the most painful way possible."

She runs a hand down her cheek and over her elegant throat. "Don't get me wrong: I'm ready for death, Willow," she says softly. "I've been ready for death since I lost Pavel. But I don't want to deal with any more pain than I already have. Every time that monster touches me, I suffer enough."

I'm not sure I'll ever be able to look at Ariel and forget Brit, but right now, I can at least see why Leo respects her so much. There is strength in there. Fire. Admirable fire.

"Have you thought about what happens after?" I ask.

"After?"

"After you get what you want? After you get your revenge?"

She looks towards the windows. "I have no fucking clue. I've been in this so long that sometimes, it feels like it'll never end."

"It'll end. Everything does."

The way we're talking, I expect there to be tears in her eyes when she turns to me. But her blue eyes are bright. Her face is smooth, unbothered. She's perfected the mask Anya tried and failed to teach me to wear.

"How did you get to be this way?" I ask in awe.

She raises her eyebrows. "Evil?"

"No," I say. "Strong."

She laughs. She clearly wasn't expecting that. "I'm a good actress, I guess. Turns out that when your soul is broken, you can become anyone you want to be."

We sit like that for a long time. We don't talk, but it doesn't really matter. The silence between us is no longer uncomfortable. It's no longer bristling with tension and distrust.

After a long while, I smile and shake my head. "I can't believe I'm just… sitting here with you."

"Do I make you nervous?"

When she smiles, her white teeth gleam. I shiver without meaning to.

She arches a brow, still smiling. "Don't worry: you're safe from me. Your brute of a husband would skin me alive if I hurt you again."

"He can't have anything happening to the Mikhailov princess," I scoff sarcastically.

She snorts. "Don't play dumb, Willow. It doesn't suit you."

"What is that supposed to mean?"

She leans in, her blue eyes sparking with something that looks suspiciously like sincerity. "Don't you dare waste what you have, Willow. The man you care about is alive. He's right in front of you. Make the most of it."

I frown, bristling at the implication. "It's not enough that I care about him. He has to care about me, too."

She gives me an appraising look, as though she's wondering how much she should say. "Pride," she says at last. "Such a fucking waste of time."

Now, it's my turn to snort. "Have you told *him* that?"

She laughs and surveys me. "You know, I didn't get it at first. But I do now. You're a match for him."

Again, my expression reveals more than I mean to.

"Don't get offended," she shrugs. "He needs a strong woman, and the woman I was holding hostage for Belov didn't strike me as strong. But you're different now."

I wrinkle my nose. "I'm not sure that's enough of a compliment for me to thank you for it."

Ariel smiles. "It's a shame, really."

"What is?"

"In another life, you and I might have been friends."

My first instinct is revulsion. But it transforms quickly when I realize that she's right. Of all the women in the world, only she knows what it's like to be with a Solovev don.

"That depends," I venture.

"Oh?" she asks, arching one perfect eyebrow. "On what?"

"On how close you got with Leo after Pavel's death."

It's a dangerous question to ask, but I figure, fuck it. We're having an honest conversation. And I definitely don't want to bring this topic up again with Leo.

Ariel seems only mildly surprised. "Does that worry occupy a lot of your thoughts?"

"Less than it used to," I admit.

She nods. "The truth? There was a time when I was so deep in grief that I thought Leo could replace Pavel. I was desperate for relief and Leo was there. He was sympathetic, he understood my pain. And in the right light, he even looked a little like his brother."

I listen with bated breath, waiting for the other shoe to drop.

"I tried to kiss him one day," she tells me. "And amazingly… he let me. At least long enough to allow me to realize what a huge fucking mistake I was making. I broke away and apologized. He told me not to worry. Then he left the room and we never spoke of it again."

The consuming jealousy I expect doesn't come. Instead, there's sympathy. Something I never thought I'd feel for the blonde bitch who laughed at my pain.

Before I can admit to any of that, we hear thundering footsteps coming down the hall. A second later, Gaiman bursts through the door. "There you are," he says, but he's looking right at me.

"Jesus Christ," Ariel snaps, leaping to her feet. "Is the sky falling down or something? What's going on?"

"Leo's office," he says. "Now."

22

LEO

Gaiman walks in with both Willow and Ariel in tow. I'm so angry I can't even look at her.

"I fucking knew this was going to happen," I growl. "I motherfucking knew it."

"Leo?" Willow sounds worried. Part of me is glad. She should have been worried this entire time.

"I fucking knew this was going to happen, and yet I wasted time trying to convince you."

Ariel knows better than to say anything. She stands back, waiting for my cue. But Willow charges right into the line of fire.

"What's going on?"

"Spartak fucking Belov is what's going on," I spit out, finally meeting her eyes. "He launched an attack early this morning."

Ariel inhales sharply. "He's not supposed to be back in the country until tomorrow night."

"Plans have changed, obviously."

She doesn't deserve my anger, but I'm too furious to rein it in. Anyone in my way is going to feel the heat.

If anyone can handle it, Ariel can.

"Where did he hit?" she asks. My spy understands her role. She's trying to get all the facts.

I face Willow while I answer Ariel. "You misunderstand. The Solovev Bratva was not his goal today."

Willow's brow furrows. She can feel the truth coming toward her like a runaway train; she just doesn't know quite how bad it's going to hurt yet.

Ariel shakes her head. "Then where did he—"

I lean in. "He attacked Anya Mikhailov's compound."

Willow's face drains of color.

"No," Ariel breathes. "He hasn't been able to find—"

"Well, he found her. But that isn't all he found, is it, Willow?"

"Pasha." Our son's name is a breath, barely loud enough to hear.

"I told you," I say accusingly. "I told you, Willow."

She shakes her head. "No… Anya has ways out of the compound. She would have escaped—"

"Oh, she did escape," I say. "But like the snake she is, she chose to save herself."

She wobbles where she stands, but she's still shaking her head. "No. She wouldn't. She wouldn't do that."

"Your mother decided to run and left our son—her own grandchild—behind to be taken."

"No," she says, sucking in a breath. "She told me she would protect him!"

"How many times do I need to repeat myself before you get it? *She lied.* Anya Mikhailov has and will always put herself first."

Willow is trembling, working hard just to stay upright on her own feet. She looks around the room for support, for comfort, for *something.* She finds none of it.

"How do you know Belov has Pasha?" she chokes out.

I turn and grab a little black box from my desk. "He sent a gift. Similar to the one he sent after you were taken."

I hand her the box, but she just stares at it.

"Being a coward won't change what's in here," I snarl.

She flinches. I know I'm being hard on her, but that's exactly the point —I've been too easy on her up until now. I should have forced her hand. Because at the end of the day, one thing has proven itself to be true time and time again: I'm always fucking right.

I open the box and fling the lid across the room. Then I pull out the thin lock of hair that's lying inside.

It's dark, just like mine. But the strands are thin and wispy, curled up at the ends. Baby soft. Baby delicate.

The moment Willow sees what I'm holding, she crumbles to the floor.

"No," she keeps whispering to herself, over and over again. As though that'll change anything. "No, no, no, no… this can't be happening."

Willow is staring down at the floor. I kneel down, grab her jaw, and pull her chin up to face me. "There's no hiding from this, Willow. This was the choice you made."

"Leo."

My eyes snap to Ariel. She's standing just behind Willow, looking at me with her calculating blue eyes. But the usual fire in them has been replaced by something else. Something I didn't think she was capable of anymore.

Empathy.

"Blaming her is not going to get your son back," Ariel says cautiously.

"She needs to understand the consequences of her choices," I snap. "She needs to know that in the Bratva, the consequence is usually death."

Willow lets out a horrible sound, a nightmarish cross between a cry and a scream. Ariel rushes forward and wraps an arm around her waist.

"You're being too hard on her."

I raise my eyebrows and straighten up. "Oh, I see. The two of you have made friends now. So you think it's appropriate to stand up to me."

"Leo, I—"

I shake my head and she snaps her mouth shut immediately. Gaiman moves forward and puts his hand on Ariel's shoulder. It's a light touch. A reminder.

"Come on," he tells her.

"No," I say harshly. "Ariel stays. Take Willow. Put her back in her room. Make sure she stays there."

Willow doesn't move. She doesn't give any indication that she's even heard me speak. She just stays on her knees, staring at the carpet like there is a way to turn back time woven into the pattern.

It's only when Gaiman grabs her and helps her to her feet that she snaps out of it. "Wait. Leo."

I turn to her, my expression dark. She takes one look at my face and I watch the regret ripple across her features. But I don't have it in me to be anything other than angry.

"We have to get him back."

I nod. "I will get him back. And I'll do it on my own."

I give Gaiman a curt nod and he pulls her from the room. "No," she says, pleading. "Leo, I—"

But I turn my back on her and wait until I hear the door click shut.

"Was that necessary?" Ariel asks when we're alone again.

I whirl around. "Excuse me?"

She raises her hands like she's surrendering, but I know better. Ariel doesn't back down even when she should.

"She's a mother who just learned that a monster has her kid," she says. "I'm just pointing out that maybe you were a little… insensitive."

"You realize that's my kid, too?"

"It's different."

"Why?" I demand. "You think I don't care about him as much?"

She sighs. "Spartak isn't going to hurt the baby."

"Can you guarantee that?"

"As soon as I get back, yes," she says confidently. "I'll make sure nothing hurts that little boy."

"And if he orders you to hurt him?"

"I'll find a way around it."

I shake my head. "Even you won't be able to talk yourself out of a direct order, Ariel."

"I'm not one of his men," she says defensively. "He considers me his partner."

I stare at her in disbelief. "Please don't tell me you believe that."

"He trusts me more than anyone else in his life."

"That doesn't mean he trusts you."

"I've survived for years by his side. I've earned his trust, Leo. And I thought I'd earned yours."

I grit my teeth. She does have a point, as much as I hate to admit it. "I don't want you to get complacent."

Her eyes blaze with anger. "Complacent?" she repeats. "Do you really think I would ever get complacent with the man who murdered my fiancé? This isn't a game for me, Leo, and even if it was, I'm no fucking amateur. Don't treat me like one."

I bite my tongue, but it's not to be kind. Nothing that happens here will change the fact that Ariel has to go back to Belov. And nothing will change that, for now, she is the only thing that stands between my son and safety.

"You need to go," I tell her.

She nods. "I've been packed for the last two days. I'll be back with him by nightfall."

"He's going to want to know where you've been."

"And I have a whole itinerary ready to show him."

"Proof?"

"What do you think I am?" she asks. "An amateur?"

I don't answer.

"He's not going to be worrying about where I was, anyway," she continues. "He's going to be high off this victory."

"Don't make assumptions."

She smiles. "I know the man."

"But where my son is concerned, I want to make sure you're prepared for any possibility."

"Your son is going to be under my protection," she says. "And anyway, Belov needs him alive. You already know that."

I nod. "You're right."

She puts her hand on my shoulder and gives me a reassuring squeeze. "I might not be able to make contact once I'm back."

"I know."

"Don't let that worry you. Just because you don't hear from me doesn't mean anything is wrong."

I nod. "But if you do get the opportunity—"

"I'll make sure I send you a message at the very least," she promises.

I nod again, and she takes a breath. I can already see her shifting, morphing from Ariel into Brit. Her jaw hardens. Her fists tighten. The light in her eyes dims and dims until it's gone, and only dark blue ice remains.

"We're in the home stretch here," I remind her.

She nods. "See you on the other side."

Then she turns and walks out the door, leaving it open for Jax and Gaiman to walk through.

"Everything done?" I ask.

"She's in your room," Gaiman confirms. "She… doesn't seem to be in a good place."

"Can't blame her," Jax mutters.

"Actually, I can," I growl. "She's responsible for this mess. If she hadn't fought me so goddamn hard, Pasha would be here with us. Belov wouldn't have found anything when he invaded Anya's compound."

Gaiman and Jax exchange a glance, but neither one says anything. Both of them are smart enough to know that this is not the time to defend Willow.

I'm sick of talking about it, anyway. The blame game solves nothing. It's time for action. For violence.

It's time for what I do best.

"What have you got for me?" I ask Gaiman.

He straightens up and clears his throat. "I had a team follow Anya's tracks out of the city, but we lost her about two miles out. She's probably in one of her safehouses somewhere, hiding."

"Find her," I say. "It's about time we spoke face to face."

Gaiman looks wary. "It might take a while. She's no slouch. She knows how to hide, how to cover her—"

"I don't give a flying fuck," I interrupt harshly. "When I ask you to do something, I don't want to hear excuses. I want results. Do you understand me?"

"Yes, sir," Gaiman says. "I'll see what I can do."

He's about to leave the office when the door cracks open. "Boss?"

"Connor," I say to the young guard. "What is it?"

"It's… um… Mrs. Solovev, sir," he says uncertainly. "She's banging on the door. Says she needs to speak to you."

I snort. "Ignore it. And next time, don't waste my time with that shit."

His eyes dart around the room. There's clearly something else he hasn't told me yet, but he's trying to determine just how important that information is.

Jax moves forward. "You heard him. Get out."

"Wait," I say. My instincts are prickling. "What else did she say?"

He looks relieved that I've asked. "She says she knows where to find her mother."

23

WILLOW

Pasha clings to my breast but he refuses to suckle. "He's not latching on," I whisper. "Come on, little man. Just drink. Please?"

"It won't matter even if he latches on," Anya points out. "You don't have milk."

"I'm guessing you didn't breastfeed me?"

She looks almost embarrassed that I would even think to ask the question. "Of course not."

"How old was I when you gave me up?"

"A month," she says.

"You could have breastfed me until then."

"But I didn't want to," she says curtly. "That's all there is to it."

I focus on my son in order to keep my resentment from spilling out. She adjusts in the chair, and I can feel her eyes on me.

"You're expecting more from me than I can give, Viktoria," she remarks. "I was not meant to be a mother. That was one of the reasons I gave you up."

I laugh bitterly. "That may be the first honest thing you've said to me in a while."

"Don't be dramatic."

I shrug. "Just telling you how I feel."

She sighs and crosses her legs. "That's the one thing I regret about letting you go: so many fucking feelings. They formed you in their image, and that image was weak."

"If you're talking about my parents, they're the best people I know."

"They are weak. They think feelings matter. They think that's how you decide things—how you *feel* about them. Pah! Pathetic."

"Some would call that love."

She snorts, and her eyes dance with irritation. "They didn't approve of the man you were with. And what did they do? They said their piece and that was it. They couldn't stop you from making a choice they knew was wrong."

"What would you have done?" *I ask impatiently.*

"I would have gotten rid of him."

I stare at her in disbelief. "Are you serious?"

She nods. "Why would I joke?"

"You realize that your father killed the man you claim to have loved," *I point out.* "And you hate him for it."

Anya sighs. "What I'm saying has nothing to do with Mattias. It's about control, Viktoria. He tried to control my life when it was not his to control. I needed to take back power. I needed to show him that he couldn't interfere in my life."

I stare at her for a long time, wondering how we could be related. "I don't understand you."

"You will," *she says.* "When everything you love is burning."

"Jesus..."

"You think we're on vacation here?" she asks bluntly. "We're not hiding out, Viktoria. We're preparing. They'll come for us. And when they do, we need to be ready."

"I really wish you'd stop calling me that."

"It's your name."

"My name is Willow."

"Do you know why they want you?" she asks angrily.

I sigh. "I don't want to do this again."

"Too damn bad. Say it."

"They're coming for my name," I recite. "And everything that comes with it."

Anya nods. "Exactly. It's the most valuable thing about you. So you might as well own it. Because you very well could end up dying because of it."

"Great," I say tiredly. "Good mother-daughter chat."

"You'll thank me one day."

Doubt it, I think to myself. But I say nothing out loud. I just look down at my son and marvel at how much he looks like his father. When I spare a moment to think of Leo, my heart clenches.

Every. Single. Time.

I'm hoping it'll pass with time.

So far, no such luck.

~

The door opens and Leo walks in. I rush to him, stopping just out of arms' reach. "I think I know where she might be."

"Tell me."

I take a breath. "Leo… I know I messed up. You have every right to be angry at me."

"Thank you for your permission."

The way he's looking at me is so different from this morning. So different from last night. Can all of that really have been in the last twelve hours?

"Leo," I plead. "Please let me come with you. I need to speak to her."

He stares at me. I'm expecting to do more begging, but he nods curtly. "You have five minutes to get your ass into my jeep or I'm leaving without you."

He turns and leaves the room. I dress as warm as I can, grab a coat, and run out after him. By the time I trudge the snowy path down from the cabin, there are a trio of jeeps parked along the road. Leo, Jax, and Gaiman each sit behind the wheel of a different car.

I head towards Leo's, despite the look he gives me.

"Get in the front seat," he instructs. "If there are guards posted out front, I want them to see you."

Nodding, I get into the passenger seat and put my seatbelt on. There are four men in the back of the jeep, but Leo puts the partition up so they're essentially cut off from the front of the vehicle.

"Show me," he says, tapping the screen where a map of the territory is waiting.

I scan for a while to get my bearings, then point to a mountain pass that's barely marked. "The safehouse is there." No address pops up on the screen, but then, there wouldn't be.

"How do you know she'll be there?" he asks.

"She mentioned that if the compound were ever attacked, we would evacuate to this safehouse," I explain. "She had a secret passageway out of the compound."

He falls into silence again. No matter how many times I look his way, he doesn't offer me a single glance.

"I regret leaving him with her," I finally say when the silence gets too oppressive. "I never should have trusted her."

"You didn't trust her," he says. "And you didn't leave Pasha with her because you thought she'd be better for him than me. So tell me why. Tell me the real reason why."

I frown. "What do you—"

"I know who Anya is. I know what she's like. And despite your choices recently, I know you're not stupid. So, what's your reason?"

I shake my head. "I don't know what you mean."

"If you don't start telling me the truth right now, Willow, I'm going to pull this vehicle over and kick you out."

I gape at him, wondering if I should call his bluff. Then he glances at me and that one look is enough to tell me what I already know: Leo Solovev always keeps his promises.

I close my eyes. "I was trying to… to hurt you."

He nods, satisfied. "Keep going."

"You used me for my name," I say, trying to push back the sobs that threaten to derail my composure. "You married me to gain more power, to gain a hold over the Mikhailovs. Do you know how that made me feel?"

"About the way I feel right now," he snarls. "Was that the goal?"

"I never meant for this to happen."

"And yet here we are."

I turn towards him. "This would never have happened if you'd been honest with me from the start."

His grip tightens on the wheel. "Right, because you could have handled the truth?"

His tone is cutting. It makes me feel the way I felt all those months with Anya. Like I'm a disappointment. Like I'm not good enough.

"You don't know that I couldn't. You just assumed."

"Jesus Christ, Willow. Do I really need to remind you?"

"Remind me of what?"

"Of the woman you were before I walked into your life?" he demands. "You were living with a man who was abusing you. You had nowhere to go and no money of your own. I saved you from that hell. Never forget it."

My words cut off with every new wound he leaves on my soul. It's like he's become that little voice in my head, whispering back all my weaknesses. All the qualities I hate most about myself.

It hurts most of all because I know he sees strength in me, too. He's said as much. So which is it? Does he love me or hate me? Respect me or pity me?

His hand closes over mine as I'm lost in thought. When I look up, his eyes are searching mine. The temper recedes, the edges soften. "We're getting him back, Willow," he rasps quietly. "We're getting our son back."

Then his eyes go wide. He whips his head around to see something out the window, but before I can follow his gaze, he wrenches the car hard to the right.

If it weren't for my seatbelt, I might have flown into the window. "What the—"

"We almost missed the pass. The safehouse is close now."

"Shouldn't we duck or something?"

"The glass on these jeeps is bulletproof. What does Anya's security look like?"

"Fully armed and all over the place. But you already knew that."

As we turn into the rocky road that leads towards the safehouse, I spot a line of guards. Their weapons are out and drawn. Apparently, they've already caught our scent.

I'm not surprised. It's quiet up in the mountains and we're in a caravan of jeeps. Not exactly subtle. Before Leo can bark an order at me, I unbuckle and open the passenger side door.

"Willow—"

I jump out of the jeep and slam the door.

"Hold it! Don't come any closer."

I recognize the voice instantly. "Armand."

"Fucking hell," he breathes. Immediately, the guns come down. Of course, that lasts only until Leo climbs out of the car.

"Ms. Viktoria, you brought him here?"

I'm about to apologize, but I stop myself. I have nothing to apologize for. I came here to see the woman who promised to protect my son.

I said a long time ago that I don't want to be a victim anymore.

It's time I started acting like it.

I draw myself up tall. "Where is she?" I demand.

Leo moves in next to me. I'd be lying if I said his presence didn't make me stand a little taller.

"Ms. Viktoria, I can't let you in. Not with him."

I look towards the house. It's a cabin, but it's nothing like Leo's. Where Leo's is open with large windows and natural light, this cabin is just like its owner: cold and closed off. The small windows dotting the sides are covered with black curtains. There's not a crack of daylight getting through anywhere.

It could just as easily be a prison.

Which is how I know she's in there somewhere.

"Anya Mikhailov!" I scream at the top of my lungs. "Come out here and look me in the eye!"

The men look towards the house, concern written in the way they hold their guns, not sure whether to lower them or aim to kill.

They know the woman they work for. If I was anyone else, I'd be dead already.

But I'm not just anyone else. And they don't know how she'll react to me.

Truthfully, I don't know how she'll react to me either. She may have given birth to me, but this woman is not my mother.

"Anya!" I roar again.

The door to the cabin opens. I see one thick-heeled boot hit the snow-dusted wood on the front porch. Then she emerges.

She's dressed in dark colors as usual. Gray tights, a black sweater, a black coat that falls to her ankles. Her hair hangs long and loose around her face.

"You should have known better than to bring the enemy to my door," she hisses.

"I should have known better than to trust you with my son."

"The attack was fast, Viktoria—"

"My name is WILLOW!" I scream.

I can feel everyone's eyes on me. I have no idea what they think of me. Maybe they think I'm weak. Maybe they think I'm pathetic. Maybe they think crazy.

Hell, maybe I am all of those things.

But for once, I don't fucking care.

24

LEO

I didn't think she had it in her.

But watching Willow stand in front of a woman that even grown Bratva men are scared of, I can't help but feel proud.

She's confident, operating on the edge of fury as she stares down the Mikhailov bitch. She's doing such a good job that I'm content to sit back and watch.

I glance over my shoulder and notice that Gaiman and Jax are standing next to their respective jeeps, watching the show with brazen enthusiasm. Well, Gaiman just looks mildly interested, but that counts as enthusiastic for him.

"Enough," Anya snaps. "You're making a scene."

"Me?" Willow scoffs. "You promised to protect my son. And instead, you handed him over to Spartak fucking Belov!"

I can feel the rage pouring out of her. She takes a step forward, and I go with her. Anya's men raise their guns immediately, reacting to me. But since Willow is at the forefront of this confrontation, Anya raises her arm, ordering her men back.

"You're his grandmother!" Willow continues. "I thought he'd be safe with you. I thought you were strong. But all you are is an old woman who's out of her depth."

Well, *fuck me*. The girl's got balls.

Anger flashes in Anya's eyes. "It wasn't as simple as you seem to think it was."

"Explain it to me, then."

"The attack was fast," Anya says. "By the time the alarm was sounded, they were already in the compound. Pasha's room was all the way in the west wing. Going to get him would have meant we were both captured."

"Then you should have been captured," Willow snarls. "He wouldn't have killed you. You're Semyon's daughter."

"Don't be a fool, Willow. He'll keep the child alive as insurance. He'd keep you alive as a weapon. But me? I'm more valuable to him dead than alive."

"So there it is. You chose to save yourself," Willow says. "I don't know why I expected anything different. You always come first, don't you? You were even too much of a coward to keep me. Though I should probably thank you for that."

The venom Willow is spewing Anya's way is intoxicating. I can't take my eyes off her.

"Enough!" Anya bites out. "You're not a child and this isn't a fairytale. This is the Bratva. Hard choices have to be made."

"And whether or not to trust you is no longer one of them."

"So your answer is to trust *him*?" Anya glowers at me.

I take a step forward, ignoring the dozens of guns aimed at my head. "No matter what, I keep my promises. Can you say the same?"

"I don't answer to you, Solovev."

"I think you'll find you do." I place my hand on my gun. The guards tense in front of me, and I hear Jax and Gaiman advance into position.

"Stop!" Willow says, putting herself between the brewing fight. "For right now, we have one common enemy."

"That doesn't make us friends," Anya says.

"Not by a long shot," I agree.

Willow sighs. "So you two are going to go head to head and then whoever's left is going to take on Belov. Is that it?"

"I don't intend on taking on my father or Spartak," Anya says.

"I do," I say, looking Anya right in the eye. "I intend on gutting them both."

She pulls her teeth back, bearing them at me. "I know what you want, Leo Solovev. But the Mikhailov Bratva is rightfully mine."

"Is it?" I ask. "Because it seems like you're not willing to do the work it takes to get it back."

That stops her in her tracks for a moment.

"Anya," Willow says into the tense silence, "let's face it: you don't have the manpower to take on Belov. But Leo does."

"And after he is dead?" Anya asks. "What then, Willow? Leo is going to be the leader of the Bratva that is rightfully mine. Rightfully *yours*."

"And after you and I are gone?" Willow asks. "Who takes over then?"

She frowns.

"Pasha," Willow says coldly. "Half Mikhailov and half Solovev, that boy is the future of both Bratvas. And he's with Spartak Belov right now. So I, for one, don't understand what we're standing here fighting about."

Anya looks skeptical, but it's clear she's losing her own argument. She's clinging to a power that no longer exists. And she's starting to realize that it may never have existed at all.

"Did you even see them take him?" Willow whispers suddenly.

"No."

Willow's expression turns deadly. For a moment, I think she might run past the guards and throw a punch. I wait for it. She might be the only person in the world who can get away with that shit.

I can't touch Anya without a full-on war breaking out between Anya's men and my own.

But Willow? Willow can spread pain as she sees fit.

Instead of fighting, though, she walks away. Away from Anya, away from her men and the cabin, away from heartbreak and fear. She heads into the trees.

"Boss…" Jax says, coming forward.

I hold up my hand. "No. Let her go. She needs time."

I look up at her mother, standing in the snow with fists clenched. Anya meets my gaze, one eyebrow arched. Then she sighs. "No point in standing in this godforsaken cold. Come in. Your men can freeze. Mine, too, the useless fucks."

I nod and follow her into her cabin.

Unsurprisingly, it's just as bleak on the inside as it is on the outside. No decor, no finish, and what little furniture there is is a bone white. It feels like I'm walking into a hospital room. Maybe the psych ward.

Seems fitting.

"I like what you've done with the place."

She glares and gestures towards the white, L-shaped sofa. "Sit. I'm not going to offer you anything to drink."

I snort. "I wouldn't drink it even if you did."

"Worried I'll poison you?"

"You wouldn't dare."

She meets my gaze. I can tell she's sizing me up. "She's in love with you," she says suddenly, making a sharp detour.

"I know."

"Do you?" she asks, raising an eyebrow. "Can't say I'm surprised. Men believe women are in love with them even when they're not."

"I can't imagine any man has been foolish enough to make that assumption about you."

She smiles. "That almost sounds like a compliment."

"It might have been. Haven't decided yet."

She brushes her hair out of her eyes. "Let's not beat around the bush, Leo," she says. "Why bother coming here? What do you want from me?"

"Information," I say.

"And what do I get in return?" she asks, tilting her head to the side.

"Your life."

She laughs. It's a harsh, grating sound, like rocks scraping down sheets of ancient ice. "You really think you can kill me if I say no?"

"I know I can."

"There are quite a few men who have tried in the past," she says. "None of them have succeeded. I'm like a cat, but with more lives."

"No one can live forever," I tell her, without breaking eye contact. "Especially after they meet me."

"I bet men quake in their boots when they meet you."

"Women, too," I add, glancing down at her boots.

She laughs. "Cockiness is a young man's game, Leo. But you play it well."

I lean back on the sofa and drape my arm over the cushion. "I like you, Anya. I'll admit, I didn't expect to."

Her response is whip-quick. "You may have won over my daughter and made me a grandmother, but that doesn't mean I give a shit what you think of me."

"And I wouldn't expect you to," I say. "But what I do expect, I will get."

"You can't make me talk by threatening my life."

"Then why did you run from Belov?" I ask. "Seems like threatening your life is the way to get results with you."

"I wasn't about to let Belov win."

"So that's what this is about? Winning?"

She raises a brow. "Isn't that what it's always about?"

"No," I say coldly. "For me, this is about getting my son back."

"At the cost of your Bratva? Your life?" Anya asks. "Somehow, I don't think so. You can always make another baby, Leo."

I get to my feet and approach her. She doesn't appear to be worried, but I know the truth.

She's fucking terrified.

"Don't worry," I tell her. "You won't need to use that gun you're hiding."

Her eyes spark with annoyance. She actually believed that I hadn't noticed. Stupid woman.

"You don't know me, Anya. So let me explain something to you," I say. "My Bratva means everything to me. But so does my family. Luckily for me, they're one and the same. My Bratva is my family. My family is my Bratva. I won't have to sacrifice my son for my empire, or the other way around."

I lean in, forcing her to scrunch back against the hard, white sofa cushions.

"But even if I have to choose between the two, know this: I would burn my Bratva to the ground before I let anyone hurt my family."

She matches my gaze, trying to determine just how serious I am. When she doesn't find the chink in my armor that she's looking for, she sighs. "Does that include Willow?"

"What do you think?" I ask calmly.

She gets to her feet. Even at full height and wearing high heels, she only comes up to my mid-chest. She hides her intimidation well, but I can see uneasiness in her eyes.

"I always thought I'd be in charge of the Mikhailov Bratva one day." She hides her anger behind another resigned sigh. "But it's a man's world."

I shake my head. "No, it's my fucking world. So the smartest thing you can do right now is pick the right side."

One corner of her mouth turns up. It's not quite a smile, but I figure it's the closest thing I'm going to get to one. Jax would be proud.

"I have to say," she remarks, "I can see why she made the mistake of falling in love."

"Indeed," I murmur.

But in my head, I'm thinking, *She's not the only one who fell.*

25

WILLOW

It's cold, but nothing compares to how I feel on the inside. I know I'm not far from the cabin, but I walk until I can't hear the engines rumbling in the distance. Until the trees and snow smother all outside sound.

I walk until I feel like I'm alone.

Only when I feel like the last person on earth do I stop. I drop down next to a large boulder, the dappled surface blanketed in fresh snow. I put my head in my hands and I don't look up for ten, fifteen, twenty minutes.

Or maybe it's longer. I lose track of time as I sit there, contemplating every decision I've made. Every wrong instinct I've followed.

I'm sorry, Pasha. I'm so sorry...

"Torturing yourself won't bring him back, you know."

"Jesus!" I jerk my head up and see Leo standing between the trees. He keeps his distance, and honestly, I don't blame him. I wouldn't want to be anywhere near me, either.

"Come on," he says. "Let's go."

"Go where?"

"Back to the cabin."

Disappointment curdles in my stomach. Irrationally, I had hoped for something different. Some words of comfort, though I don't deserve them. Maybe even an accusation would be nice. If Leo yelled at me, maybe I'd stop feeling so guilty.

"I'm not done being alone," I say stiffly.

"I think you probably should be done with it."

"Did you talk to her?"

He nods. "I did."

"And?"

"And we're leaving now."

I run a hand over my face. I've never felt so bone-tired before. Leo squats down in front of me, forcing me to look up and meet his eyes.

Suddenly, everything comes into sharp focus. It's all clear and it's making my head hurt.

"Please," I say, shaking my head. "I just need some quiet. I just need to sit for a minute."

"Sitting here is not going to bring Pasha back, Willow."

I look down and grit my teeth to stop the tears from coming. "I know. I know I fucked up badly. You don't need to tell me that."

"I wasn't planning on it," he says.

We stare at each other silently for a while. But it isn't long before I get antsy. I want off this rock, I want out of these woods, I want to leave these mountains behind me and never, ever come back.

Either that or bury me here now. I can't take much more of this.

"Fine then," I say, getting to my feet. "Let's go."

We make our way back to the cabin together, him following just behind me. The whole time, I'm intensely aware of his presence.

I long for his touch. But he keeps distance between us as we walk. The intimacy we shared recently seems like ancient history. I barely remember how it feels for him to look at me with anything but resentment in his eyes.

When we emerge from the trees, Anya is waiting for us. Guards surround her, bristling with guns.

As I walk towards her, I stand taller. The time to collapse in the snow and mourn is over. Now, I lift my chin and square my shoulders.

"We're leaving now," I state.

She nods. "You are."

"What are you going to do?"

"Stay here until the danger has passed," she says. "And then I'll go back to the compound, rebuild and reinforce."

"Right. Back to business, huh?"

"There's no changing what happened, Willow. You need to be strong enough to move forward."

"Pasha is my son. I don't move forward without him."

"And you'll get him back," she says confidently.

"How can you know that?"

She glances over my shoulder towards Leo. "I don't say this about many men. But… this one is impressive." I have to force myself not to look at him. "If anyone can get Pasha back, he can."

"Lucky me," I mutter.

The insult doesn't land like I want it to. She simply gives me a knowing nod, it's as much a dismissal as a goodbye.

Fine by me. I put my back on the woman who abandoned me and stride out in search of the son I refuse to abandon.

Leo's men are waiting by the cars. Jax helps me into the front seat of one. Out through the windshield, I'm distantly aware of Leo crossing over the snowy ground to Anya. I can't hear what they're saying, but they exchange a few words. It seems oddly civil for the two of them.

Then Leo walks towards the jeep and gets in next to me. I don't look back as we drive away from Anya's cabin.

Neither of us says a word. It's too quiet in the car. Too much time and space to think.

By the time the car stops, my mind is a whirlwind. Thoughts and scenarios whirl around faster than I can grab them. I feel dizzy and nauseous.

I jump out of the jeep and rush inside. I'm in the living room, gulping in deep breaths, when Leo approaches me from behind.

"You need to calm down, Willow."

"What did you say to Anya?" I rasp. "Right before we left?"

"Take a breath," he says, ignoring me. "You're having a panic attack."

I know he's right. I can barely breathe. And no matter how many breaths I take, it doesn't ease the ache in my lungs.

"Sit down," Leo orders. "Put your head between your legs."

I can barely hear him, but I feel his hands on me. Gently, he tucks me into a ball and the pain in my lungs eases. His large hand smooths circles on my back. That, more than anything else, helps me calm down.

I straighten up slowly. Leo is sitting beside me on the couch.

"Better?"

I laugh out loud. "Not remotely."

"What happened to the confident woman I brought up here?" he muses.

I shake my head. "I thought I could do this. Become more like her. But Leo… I'm not Bratva. I'm not like her. I'm not like you."

"Is that it, then?" he asks. "You're just giving up? Let Belov do whatever he wants with Pasha?"

"That's not what I meant and you know it!" I snap, pushing off the sofa and turning to face him.

"Isn't it?" he counters. "You're sitting here, claiming defeat before the battle has even begun. Belov may have Pasha, but as long as our boy is still breathing, there's hope we can get him back."

"And what makes you so sure… sure… he… he's… oh God…"

Nausea and fear come together like old friends. I'm about to hit the floor when Leo's arms find me and keep me upright.

He grips my shoulders hard and looks me in the eye. "You have to get a hold of yourself. For Pasha. The only way to save him is to stay calm. To stay in control."

"Easy to say. You've never lost control once in your life."

He shakes his head slowly. "You're wrong. Once and only once. After it was over, I promised myself: never again."

"Was it Pavel?"

He nods. "I was lost in a stupor for weeks. And then Jax and Gaiman made me realize that denying Pavel's death wouldn't change the fact that he was dead. So I made a vow to myself. What I could change, I would. What I could control, I would. And that is the code I have lived by since that moment."

My voice trembles when I speak. "I'm not you."

"Then maybe it's time you learned to be. Because Pasha needs your best, Willow."

I cling to Leo's strong forearms with weak fingers. He's the only thing keeping me upright. "If he dies, it'll be on me," I whisper.

"I won't let that happen."

"But what if—"

"Stop," he says harshly. The anger in his expression freezes me in place. "I'm not talking in what ifs. There's no point. Either you're going to help me rescue our son, or you're going to stay out of my way while I do it myself. Which is it going to be?"

I stare at him for a long time, trying to find the courage to tell him what he wants to hear. What I wish I felt.

I open my mouth, but before I can say anything, Jax steps in. I'm secretly relieved. I need a moment's respite from Leo's piercing gaze.

"Boss, sorry, I…" He tapers off, realizing that he's just interrupted something. "Should I come back?"

Leo shakes his head. "What is it?"

"Ariel left shortly after we did. She'll reach Belov in the evening, but she left a note for you."

Jax walks in and hands the note to Leo. Then he leaves quickly, without being told to. I'm guessing that's a first. I watch as Leo unfolds the letter and reads through it. It must be a short one, because in next to no time, he offers me the paper.

"Here."

I take the note and look down at the few untidy sentences scrawled across the white piece of paper. Ariel's handwriting is nothing like her. It's messy, inelegant.

I'll protect him with my life. Make sure that wife of yours gets her shit together. She's got fire when she puts her mind to it.

"Do you see?" Leo says patiently. "You're not alone. Pasha is not alone."

I whimper. That's all I can think of to do right now. Maybe Ariel is right and there is some fire in me, deep down, and I'll be able to find a way to summon that up and use it to save my son.

But maybe I'm wrong, and the one thing I've loved more than anything else in this world is lost to me forever.

Leo must see something he was looking for in my face, because he nods and rises to his full height. Towering over me, he looks down and says, "You have until tomorrow morning to get yourself together."

"What's happening tomorrow morning?" I ask warily.

"Your training starts."

I raise my eyebrows. "But I already trained with—"

"That training is bullshit," he says. "Anya trained you to be like her, but she's the reason Pasha is gone in the first place. You don't want to be like her. You need a new trainer."

"Who's going to train me?" I ask.

Leo fixes me with a smirk. "Me."

26

LEO

I walk into the office, sweat dripping off my body. "I was in the middle of a training session," I scowl. "What is so important?"

I woke Willow up at the crack of dawn to begin. We don't have a second to waste. But I also know that if I give her a second to start thinking, she'll fall apart again. And I need her focused. Even being away from her for a few minutes has me worried.

Gaiman is waiting by my desk, his body rigid with tension. "I know. I wouldn't have interrupted except… Belov."

I freeze. "What about him?"

He holds out the phone. "He wants to talk to you."

The fucking nerve.

I march forward and put the call on speakerphone. Jax would want to be here, but I'm not going to take the time to call him in.

"Belov," I growl.

"You don't sound happy to hear from me, old friend." Belov's voice is as slick and smarmy as I remember.

"You're no friend of mine."

He chuckles darkly. "You never have learned the art of diplomacy, have you? If an enemy had my son, I would do my best to play along, make nice."

"What's the point of being disingenuous?" I ask. "We both know where we stand."

"Hostility is so ugly, so unnecessary. We're both adults. We can talk things out, can't we?"

"Cut the shit, Belov," I hiss. "Where's my son?"

"Oh, don't worry. He's with me. Safe and sound."

"I assume you called because you want to negotiate."

"Negotiate?" Belov repeats. "With the man who took down two of my buildings in a matter of seconds?"

"I warned you."

"You did," he says after a small pause. "And if I had suspected you were serious, I would have warned you: I'm an artist and revenge is my medium."

I roll my eyes, but bite my tongue. Belov isn't wrong. He has my son, and I don't want to poke the bear.

"Then what's this about?" I ask.

I wonder if Belov is alone right now or if Ariel is right there beside him. It's comforting to know that the person he trusts most is a person whose allegiance lies with me. I long for the day I can rub that in his face.

"I think it's about time we meet," Belov says. "Face to face." He knows I can't turn him down.

"Name the time and place."

He rattles off some details, none of which trigger any alarms in my head.

"Fine," I grunt when he's finished.

"See?" he croons. "So much nicer when we act civilized. I do look forward to seeing you, Don Solovev."

"Civility is for cowards," I snap. "I don't have the time or the patience for it."

He sighs, feigning disappointment. "Sometimes, I wonder how a man like you managed to gain such a loyal following. You're not exactly charismatic."

"Noted."

"Now, your pretty little wife, on the other hand... She's someone I would love to get to know better. I do hope you bring her when we meet."

"You must not have learned your lesson last time, Belov."

"And what lesson is that?"

"Anyone who touches her dies."

I slam the phone down, huffing furiously. My fists are balled tight and my muscles are tense, ready for battle.

Gaiman rounds the table and sits down in front of me. "Do you think we can trust him?"

I sigh and slump into a seat. "Of course not. But we can't reject the invitation. It's the best opportunity we have to get close to him."

"And Pasha?"

"He's not going to bring a baby to a Bratva meeting."

Gaiman shrugs. "I wouldn't discount it. Fucker is insane."

"Ariel is there now," I point out. "She's going to make sure nothing hurts Pasha."

"How sure are we that her identity is secure?"

"She's been at his side for years," I point out. "If Belov suspected anything, she would already be six feet under."

"Fair point," Gaiman concedes. "Are you going to tell Willow?"

"I have to. But she's not coming with me."

"I bet she fights you on that."

"I bet you're right."

I leave Gaiman to sort out details of the upcoming meeting while I head back outside to where Willow is waiting for me. My men have cordoned out a section for us just behind the cabin, where they've cleared the snow so that we have a flat, dry surface to work on.

I expect to find Willow resting when I get there, but instead, she's down in the snow doing push-ups.

Her body is tight. The all-black, skin-tight sweat suit she's wearing highlights her new muscle. She doesn't stop the push-ups even when she notices me.

After she hits fifty, she twists around and sits on the cold, packed earth.

"Everything alright?" she asks.

"Good enough."

She raises her eyebrows. "Gaiman looked concerned when he called you in."

"Did he?"

She narrows her eyes, clearly annoyed with my evasiveness. "Is there a reason you're being sketchy?"

"I'm not."

"Leo."

"Willow," I counter, "you should have been resting. We're not done with our training session."

"I didn't think we were. But that was how I rest."

"Are you trying to impress me?"

She gives me a sly smile, but under no circumstances do I believe she's been distracted. Her gaze skims over my body. "Aren't you cold?"

I discarded my shirt an hour ago. The heat of training had made the extra layer unnecessary. The added benefit was watching Willow try not to stare.

"Am I distracting you?"

She rolls her eyes. "I think you're projecting. You're the one trying to distract me. What's up?"

"It was Belov."

She freezes immediately. "What?"

"Belov," I repeat. "He called."

"Are you serious?" She jumps to her feet. "Why do you sound so calm? And why didn't you bring me in to listen?"

"Because he called me," I growl. "Not you. I'm training you so that you won't be a sitting duck if it comes to a fight. That doesn't mean I'm going to take you into one."

She stops short, her expression calculating. "He asked for a meeting, didn't he?"

She's more perceptive than I've given her credit for. "Something like that."

"I'm coming."

"No, you're not."

She stares at me in disbelief for a moment. "You're really going to leave me behind?"

"Yes."

"You bastard," she snaps. "He is my son. Pasha is *my* son. I won't be left behind."

"There's no point fighting me on this, Willow," I say. "You won't win."

I move towards the cabin. She runs ahead of me and blocks me before I can reach the door. "Oh, no, you fucking don't," she hisses. "You can't just walk away from me."

"Go to your room. The session is over."

"Like hell it is. Why can't I be there?"

"Because my job is to keep you safe."

I try to push her out of the way, but she clings to me. Her limbs are tangled up with mine so I don't even know where to start peeling her off.

"Since when?" she asks. "You used me as bait before. Let me go with you."

"That was different."

"How was that—"

"You ran off," I remind her. "You got captured and put me in a bind. I didn't have a choice."

"Well, now you do. And I want you to choose to take me with you."

"No."

"Why not?!"

"Because I can't lose you both!"

Her eyes go wide as the words settle between us like fresh snowfall. Her anger doesn't exactly melt away, but it shifts. Her eyes narrow in on me. My mouth.

Then, without another word, she kisses me.

It's a vicious, crushing kiss, and I give back in kind. I walk forward until her back is pressed against the wall, and then we're ripping each other's clothes off. Even against a wall, we're still out in the open. But I'm not in a position to stop this. And Willow doesn't seem to care anymore than I do.

Her fingers slide into the waistband of my pants. She pulls my cock free and starts rubbing her hips against mine.

"I want you inside me now," she breathes.

This request, I see no reason to deny.

She wraps her legs around my waist, and we slide together in one thrust. *"Blyat',"* I curse in Russian as I sink into her.

She's wet and only getting wetter by the minute.

"Yeah," she moans as I press deeper inside her. "Fuck me, Leo."

I pound into her until it feels like the whole cabin might collapse around us. Her pussy tightens around me as her orgasm quickly crests and then breaks around me.

She screams my name as she comes, and it's so hot that I don't want to hold back. I erupt inside of her, driving into her until I'm completely spent.

Breathing heavily, I lean my forehead against the wall with Willow trapped between my arms.

Her hands smooth up and down my naked chest. Steam rises off our bare skin in spiraling columns.

"That was fast," she says, eyes flashing with laughter.

I narrow my eyes at her. "I got the job done, didn't I?"

Then she pushes at my chest to give herself a little more breathing room. She zips herself up again.

"You can't always control everything, Leo," she says softly. "You know that, right?"

The moment has passed. We're back to business, back to the endless chess game that is my life.

"I've managed so far."

"We can't trust Belov. If he's called this meeting, it's because he's got something up his sleeve."

"And you think I don't know that?"

"I'm just saying we could be a team, you and I."

"If we are a team, then putting ourselves in danger at the same time isn't the smartest move, is it?"

"Now isn't the time to pull punches. We should both be there."

I smile. "Believe me, I'm not pulling any punches. I've got the knockout blow in my back pocket ready to go."

"Ariel," she whispers.

"Exactly."

"I know you trust her, but I'm not sure anyone can be as ruthless as Belov."

"Maybe not," I admit, "but he doesn't suspect her. She's the secret weapon and as long as her identity remains hidden, we don't have anything to be worried about. She will protect our boy."

She lets that sink in for a moment. Then her face softens. "Our boy." Her eyes lift and she meets my gaze. "You haven't even held him… you haven't even seen his face."

I brush a strand of hair away from her face and tuck it behind her ear. "I don't have to hold him or see him to know he's mine."

"Are you sure Belov won't hurt him?"

"Yes. Whatever the fucker says, he's scared. The last time he underestimated me, he paid for it. I took down half his empire with the push of a button. He won't make that mistake again."

She bites her lower lip and looks up at me from beneath long lashes. "You're ready, aren't you?"

I take her hand. It's cold and clammy. She is even more nervous than she's letting on. "Do you know how long I've been planning this take down?"

"Since Pavel?

I nod. "Eight years, I've been waiting for my revenge. You better fucking believe I'm ready."

27

WILLOW

Leo thinks he knows me. At this point, I can't deny that he does.

But I know him, too. And I know that arguing with him is pointless.

So how do you get your way with a man who *always* gets his?

Easy.

You lie.

I'm reaching for my sports bra when Leo walks into the bathroom. We're back to sleeping in his bedroom. In his bed. Together. Almost like a real life couple.

Except that it still doesn't feel quite right. We both have too many secrets we're protecting.

"Excuse me," I say. "Changing here."

"Like I haven't seen it all before," he says with a raised brow. "Back at it again so soon?"

I shrug. "I wasn't satisfied with my last round. I need to work on my upper body strength."

"You're pushing yourself too far."

"No, I'm not."

"Willow—"

"I hate it when you say my name like that," I snap. "I'm not a child, Leo. Stop treating me like one."

"There is such a thing as burn-out, you know? But if you can't restrain yourself, then I'll have to do it for you." He snatches my sports bra out of my hand.

I whirl around to face him, venom in my glare. "Oh, very mature. Give that back."

He doesn't move an inch.

"Fine. I guess I'll just train without one," I say. "That should give your men a real show."

His eyes flash, his knuckles whiten, and the next thing I know, I'm pinned against the bathroom wall with his breath in my face.

I push on his chest and try to keep a brave expression. "You're the reason I need stronger arms, always pinning me against walls."

"Only because you ask for it."

I push him off me again, successfully this time, but only because he lets me. "You're infuriating, you know that?"

"I have your best interests at heart. You're going to injure yourself if you keep this pace. It's not healthy."

"I can handle myself."

"Why do you have to be so damn stubborn all the time?"

"Probably the same reason you are," I retort.

He rolls his eyes. "Life would be easier if you'd admit that sometimes I know better than you do."

"Leo," I say, my voice dropping, "I have to do something, okay? If I don't train, I think. And when I think, I keep dreaming… I imagine the worst possible scenarios."

He sighs. "Willow—"

I shake my head and cut him off. He needs to understand this. "You can talk all you want about your plans and your power, but until Pasha is in my arms again, I can't have faith in anything."

Leo sighs. His face falls, from that ever-present crackle of arrogant tension to something softer, more vulnerable, more malleable.

"Come here," he says quietly.

I shake my head again. "I'm drowning, Leo. It's crushing me. The worry, the guilt. I feel like I can't breathe. But as long as I'm moving, then I can handle it. So I can't stop. I have to keep moving."

I try to walk past him, but Leo stops me. He grabs my face between his huge hands. "Stop for a second. Just stop."

And I do.

But not because he told me to. The days of me accepting Leo's orders at face value are over. I stop because there's a catch in his voice that matches the softness in his eyes.

It isn't a command. Not this time. It's a request, made from one person to another based on respect. Based on affection. Maybe even based on love.

The warm glaze in his eyes bolsters me. It gives me something to hold onto, a life raft in the storm.

"All this worry…" he murmurs. "What will it change?"

"Not a damn thing. But I can't help it."

"Yes, *kukolka,* you can. You can't control this situation, but you can control your reaction to it," he says. "That's your lesson for today. Be the master of your own mind."

"Is that lesson supposed to distract me from the fact that your meeting with Belov is today?"

He smirks. "Don't worry about Belov. I can more than hold my own."

"I'm not worried about that."

He lets go of my face, but doesn't step back. "Then what are you worried about?"

"Will he bring Pasha?"

"Unlikely."

I bite down on my bottom lip. "What about Ariel?"

"She's Brit now, Willow," he reminds me. "We can't give Belov even the slightest hint that she is not a hundred percent on his side. Even if she is there, I can't ask her how Pasha is. She won't be able to tell us anything. Not in his presence."

"I just need to know that Pasha is okay," I whisper desperately. "I wish I could come with you."

His expression grows wary. I know he's expecting me to try and convince him to take me. But I'm done with begging.

"It's best this way," he says instead. He steps back, then moves past me into the bedroom.

Now, it's my turn to follow after him. I walk up behind him and trace my hand down the rippling muscles lining his back.

He flinches at my touch. Stiffens. Then he rotates slowly, letting my fingers trail over his skin until my palm is against his chest. I skim over the muscles there, the defined lines of his abs, the winding tattoos that snake over his skin.

"I've never asked you about your tattoos. What's this one?"

"The sigil of the Solovevs," he says, pointing to the dragon with the flaming eyes.

"And this one?" I point to a tall, thin tree that sits in the middle of his chest. Twisted branches stretch out in every direction, bare and forlorn.

"I got it right after Pavel's death."

It's a lonely image. Even before I'd known who it was for, I sensed the sadness.

"It's beautiful. Sad, but beautiful."

Our eyes meet. Heat flares between us.

It seems to always be there, burning and growing despite our loss and grief. Sometimes, I think it feeds on those things.

The pain brings us closer together. Makes me crave the comfort only he can provide. And maybe it does something for him, too. Maybe, in some small but powerful way, I lighten his burden.

Right now, I can tell we both want that. Desperately.

"You make me want to do things I've never done before," I whisper. It doesn't sound like my voice or something I'd say. More like something out of a dream.

Leo smiles mysteriously. "What's stopping you?"

My pussy is already thrumming with need and my body is slick with desire. I've been so tense with nerves that anything that can divert my attention is welcome.

But it's more than that. I want *him*, too. And I've finally given myself permission to admit that out loud.

I lean in and run my tongue over his left pec. I graze over his nipple. As I slide my tongue down his stomach, I can sense his erection growing.

I get onto my knees in front of him and pull down his boxers. His cock hits me in the face, already half-hard. I lean forward and slip his tip into my mouth.

I'm in control for a few minutes before Leo reaches down and pulls my towel off. I shudder at the onslaught of cool air, but it doesn't take long before the heat of my pleasure crowds out the chill.

Leo curses under his breath as I work his length. After a few more minutes, he pulls back gently and lifts me to my feet.

He kisses my neck and my chest while he walks me back towards the bed. Just as I reach the edge of the mattress, he spins me around and grips my hips.

I arch my back, giving him an invitation. He wastes no time accepting.

Leo slides into me, moving deeper inch by inch, so slowly I feel like it will never end. My body stretches around him, and I moan into the mattress.

He fucks me with slow thrusts that make me squirm, aching for more, even as I feel like I can't take another second of this beautiful torture. His fingers dig into my skin, pulling me against him to match his movements.

The build-up inside of me is steady, its heat doubling and coiling in on itself until I'm trembling with the need to unleash it. When I finally give in, I grab fistfuls of the blankets, trying to anchor myself to the earth, to this moment, to remember how it felt for everything to seem like it might be okay.

I cry out, and Leo runs a hand down my spine, soothing me as I lose control.

It rips through me like a wave of electricity. I can't feel my fingers or toes. Rainbows dance past my closed eyelids.

I don't know how long I lie there afterwards, limp and sated, until Leo rolls me over. I didn't even realize he hasn't come yet until he twists me around to face him. He climbs my body and positions himself right over my face.

Then he presses his cock between my lips until I open for him. I swallow him just as he shoots off inside my mouth and I feel him slide down my throat.

When we both have nothing left to give, he collapses onto the bed next to me and throws an arm over my torso.

"That… that was…"

"Just what we needed?" he suggests.

I smile. "Yes."

He nods and sits back up.

"Where are you going?" I ask.

"I have work to do before we leave," he says vaguely. "Why don't you get some rest? After that, you'll need it."

I frown. "Is that what this was? You trying to exhaust me before the meeting?"

"I didn't say that."

"You didn't have to."

"Are we fighting again?" he teases mildly. "Because I can always pin you to another wall."

"Just get out," I snap, half serious and half joking.

"Are you still planning on going down to train?" he asks.

I roll my eyes. "No, you won. As per usual. My legs are so shaky I can barely walk."

He gives me a triumphant smile and gets to his feet. I watch him dress, marveling at how easy this feels. How intimate things have become between us. How willingly I give myself up to him, time and time again.

Then he's gone, with nothing more than a glance on his way out, although even that tiny little gesture sears my skin like he's branded me.

I lie naked on the bed for a few minutes longer, waiting for my legs to turn solid again. Once I feel up to walking, I slide off the bed and stagger over to the window.

I watch as the men prepare outside in the snow. Weapons are passed from hand to hand and stored in trunks. Gaiman is at the forefront, issuing orders and directing traffic. Jax is less integral in the management of things. He sits opposite the cabin, leaning against a tree and smoking a cigar.

I watch until I see Leo appear. All the men turn towards him automatically. He says a few words and everyone disperses.

I check the time. They're not set to leave for another forty minutes. Which means they won't start loading into the jeeps for another half an hour at least.

It's early, but now's my only chance to make this happen.

I pull on a pair of black jeans and a black thermal shirt. A jacket or coat would be too bulky, so I don't bother, even though I'll be cold. The only other thing I need is my boots.

Once I'm dressed, I arrange my hair into a tight knot at the back of my head. Then I check the windows once more.

Gaiman has disappeared down the path that leads to the smaller cabins scattered down below. Some of the men have gone with him, which leaves only a handful of Solovev soldiers crowded around Jax. Their body language is relaxed, which means they're probably just shooting the breeze before they need to leave.

Ancient pines are clustered along the left side of the road. Thick and tight enough to hide anything from view.

Including me.

I can pick my way between the trees and slip inside one of the jeeps while they're being queued up for departure.

I have no idea if this will work, but I'm not willing to just lie down and be the obedient wife.

This is the Bratva. You have to take what you want.

And that's exactly what I plan to do.

Getting out of the house turns out to be surprisingly easy. The staff are congregated in the kitchen, so I skate past the room as silently as possible. I use the back door to get out and it takes only a short run into the trees before I'm hidden from view and hiding in plain sight.

The creeping walk through the alpine forest is far more nerve-wracking. Mostly because I assume every snapping branch and whistle on the wind is Leo at my back, coming to drag me back to my room and lock me there.

But no one comes. Nothing stirs or makes a noise. The snowfall muffles my footsteps and my breathing remains quiet.

I see the shape of the vehicles through the trees. Steam rises up from the tailpipes as they idle in place, lined in a column along the rough road.

I reach a vantage point behind a massive fir and sit to wait.

Still, no one comes.

"Now or never, Willow," I mutter to myself.

I choose now.

Rushing out into the open, I sprint to the closest jeep and jump into the trunk. I tuck myself beneath a tarp and pray that no one accidentally crushes me to death with anything else they load in.

Soon, my labored breathing stills and the silence of the mountains takes over again. I wait, and wait, and wait for what feels like forever, until I hear the distant sound of voices and footsteps.

It grows louder. I can't see, only listen, as the Solovev army tromps forward and clambers into the vehicle. I smell sweat and metal as the men buckle in. The jeep sags under their weight.

The engines purr to life within seconds of one another. Like a pack of wolves all howling at once. I feel a violent surge of relief as I start to wonder if maybe this just might work.

We pull out. The drive feels both rough and long. Half an hour in, I find myself cursing the driver, who seems intent on driving over every fucking rock and pothole he can find.

I didn't anticipate being so hot, either. But the engine, the glow of bodies, and the thickness of the tarp all contribute to the nausea roiling in my stomach.

The one good thing is that it prevents me from worrying too much about what's going to happen when we actually reach the meeting spot. I don't have time or the presence of mind to stress or obsess. I just lie ensconced in darkness and try not to think about anything else.

When the engines finally come to a stop, I feel an intense burst of relief. We're here. I made it. I actually managed to fly under Leo's radar.

I wait for the men to pile out of the jeep. The second I know it's empty, I crawl out from under the tarp and suck in air greedily.

I'm here.

I'm alive.

Everything else remains to be seen.

28

WILLOW

I'm spotted as soon as I step out of the jeep. A dozen men gawk at me like I'm a ghost, too dumbstruck to move or respond.

Leo hasn't been dumbstruck a day in his life, though. When he sees me, he flies over, rage etched across every feature of his face.

"What the fuck do you think you're doing?" He grabs my arm and tries to pull me away from the men.

I slip free of his grasp with a practiced move and spin around, taking in the surroundings.

They've parked the jeeps on the side of a wide dirt road. Just ahead are chain-link gates, thrown wide, and beyond that, rows of boxy gray buildings.

"Is this the meeting spot?" I ask. "Looks kind of bleak."

"Jesus." He sighs and pulls me away from the men and into a private corner. As soon as we're far enough away, he rounds on me. "Are you kidding me with this shit, Willow?"

I stand my ground. "You refused to bring me. I had no choice."

"You had the choice to listen to me. To stay at the cabin."

"I've told you already: I'm done being a damsel in distress."

"What you're being is childish."

I shrug. "I'm staying. There's nothing you can do about it now."

"I can tie you up and lock you in one of the jeeps," he argues.

"Great plan. Leave me alone, incapacitated, and defenseless so I can be kidnapped again."

He narrows his eyes. "I'll leave a few men to watch you."

"Doesn't seem smart to waste men when you're going up against Belov."

"*I've* told *you* already: I can hold my own."

"I'm not so sure. You've already underestimated one person today."

He grinds his teeth together, but I can't help but revel in his anger. This is the first time I've actually managed to get my way with Leo.

It feels good.

"Stop looking so goddamn smug," he snaps. "Do you think this is a game? Do you think you showing up here is some funny prank? Because it's—"

"You're the one who told me to go after what I want," I remind him coldly. "You told me to fight. That's what I'm doing. Now the only question is: am I fighting with you or against you?"

He stares at me for a few seconds, eyes roaming my face. "*Blyat*'," he finally growls. "Fine. You can come. But you stay behind me the entire time and, from this moment on, you follow my orders. Do you understand me?"

"I'm not some—"

His eyes freeze over. "I don't give a fuck what you think you are. Not here. Not now. From now on, I am your don. My word is law. So answer the question. Do. You. Understand. Me?"

Looking into his face now, I can see why so many men are willing to follow him to the ends of the earth. To die for him.

His eyes are glowing, wreathed in fire and fury. His jaw clenched cruelly tight, eyebrows arrowed downwards. He looks like a king. He looks like a god.

He looks like a don.

"Fine," I croak.

"If I say run?"

"I run."

"If I say hide?"

"I hide."

He smirks. "Bit by bit, you're learning."

"Now, who's smug?" I grumble.

Leo ignores me. "Jax!" he barks. "Get her a vest and a weapon. She's coming with us."

"Seriously?" Jax calls.

I tilt my head to the side. "Questioning the don, are we, Jax?"

He raises his eyebrows while Gaiman suppresses a laugh. A minute later, I'm being fitted with a bulletproof vest and a gun.

"Is this really necessary?" I ask as I pull the heavy vest over my head.

Jax is a little gruff, observing me as I fiddle with the straps to try and get it to fit right on my torso. "Unless you like bullets in the chest," he says, "then yes."

"Are you wearing one?"

"I don't need one."

"Why?" I demand. "Are you bulletproof?"

"I'm not an amateur."

"Neither am I. I've been training hard for months."

"Training and actually being on the ground are two different things," Leo interjects. "This is the real world, Willow. When you get knocked down, there might not be anyone to pick you back up again."

Gaiman joins us, flanking Leo on the other side. I have to admit, the three of them make an impressive group. I wonder if Belov knows quite what he is up against.

"Fine," I concede. "I'll wear the damn thing."

"Great," Jax drawls. "Now, could you take it off and turn it around? It's backwards."

I look down and realize that's why the damned thing won't sit right. "Jesus," I mutter.

"Here." Gaiman moves forward. "Let me help."

I expect Leo to stop him and take over. Instead, he turns his back on me and starts barking orders to his men.

It's almost unnecessary, though. The soldiers fall into formation like they were born knowing how to do it. I watch them as Gaiman fastens the vest on me.

"Thanks," I say quietly, avoiding his eyes.

"Leo is right, you know. This situation is dangerous. You need to stay close to us. And if shit hits the fan, you need to be able to listen."

I frown. "I already got one lecture from Leo."

He almost smiles. "My observation has been that you don't do well when you're given an order."

"I can follow orders!"

"If that were true, you'd be back at the cabin, safe and sound."

"I'm not interested in 'safe and sound' anymore," I whisper mournfully. "I just want my son back."

"Did you ever think that being here might compromise that?" he suggests.

Leo is watching us. Our conversation is whispered, but I'm certain Leo can hear. The bastard knows everything.

"How?" I ask defensively.

"If Belov decides to open fire and make this an all-out war, have you thought about what would happen if we don't win?" he asks. "He'd take Leo out. He'd take you out. And he already has your son. Who is left to oppose him then?"

I've already thought about all of this. Every worst-case scenario has been floating around in my head for days. I don't need Gaiman to remind me of them.

"I guess we only have one option, then."

"And what's that?"

"Don't lose."

He stares at me for a moment and then he smiles. "You'll make a fine Bratva queen one day."

"Let's cross that bridge when we come to it," I say. "One horrifying situation at a time, okay?"

He chuckles and falls into line behind Leo. The rest of the men are already heading for the building. Leo, Jax, and Gaiman are hanging back, waiting for me.

I tuck my gun in the waistband of my pants and turn to Leo. "Okay. I'm ready."

He nods grimly. "Stay behind Jax and Gaiman."

I fall into step behind the two men, despite my personal preference. I should be walking in by Leo's side. I'm his wife. Pasha is my son, too.

But I bite my tongue and follow orders. The only thing that matters is getting Pasha back.

The Solovev army has set up a straight line in front of the entrance of one of the bleak buildings. They part as Leo arrives. We pass through and emerge on the other side to see what's waiting for us.

The Mikhailovs have set a similar line opposite us. They're right in front of the decrepit building. The door behind them is closed, but I'm certain that Belov is inside. I can feel his presence on my skin like ocean air.

It doesn't take long before the door slides open.

But the man who appears, I don't recognize. His grizzly expression lands on Leo. He gestures for Leo to approach, but Leo doesn't move.

The man moves forward, instead. "Good evening, Mr. Solovev."

"Don Solovev," Jax corrects with a violent growl.

"Forgive me," the man says, inclining his head. "Don Mikhailov is inside waiting for you."

"Don Mikhailov?" Leo asks. "Has he finally dropped the pretense, then?"

The suited man just gives him a secretive smile. "Please come with me."

"Not until we dictate terms."

He raises his eyebrows. "What do you suggest?"

"Your men can take the west wall," Leo says. "My men will take the east."

The man nods. "Very well."

He's being so… reasonable. It's making me nervous. But Leo seems perfectly calm. Unaffected by all the guns pointed right at us.

Jax barks the orders in Russian and the Solovevs do as instructed. Across from us, the Mikhailovs move as well, smooth and flawless as a watch mechanism.

Only once the men are each standing against their appointed wall does Leo move forward.

I follow behind Jax and Gaiman. But as we enter the building, Gaiman shifts in front of me and Jax moves behind.

The building is similar to the one where Leo and Belov faced off last time. Except, last time, I was standing behind the wrong man.

It's been a year since that day, but the memory is clear in my mind. The dusty warehouse is rife with reminders. With every step, it becomes harder to ignore the sense of foreboding in my gut.

A table waits for us in the center of the space. Belov is at the head, with Ariel standing just behind him.

Except, no—that's Brit. The gleam in her eyes is deadly. Even knowing what I know about her story now, I fight the urge to reach for my gun.

Next to Belov is another man. He's overweight and sallow-skinned. Clearly unwell. He's sitting in a wheelchair with gilded handles. A uniformed nurse stands beside him, skinny and forgettable.

All of which can only mean one thing…

The man in the wheelchair is my grandfather.

"Ah, Leo!" Belov says, clapping his hands together. "You brought your dear wife. I cannot even begin to express how happy that makes me."

Leo drags out the chair on his side of the table and sits down. "Let's get this over with, Spartak."

I notice how the old man looks at Leo. He may look like he's got one foot in the grave, but his eyes remain sharp.

Then slowly, those eyes turn to me. My face burns, my stomach churns, and I look away immediately.

Leo pulls out the only remaining chair next to him.

"Willow," he offers.

I move forward as confidently as I can and sit down next to him. The old man's eyes still follow me. Despite myself, I hear Anya's voice in the back of my head.

You can't show fear. Powerful men are trained to pounce on it. Don't let them.

So, drawing in a breath to steel myself, I look him right in the eye. I expect to be confronted by a monster.

But instead, I see only a sick old man.

He doesn't look like the kind of person who'd murder his daughter's first love in cold blood.

He doesn't look like the kind of man who would abduct his own grandchild and hold him for ransom.

I realize, as I'm staring back at him, that I feel no tug in my chest. No desire to want to know him or question him. I don't care about his motives or his reasoning.

The only thing I want from him is my son.

If he dies in the process, so be it. Just one less problem to deal with in the future.

I don't have time to ruminate on what that lack of emotion means because just then, Belov turns to me with a sickly smile. The turmoil in my stomach intensifies.

"I'm so glad you decided to join us, Viktoria," he says. "We set up this meeting for you, after all."

My eyes flicker to Ariel for a second. She's standing silently behind him. It's only been a few days since I saw her last, but she looks unrecognizable. A million tiny little differences in her posture, her hair, even the light in her eyes, serves to turn her into a stranger. Into a monster.

Her eyes find me. There is such vivid dislike in her gaze that I question how much of the last few days has been in my head. Was our fledgling friendship real or just another trick?

"Does that mean you're going to return my son?" I ask, proud of the fact that my voice never wavers.

"Return him?" Belov asks. "Why should I return a child who is exactly where he belongs?"

"He belongs with his mother," I hiss. "With his parents."

Belov glances towards Semyon, who still hasn't taken his eyes off me. His gaze is direct, but I refuse to let him intimidate me.

Anya stood up to him a long time ago, and she's been standing up to him ever since. I might not agree with her methods, but I can certainly hold my own… in my own way.

Semyon mumbles something, his words slurring together so that their meaning escapes me. The moment he finishes, drool dribbles down the side of his mouth.

His nurse steps forward to wipe away the spittle with a practiced efficiency. She works gently and moves back to her spot behind him without so much as a single noise.

Belov must have understood what Semyon said, because he smiles. Or maybe he's just pretending to humor the dying old man. It's clear which of them calls the shots now.

Spartak clears his throat. "What Semyon is trying to say is, your son has a vested interest in the Mikhailov—"

"He may be the great-grandson of the don of the Mikhailov Bratva," I interrupt harshly. I'm looking at Belov, but as I continue talking, my gaze veers to the old man. "But he's the *son* of the Solovev don. I think that trumps whatever claim you think you have."

One half of Semyon's palsied face goes up in what looks like a smile. It's not terrifying at all. In fact, all it does is make me feel pity for the once powerful man he used to be.

Now, here he sits, nothing more than a glorified puppet, dancing to the tune of his inferior. It's not something that Leo would ever tolerate. He'd rather die than let anyone else be his mouthpiece.

"Young Viktoria—"

"My name is Willow," I hiss. "Don't make that mistake again."

His mouth tightens in frustration. I know he's not used to being cut off, particularly by a woman. But he's playing a part today, and he looks determined to see his plan through.

I'm just waiting to hear what that plan is exactly.

"Willow, then," he says. "I thank you for coming. But you seem to misinterpret your position here. The fact is, you don't have a leg to stand on. We have your son."

I ignore Belov and look towards Semyon. "You've run your daughter out of your life. Are you really going to do that to me, too?" I ask. "To your great-grandson?"

Semyon's eyes dart from me to Leo and then back again. He mutters something under his breath, but none of us manage to catch it. Not even Belov pretends to understand.

"Semyon is overly tired," he says instead. "Nurse, I think it's best you take him back to the vans and get him home. He needs to rest."

I'm not sure if the dismissal is meant for Semyon, or if it's a signal to someone. But the nurse obeys immediately and wheels Semyon out through a small, rusted door on the opposite side of the building.

A space sits vacant next to Belov now, but Ariel doesn't bother to shift her position. She just stays put at his shoulder. She looks more like an object than a person.

She must hate this. Living like a heeled dog, slave to the beck and call of a man who murdered the love of her life.

I wish I had half her strength.

"I'm glad you got to see your grandfather," Belov says. "Don't let his appearance now color your view of him. He was a mighty man once."

"So they tell me."

"Hearing stories is not the same as understanding."

"I don't have any desire to understand him."

Belov sighs. "That's disappointing. Because he desperately wants to know you."

Leo is tense beside me, but he is being curiously quiet. I look at him, but he doesn't meet my eyes. His gaze remains fixed on Belov.

Spartak gives me a smile. "If Don Solovev is keeping you against your will—"

Leo slams his fist down on the table so hard I'm surprised it doesn't crack. "That's enough, Belov," he growls. "I'm done with your games. Why did you call this meeting in the first place?"

"I hoped we could have some civil discourse. A rousing bit of conversion before—"

Leo's growl cuts him off.

Belov sighs. "Very well. I'll jump right to the chase then. I have a proposition for you."

The thing is, he looks right at me when he says it. I blink in surprise. But I do my best to hide it.

"We're all ears," Leo drawls viciously.

"It's simple, really," Belov says. "You can have your son back immediately. I'll place him in your arms myself. All you have to do… is renounce the Solovev and come with me."

I laugh out loud. This can't be a real offer. But I humor him. "What's to stop you from killing me the moment I'm on Mikhailov property?"

"Do you think so little of me, Willow? You're Mikhailov royalty. I have too much respect for Semyon to even consider such a thing." He shakes his head like he's offended by the mere question.

There's a catch coming, though. I can feel it in the air like a storm on the horizon. The crackle of static electricity. The whisper of a cold wind.

Then Belov leans forward.

His eyes are locked on mine. I feel like we're the only people in the room, in the worst possible way. He tips his head to the side and his mouth curves into a smile.

"Besides," he adds, "I would never harm my future wife."

29

LEO

If I lunge across the table and strangle Belov, Ariel and Willow will be caught in the middle of the ensuing fight. That tiny, inconvenient little fact—that I'd have to risk both of their lives to kill this motherfucker—is the only thing that keeps me seated.

Lucky him.

"You've really gone soft in the head since I brought down your buildings, haven't you?" I snarl instead through clenched teeth.

"If you think I've forgotten dear Viktoria here is already married, you're wrong." His smile gets wider. "If memory serves, you attempted the same daring move not so long ago," he says, his gaze flickering to Willow. "Weren't you married to another man when Leo arrived on the scene?"

Willow is sitting stiffly. She's not looking at me. I wonder if that's a good sign or a bad one.

"Let's say I divorce Leo and marry you," Willow says abruptly. "What's to stop you from killing my son the moment I'm legally bound to you?"

Belov's eyes spark with admiration. "You're smart." He looks back at Ariel, the first time he's acknowledged her presence. "See, Brit?" he asks. "She's not stupid at all. Not that I ever really doubted. I knew the daughter of Anya Mikhailov would be one to watch."

"Forget my mother," Willow interjects. "I was one to watch regardless."

Willow is sparring with one of the most dangerous men in the underworld. If I wasn't vibrating with rage, I'd be proud.

She doesn't even give him the chance to respond before doubling down. "Answer the question, Belov."

Spartak raises a brow. He doesn't like being talked down to. And he certainly doesn't like the proud, easy way in which Willow barks out orders.

"Your son will never have to fear me," Belov says. "Because I plan on raising him as my own."

I do a double-take. "Excuse me?"

"I know it might be hard for you to believe, but I'm not the brute savage you seem to think I am. I'm perfectly happy to raise your son as my own."

He says it boldly, confidently, like I'm the naive asshole. But I see the way he shifts ever so slightly in his chair—he's hiding something. It doesn't take a genius to guess what it is.

"You're impotent."

Belov flinches. And it's all I need to see to know it's true.

"I think that's nature's way of telling you that your bloodline needs to end, Belov," I growl.

"Right now, your bloodline is in my possession," Belov snarls, finally dropping his nauseating smile. "I'd be careful if I were you, Solovev."

"You already stole Semyon's Bratva. Now you want to steal his grandchildren, as well?" I ask. "And how do you plan to make more heirs? Pimping out your wife because you can't get her pregnant doesn't exactly speak to strength."

Belov is shaking. Apparently, I've touched a nerve. He's revealed a vulnerability, showing me his naked neck.

And I'm trained to rip out his throat.

Perhaps he's not so lucky after all.

"The Mikhailov Bratva must go on," he says haughtily. "I will do whatever is necessary to ensure that happens. *That* is strength."

"You could have picked anyone," Willow says. "You don't need my son. Why choose him?"

"Because he's having trouble keeping his men in line," I answer before Spartak can. "Isn't that right, Belov? Are the Mikhailov loyalists giving you a hard time? You did let two of their buildings get turned into smoking craters. Maybe they've decided they don't want to be led by an incompetent outsider who can't even get his own fucking sperm to follow orders."

He grinds his teeth. "I have control over my men."

"Really?" I ask. "Because from where I'm sitting, it doesn't even seem like you have control of yourself."

"Look down on me all you want," he snaps. "I wasn't born with a silver goddamn spoon in my mouth. I had to claw my way up. Everything I have is because I earned it, won it, or ripped it away from people who weren't strong enough to hold it."

"You think you're being rejected because of where you came from?" I ask. "Because of your name?"

"I *know* that's why. There's nothing else it could be."

"Even all this time, you have no idea," I shake my head. "It is your refusal to respect our ways. You've spent your whole life in the Bratva, and yet you still don't understand any of it."

"Is this where you talk about your brother's death?" He rolls his eyes, and I want to gouge them out.

"A gentleman's tête-à-tête means something in the underworld, Belov. Going against those rules changed what people saw when they looked at you."

"You're right about that. I became feared."

I shake my head. "Fear is one thing. Loyalty is another."

"Loyalty can be bought." His fist tightens subtly on the tabletop. Bit by bit, he's heating up. That's good—arrogant men make mistakes when they're inflamed with rage.

"That kind of loyalty only lasts until there is a better offer."

I see doubt steal over him. He knows he's relying on paid mercenaries to take me down, which only shows how desperate he has become. But I know their allegiance can and will change with the wind—or with the dollar.

"My men are loyal to me," he says with a confidence I no longer believe.

"Then you have nothing to worry about, do you?" I lean back in my seat. Time to watch him steam up.

Belov diverts his attention back to Willow. "Your son is alive and well. But he won't stay that way if you refuse me."

"You really want to marry me?" she asks.

"Yes."

"And you really want to make my son your heir?"

"I do," he says, smiling deeply. "You will have the world and he will have the legacy I've built."

"Not much of a legacy, is it?" she remarks. "Really, you want to steal the legacy my family has built. The one that comes from *my* name."

He waves her words away. "Don't worry yourself over all the details. Just know, if you choose to obey me, you'll live a life of comfort and luxury. This arrangement doesn't have to be unpleasant."

"I'm not the kind of woman who obeys."

"I've tamed a strong woman before." He stands up and circles around Ariel. He grabs a lock of her hair. "This one was a real stallion when we first met. And now, look at my beauty! She's as timid as a lamb. She kills when I need her to kill. She fights when I need her to fight. But to me, she is pliant. Submissive. A helpless little marionette, with me holding the strings."

He brings her hair to his nose and inhales it deeply. "So lovely," he sighs. "You're happy… aren't you, my darling?"

Ariel's eyes flicker to mine. There's nothing in them but a burgeoning emptiness that she's cultivated over the years. Even now, she makes me question her loyalty.

"Yes."

The word comes out clipped and harsh, but it just makes Belov laugh. "She's a little upset with me today," he says. "She's not so happy about this scheme of mine. But do you see? She's still here, because I asked her to be. That's love. That's loyalty."

Belov plants a kiss on the nape of her neck. How Brit doesn't stab the motherfucker in the gut is beyond me. She's made of powerful stuff.

As am I.

I know he's going somewhere with this. There's no way a man like Belov would start singing his woman's praises if he didn't have a point to make.

Sure enough, he isn't finished yet. "The thing to know about me is that I'm a simple man. I only want respect and obedience. Isn't that right, Brit, my dear?"

"Yes," she intones robotically.

He smiles. "She knows me better than any other human being," he says. "And she doesn't have to worry. Even if I do marry you, her position will remain. She will always be the only woman in my life."

"Is there a point you're getting to any time soon?" I snap impatiently.

"The point I'm making is this: I'm not all bad, Willow," he says, gazing fondly at my woman in a way that makes my blood run cold. "I can feel love. I feel it for this damsel and I can feel it for you, too. I won't ever need to hurt you so long as you choose your side… and stick to it."

He remains standing just behind Ariel. He's curled her hair around his fingers and he's tugging softly. She looks detached from his touch, but I can sense that it's only because she's suppressing the urge to push him off her.

When all this is over, I'm going to have to buy her a mansion in the French countryside, a cabin in the Alps, a villa on some tropical beach. Somewhere peaceful and quiet where she can overcome her remaining demons. She deserves that at the very least.

"And what if I turn you down?" Willow asks.

He sighs. "Then your son dies."

She stiffens instantly. "You wouldn't. They'd—your men, they'd turn on you."

"Maybe," he says with a shrug. "Maybe not. But whatever the outcome, your son would still be dead. Is that a risk you're willing to take?"

Her eyes flicker to mine and I can see the panic in them. He's succeeded in scaring her. She's more than scared now—she's desperate.

I grab her hand and force her to look at me. "Don't listen to him."

"You think I'm making an idle threat?" Belov asks. "Watch and learn."

Quick as a snake, his fingers tighten around a fistful of Ariel's hair. Then he uses it to throw her face down into the table. Something snaps.

Willow screams and jumps back, and I spring to my feet as Belov pulls Ariel upright again. Her eyes are wild from the sudden attack, and I can tell this is not rehearsed. He hasn't planned or discussed this with her. Her nose is bleeding and she's got a black eye that's only going to get darker. When she opens her mouth, I realize part of her front tooth has chipped loose.

For a panicked moment, I wonder if he's found out who she really is, but I dismiss that suspicion immediately. We've been too goddamn careful. He can't know.

"What are you doing?" Willow screams.

"Making my point," Belov retorts with his signature sickly smile. "I love this woman more than anything on earth, but I will kill her if I have to. I will kill her just to make a fucking point."

The smile drops off his face instantly. As chilling as the effect is, it doesn't make the slightest difference to me. The problem is that Willow has started to break under his pressure.

"Your son is not my heir yet. He is nothing to me. And I will not hesitate to slaughter him like a rabid dog if I have to. If you *make* me."

Willow stares at him in horror. "He's a baby… a tiny, innocent—"

"Innocent?" Spartak interrupts. "He's not innocent at all. He's guilty of being born to the wrong parents. He's guilty of being born at all. But I'm the kind of man who looks for the silver lining in everything. And I'm willing to make something of his life… as long as I have control of it."

"You can't do this…"

"And he won't," I snap. "I will get my son back, you sick motherfucker—"

"Willow!" Belov bellows. "You have a choice to make."

He pulls out a knife and starts running it lightly up and down Ariel's exposed neck. She closes her eyes, and goes still. But I can see the trembling in her fingertips. She is not afraid of death. But dying like this? Gutted like a stuck pig? That enrages her.

"What are you doing?" Willow gasps.

"Showing you how far I'm willing to go to get what I want," he says.

Willow looks helplessly at Ariel and then she screams, "Stop! Please, just stop!"

"Is that your answer?" Belov asks expectantly.

"I'll go with you," Willow blurts out.

I grab her hand and twist her around to face him. "You're not going anywhere."

"I have to protect our son," she says.

"Not like this."

Then I throw her over my shoulder and start walking away from Belov and Ariel. I hear his cackle as I exit the building. But it's almost completely drowned out by Willow's screams.

"My son! Leo! Let me go. I have to go back. I have to protect him!"

I set her on her feet on the path in front of Jax and Gaiman. She tries to make a run for it, but I catch her without so much as moving and lock her against my own body.

"Bind and gag her," I tell both of them. "Get her back to the jeeps. We're leaving."

If they're curious about why my wife wants to run back towards Spartak, they hide it well as they rush to do as I told them. I turn back towards the building, just as Belov appears at the door. He gives me a smile and disappears into the darkness beyond.

I need to kill him before he makes a move that will take us all down with him.

There's nothing more dangerous than a desperate man.

30

WILLOW

"How's your training coming?" Anya asks, as she sits down beside me.

Pasha suckles at my breasts, but the milk stopped coming a long time ago. I cringe when he bites down, but I still keep him on my nipple. I can't bring myself to let him go.

"What are you doing?"

"You wouldn't understand."

"You don't have milk."

"It's all the training," I snap. *"It's all the stress. It's your fault."*

"You'll thank me later."

"For what?" I demand. *"Turning me into a weapon at the expense of being a mother?"*

"Oh, you're far from being a weapon," she says curtly. *"You've been distracted during training."*

"That's because I'd rather be here, with my son."

"He's not going to notice if you're here or not."

"How would you know?"

She gives me a tired sigh. "The only way you can protect him properly is if you're strong. And right not, you're the farthest thing from it."

"Gee, thanks. It's always nice to get words of encouragement from a parent."

"You want praise or honesty?"

"Right now? I'd rather have silence."

Anya doesn't react to that, but she doesn't leave, either. I haven't seen her in several days. This is the first time she's visited Pasha in twice as long as that.

"Who's your boy toy?" I blurt out. Last week, I caught a glimpse of her on the third floor with a young bodyguard. My age, maybe even younger. Bland, but handsome.

"Excuse me?"

"The guard you're fucking," I say casually. "He's young enough to be your son."

"I like them young," she says, without bothering to deny it. "They can be molded."

"Right. Do you always fuck the men that are on your payroll?"

"You must be missing your husband, darling," she says so sweetly I want to vomit. "I see that look on your face any time he's mentioned. You don't want to love him, but you do. And that makes you *angry*."

I try to keep a neutral expression, although it's as hard as anything I've ever done. What is Leo to me now? What am I to him? The ideal answer would be "nothing." But I'd be a fool to pretend that's an honest one.

"I'm not angry anymore. I've accepted that I was nothing more than a pawn in his game."

"But you're still his wife. You gave birth to his child not long ago. You are bound forever."

"What do you care?" I demand. "What's the point of this whole fucking inquisition?"

"The point is that I need you to focus. The longer you take to get over him, the harder that will be."

"I'm already over him."

"Your ability to lie is as bad as your focus."

"Are you going to send someone in to train me to lie now, too?"

She meets my eyes with her cold gaze. "Don't act like a petulant child, Viktoria. It doesn't suit you."

"Tell me something: how many lovers have you had over the years?"

"Countless."

"And you never want something more?"

"Never."

"Why?"

"Because the only man that ever made me feel anything was your father," she says. "And once he was gone, that door closed forever."

"So you're just hiding from reality?"

"I'm surviving. There's a difference."

Pasha starts to whimper at my breast. I pull him away and stroke his apple cheek as regret courses through me.

I used to think about having a baby, but whenever I did, I imagined a good man by my side. Or at the very least, a man I loved.

It's funny that, in the end, even love wasn't enough. But then, love was never what Leo was after. Despite my denial, I know Anya's right about me. About my feelings. About where my heart lies.

I just don't want to give her the satisfaction of acknowledging it.

"I don't want to go back to training today," I say instead.

Anya crosses her legs and scoffs, "You don't have a choice."

"Why is it that, in the Bratva, being powerful means removing everyone else's options?" I demand.

"I'm not trying to control you, Viktoria. I'm trying to protect you."

"It all feels the same from my perspective."

"What do I keep telling you?" she demands. "I've said it over and over again since you got here?"

"Lie better? Abort your child? Abandon your principles?" I rattle off. "You've given me so many gems of maternal wisdom; it's hard to keep them all straight."

She glares at me with a deadpan expression. "If you want something enough, take it. If you really wanted out of here, then you'd be back with your Bratva prince. If you really wanted to stop training, you would have stopped by now. You are like all those other ordinary people out there in the world: you love to complain, but you refuse to do anything to change it."

Her words feel like rocks being pelted at me, but beneath the harsh words, I find a small iota of truth.

"You like playing the victim, Willow," she says. "But no one will feel sorry for you here. So I suggest you stop feeling sorry for yourself."

"Willow."

I glance towards Leo, realizing belatedly that we've come to a stop outside the cabin. Right back to where all this started. The men are already piling out of the jeep and unloading their violent paraphernalia.

"Come on," he says. "Let's go."

I try to move, but my body feels completely numb, so I just slump back in my seat and stare up at the roof of the car. Instead of snapping at me to get my ass in gear like he normally would, Leo just waits next to me silently. Patiently, if a man like him could be said to do anything patiently.

We sit together until the quiet becomes too oppressive to continue. "We need to at least consider it," I whisper.

"Consider it?" Anger curls off each of Leo's words like steam. "It sounded like you were ready to do more than consider it back there."

"It has nothing to do with you. It isn't personal, but—"

"You think I'm pissed because you hurt my feelings?" he growls, cutting me off. "I'm pissed because it was a stupid decision to make. You can't trust anything he says, and you should know that."

I turn to look at him. He's as savagely beautiful as he ever is. I know he has love for me, somewhere deep down beneath the ever-present rage. I know he understands what my heart has been through, too. How badly it's hurt to love someone who might not let himself love me back.

"He has my son, Leo."

"Spartak is not going to kill Pasha," he says firmly. "He's on shaky ground as it is. If he kills the heir to the Mikhailov throne, the loyalists will have no reason to continue to follow him once Semyon is dead."

"You saw what he did to Ariel, didn't you?"

"He was putting on a show."

"He hurt her."

"That was the whole point!" He's frustrated with me, but he's trying to be gentle. I can sense him holding back his anger like it's a rabid dog on a leash. "He was trying to make you believe that he would kill Pasha if you didn't come with him."

"And what if you're wrong?"

"I'm never wrong."

"Aaargh!" I push the door open with a frustrated scream and jump out of the jeep.

I underestimated the height, so I trip on my way down and nearly fall to the snowy earth. I manage to stay on my feet, but just barely. I hear the driver's door slam behind me, but I don't look back. *Just keep walking.*

It doesn't do much good. He catches up to me in no time and plants himself right in my path.

"Stop running away from difficult conversations."

"I don't know what else to do!" I cry out, throwing my hands up in the air. "You don't listen to me."

"You're the one who's not listening, Willow. Ariel will be fine. She's been through worse. She survived that and she'll survive this, too."

My eyes go wide. "I hardly even know her and I could barely watch it. How could you?"

"You think I'm cruel?"

"Yes."

That's a lie. The truth is no. Not in the essential ways, at least, the deep-down ways.

But he's not the only one who's frustrated.

"Maybe I am." He shrugs. "But it takes a hard heart to survive in the underworld. Ariel understands that. It's why she's lasted this long in the monster's den."

"He could have killed her."

"But he didn't."

"Okay, and what if I didn't stop him? What if he *had* killed her?" I press. "Would you have been able to just stand by and watch that happen?"

He grabs me by both shoulders and pulls me forward. "Do you think this is my first day on the job?" he asks. "If I had stepped in and stopped him hurting Ariel, what do you think he would have assumed?"

"I…"

"And once the suspicion grew, what do you think he would have done?" he continues. "He would have murdered her. And not a quick-bullet-to-the-brain kind of murder. More like the torture-until-you-pray-for-death kind of murder."

I cringe, but Leo doesn't let me look away. He pins me in place.

"And then who would have protected Pasha, Willow?" he asks. "You didn't think of that, did you? You just acted with your heart, not your head. I keep trying to tell you not to do that. It's what makes me love —it's what makes you innocent. But it's going to get you killed. So yes, I did what I had to do. I thought for both of us. I got you out of there."

Leo isn't wrong, which wounds my pride more than I'm willing to admit.

"Okay, maybe you're right," I say softly. "About all of it. But I still think a man who's willing to beat up a woman he claims to love is capable of anything."

"Spartak doesn't know anything about love. He isn't capable of it."

"But they've been together so long and—"

"He gets off on the high of controlling a woman like Ariel," Leo explains. "He likes hurting her and having her come back to him. He likes watching her destroy his enemies, knowing that she's doing it to win his approval. It's a transactional relationship, Willow. It's not the real thing. He may think it is. But he's wrong."

I take a deep breath. "Okay. Fine. I'm listening and I understand what you're saying—"

"I can already feel the 'but' coming."

"*But*," I say, adding extra emphasis to the word, "that makes the case for him hurting Pasha even stronger. If he's backed into a corner and he has nowhere left to go, he *will* hurt him. He'll hurt our son, Leo. And if that happens… I won't be able to live with myself."

Leo reaches out and cups my cheek in his large hand. His thumb is rough but his touch is gentle as it brushes across my skin. "Do you trust me?"

The question is so earnest, it brings me up short.

Since the moment I met Leo, we've been on a seesaw. A back and forth, give and take relationship where it is hard to know which way is up.

I've loved him. I've hated him. I've done everything in between.

As for now? Well, I'm not sure what to say.

"Willow?" he says. "It's a simple question. Do you trust me?"

My mind whirls, but I dig deep. And Leo is right. Underneath layers of questions and fears, the answer is simple. At the root of me, I know the truth. I know what I feel in my bones.

"Yes." My shoulders collapse. I bite back a sob. "I trust you."

He runs his thumb over the corner of my lips. "Then trust that I know what I'm doing."

"I do, but… it goes both ways, Leo," I remind him. "If I have to give you my trust, then you have to do the same for me."

"What do you have in mind?"

"We tell him yes. I'll tell him I ran from you," I explain hurriedly, before he can intervene. "I'll tell him I accept his deal. I'll make sure our son is safe and when I get close enough to him... I'll make my move."

Leo's arched eyebrow tells me plainly enough what he thinks of my wild plan.

"I'm not some shrinking wallflower, you know," I bristle. "I may not be as skilled as Ariel or you, but I can hold my own in a fight. Especially because he won't see it coming."

"If it were that easy, don't you think he'd be dead already?" Leo asks. "Ariel would have killed him a thousand times over if that were the case."

"He won't expect it from me."

"You're my wife. Anya's daughter. Of course he'll be expecting it from you," he snaps. "Think, Willow. You're going to get yourself killed right along with Pasha. I can't lose you both."

I can't lose you both. His words still me. Now who's the one who's not thinking clearly? It's hard to imagine Leo being afraid. I don't think he's capable of it. But this feels awfully close.

"I'll be okay," I whisper. "It's a good plan. I know it."

I look him in the eyes. They're swimming with clouded, turbulent emotions. I'm sure mine look exactly the same.

But for one moment, it feels like we might break through. Like a ray of light is almost there, ready to burst through the storm clouds. A ray of trust. A ray of hope.

A ray of love.

Then it falters, and the storm rages on. "You don't know anything," he snaps.

I pull away from him and start towards the mountain path. He's not going to listen to me, and I can't listen to him. Especially when I know I'm right.

He strides up beside me. "You're acting like a child, Willow."

"Leave me alone."

"So you can run off to Belov and get killed?" he asks. "Fat chance."

"Like you care?" I shoot back. "You're just interested in keeping Pasha alive to preserve your legacy. You're not impotent like Belov. If he and I die, you have plenty of women willing to make you more babies."

His hand clamps around my arm and pulls me to face him. I gasp, but bite it off as he towers over me.

His face is black with fury. I was angry and I said something I didn't mean, but I can't take it back. The words are lodged in my throat.

And he can see it. He can see I'm not backing down. After all, I learned the art of that from him.

"If that's what you think of me," he hisses, "then maybe you're better off with Belov."

He drops my arm just as suddenly as he grabbed it and leaves me alone on the path.

31

LEO

"Can I come in?"

I throw Gaiman a cursory glance and a grunt that he decides to interpret as permission. He slips in and closes the door behind me.

"Is there a reason it's so dark in here?"

"The blinds are down."

He shoots me an annoyed look. "Yeah, I got that bit. You done with that drink?"

I down the last sip and hold out my glass. "You can pour me another."

"Your wish is my command," he mutters, refilling my glass and handing it back over.

Then he gets himself one and fills it halfway. We sit and drink together. There's nothing like a silent drink in good company. Correction: there's nothing like a silent drink in silent company.

That's the nice thing about Gaiman. He respects my boundaries and my moods. Jax always bounds in like a golden retriever puppy, doing tricks to cheer me up.

Only when our glasses are empty does Gaiman speak. "You okay?"

"Fine."

"Because you've been holed up in here since the moment we got back from the meeting."

"I've had a lot to think about."

"Belov or Willow?" he asks.

"It's hard to tell where one starts and the other one stops." I push my glass towards him. "Pour me another."

This time, he gives me only a raised eyebrow.

"What?" I demand.

"It's ten in the morning."

"Did I stutter? Pour the fucking drink."

With a little sigh, Gaiman pours me a stingy bit of whiskey. I snatch the bottle out of his hands, top myself off, then set it back down and take a satisfying sip.

"She's out in the backyard training right now," he tells me—a little unnecessarily, since I know where Willow is at all times. "Y'know, it's only been a year, but the two of you fight like an old married couple."

I roll my eyes. "I expect that kind of funny, gossipy bullshit from Jax. Not from you."

"I'm not trying to be funny—"

"Good. Because you're not."

He sighs and cracks his neck. "I'm guessing she disagrees with whatever plan of action you've come up with?"

"More like the other way around," I mutter. "She wants to play into that fucker's hands. She wants to offer herself up and get close enough to him to kill him."

"Sounds reckless."

"That's exactly what I've been trying to tell her."

He nods in agreement, but I can tell from his face that he has something else he wants to say. He's just looking for the right way into the conversation.

"For fuck's sake, just spit it out, Gaiman," I snap.

He exhales. "She's a mother," he says quietly. "Her first instinct is going to be to throw herself into the fire to protect her child."

"I'm not discounting that. But in order to get him back, we need to be on the same page."

"You mean you need her to be on your page," he retorts.

I cock my head to the side. "Whose side are you on?"

His face is solemn as he answers, "Are there sides?"

I'm surprised Jax hasn't come pouncing into the room to toss in his two cents. And then it hits me.

"Who's outside with her?"

"Jax." He sees me wince and adds, "It's a good thing. He's easy to talk to. Easier than you, at least."

"Did you two draw straws to see which of you had to come talk to me and who had to talk to Willow?" I grumble.

"Yep. Guess who got the short one?"

I give him the middle finger. "I don't love my Vors interfering in my marriage, ya know."

Gaiman ignores that, leaning forward to prop his elbows on his legs. "Maybe you should consider her plan, Leo."

"Did we not just establish that it's reckless?"

"Yes, it's reckless," he agrees. "But it might work. Willow isn't Ariel, but they'll be together on the inside. That has to count for something."

I clench the glass in my hand so hard I wonder if it will shatter. "You talk about her instincts, but what about mine? Sending her in there goes against every instinct I have. *That* has to count for something."

"Of course it does," Gaiman says with a nod. "You're the don, and she's your wife. But she's also the key to the Mikhailov Bratva. Isn't that what you've been saying this whole time?"

"I'm gonna go outside." I leave Gaiman before I decide to do something reckless myself. He doesn't stop me as I walk out the door.

As I pass by the living room window, I stop. Willow is working out next to Jax. He already has his shirt off, the bastard. Simultaneous push-ups. Down, up. Down, up. I watch for a good minute or two. Willow conducts herself capably. I see her arms start to tremble, her shoulders weaken, but she still keeps the pace.

Up.

Down.

Up.

Down.

If there's a metaphor about us in there somewhere, I choose to ignore it.

At last, Willow's strength gives way and she collapses into the cold dirt. If there's a metaphor in *that*, I ignore it just like the first.

Grinning, Jax offers her a hand up, but she slaps it away and swings her legs around to trap his ankles and bring him crashing to the ground next to her.

I can hear him laugh in surprise. Then they start sparring.

She's a quick study, no doubt about that. Eager to learn. Actually, make that desperate to learn.

But more than anything, she's determined. Her jaw is set, her brow lowered. She's focused. Jax may be twice her size and a thousand times as experienced, but she's in this fight to win it.

It won't happen, of course. Jax isn't one of my right-hand men for nothing. But the fact that she's even trying makes me admire her all the more.

Jax feints to the side and kicks. Willow doesn't see it coming until it's too late. She tries to dodge, but the kick catches her in the hip and sends her back onto the earth face-first.

The beast in me growls.

No one touches my woman.

I storm outside and onto the porch. Willow is already dusting herself off and pulling herself together, but the moment Jax catches sight of me, he pales and backs off.

"Hey, boss," he says as I approach down the stairs. "I… I was just helping Willow train."

"Training's done," I say firmly.

"Right. Gotcha. I'm out."

"Wait, what?" Willow says, disappointment coloring her expression. "We just started. You said there was tons more you had to teach me."

"I said training is fucking done," I say, turning on her.

"Why?" she demands, putting her hands on her hips.

"I don't have to have a reason."

"Willow," Jax says, in a low voice. "I've got shit to do and—"

"Bullshit!" she explodes at the both of us. "We're training. Are you trying to protect me from your own men now, too?"

Jax hesitates, but I wave him off. He nods and slips away.

Willow plants herself in front of me and jabs me in the chest. "Why the hell are you playing the hero?" she asks. "There was nothing to save me from."

"How about saving you from yourself?"

"Don't give me that. You always aim the attention at me when it's you who's fucked up in the head. Go on then, tell me: what's the *real* problem, Leo?"

I grab her hand and pull her towards me. She slams into my chest. "The problem is, no one touches what is *mine*," I snarl.

"I've got news for you," she spits back. "I. Am. Not. Yours."

She breaks my hold, flips me off, and stalks away down the same path that Jax disappeared into. I take another route into the forest and cut her off at the pass.

She tries to reroute around me, but I slide over and cut her off. Her eyes gleam with irritation.

"You are infuriating, you know that?"

"I do," I say. Then I duck down and kick her legs out from under her, just like she did to Jax.

She's too shocked to even cry out before she hits the pillowy snowdrift piled up at the side of the path. Before she can get back up to her feet, I jump on top of her and pin her in place.

"And *you* are mine, you know that?"

Before she can protest, I cover her mouth with mine. She doesn't even attempt to struggle. She sinks into the kiss as though she's been waiting for it this whole time.

Her nails dig into my neck as she pulls me in a little deeper. I tease my tongue into her mouth, and she moans.

When my hand slips down to the waistband of her sweats, she breaks away long enough to ask, "What are you doing?"

"Stealing your wallet," I mutter sarcastically, kissing a line down her jaw.

"Your fingers are freezing."

I nip at her collarbone. "Should I take them away, then?"

She rolls her eyes, but I don't miss how she lifts her hips ever so slightly so I can work my way into her pants.

I grab a hold of her and roll onto my back, taking her with me. She sits up, straddling me, and grinds her hips against my throbbing erection. I hiss, but it has nothing to do with the snow soaking through my shirt or the chill in the air—because inside, I'm on fire. Ablaze with need for her, with passion, with a desperate, furious love.

One look in her eyes says she feels the same.

Willow runs her fingers down my chest. Then she jumps up and sheds her clothes quickly. As soon as she's done, she moves to my pants. The moment my cock jumps free, she straddles me again. She rubs herself against me, circling her hips sensuously.

"Are you trying to tease me?" I grit out.

"Depends. Is it working?"

Fuck yes, I think. Out loud, I say, "You'll cave before I do."

She frowns in concentration and slides herself along my length. Before she can retreat, I grab her hips and press myself where I know she wants me most. Where she's been avoiding.

A shiver works through her. She tries to pull away, to regain control, but I slide my thumb there instead. She's already wet and it only takes a few brushes before she's bucking her hips against me.

We both know she's already close, but she doesn't want to admit defeat.

"Don't be stubborn," I whisper. "Do you want to come on my finger or my cock?"

If looks could kill, I'd be a dead man. But even as she glares, she lifts herself up and positions me at her opening.

I grab her hips and sheath myself inside of her in one thrust. She gasps and begins rolling her hips. She presses her hands into my chest and rides me until she's breathless and panting, her hair coming loose from its tight knot.

Willow's body trembles. When she collapses against my chest, unable to keep herself upright any longer, I wrap my arms around her and thrust into her hard. She clings to me, moaning in my ear.

"Leo, Leo, Leo…" she cries out as her body spasms around me.

I don't slow down even as she comes. I pump into her, realizing how much I needed this. How much we both needed this.

I'm on the edge of coming myself when I hear footsteps approaching.

Willow hears the same thing, because she jerks up in alarm. "Oh, fuck, someone's coming."

"Yeah—me," I growl, thrusting into her harder now. Almost there…

"Leo, stop! Someone is—fuck…!" Her words turn into moans as I drill into her.

I'm so close I'm seeing stars. Just a few more thrusts.

"Leo," she breathes. And it's the way she says my name that sends me over the edge.

I explode inside her, and she cries out, louder than she probably wanted to. She tries to scramble away while I'm still pulsating, but I hold her still, letting the tension fade and the glow of pleasure spread. She still feels too good.

"Whoever it is is going to see," she warns limply.

"Let them see."

I push into her a few more times, and finally, my body is spent. As soon as I let go, Willow rolls off me and starts pulling her pants back on.

I'm buttoning myself up when someone clears their throat. "Everyone decent?" Gaiman asks.

"What do you want, *sobrat*?" I ask impatiently.

"You've got a call."

"Is it a call I can avoid?" I eye Willow and consider a round two.

Gaiman's answer is clear. "No."

"Duty calls," I tell Willow.

She nods, but avoids my eyes. I leave her in the woods with Gaiman and head towards the house. When I enter my office, Jax is waiting by the phone.

"Who is it?" I ask.

"Ariel."

"Fuck." I snatch the phone. "Ariel?"

She sounds nonchalant, as always. "Took you long enough."

"I was… occupied. I wasn't expecting your call, either. Are you safe? What's happening?"

"I have one last burner cell and Spartak is out," she says. "I just wanted you to know I'm with your son right now. Can you hear him?"

I press the receiver tight to my ear. There's a gurgling sound and then, sharp as ever, I hear a little cry.

"Did you hear that?" she says.

"I heard," I say, unable to articulate just how strange that sound makes me feel. "Aren't there cameras everywhere?"

"What do you think I am, a rookie? I've knocked off the cameras in the nursery. It'll look like a technical difficulty. Happens all the time."

"He's okay?"

"He's okay," she replies. "The nurse needed a break, so I took over. I thought I'd take the chance to give you a call, let you hear how well he's doing."

I don't bother telling her how much this means to me. She already knows.

"Thank you," I murmur in a voice I hardly recognize. Then I clear my throat and stiffen up. "How are you?"

"What do you mean?"

"After the meeting."

There's a beat of silence.

"Ariel."

"He's on edge lately," she says at last. "It makes him cruel. Crueler than normal, I should say. But it's nothing I can't handle."

I bite down on my tongue, but I can't stop the words any longer. I should have done this a long fucking time ago. "You've done your time, Ariel. And you've accomplished a lot. I think it's time to pull the plug on your mission."

"Excuse me?"

"Come back home," I say softly.

The silence drags out for a long time. "Are you serious?"

"Yes."

"Leo, the mission is not over," she says, sounding angry now. "If you're worried that I'm not up for this, then you're wrong. I've been here for fucking ever—"

"I'm not questioning your dedication or your skill."

"It sure as hell sounds that way to me!"

"I've been worried about you for some time now. You've been with him too long."

"You're worried about the psychological impact?" she asks. "What the fuck does that even matter anymore? I've been broken for a long time. This is nothing new."

"You need to come back home," I repeat.

"Home?" She laughs at the very concept. "My home died with Pavel."

"You still have people that care about you."

"Stop trying to save me. I don't need saving."

"Ariel—"

"Have you forgotten about your son?" she interrupts. "I need to be here to protect him."

"Actually, I'm thinking we kill two birds with one stone. You come home… and you bring him with you."

"Jesus," she breathes. "I'll never get away with taking off with this guy in tow. It's not like I can ask him to cooperate with me, either, is it? Damned useless babies."

"We can work out the details," I say, though fuck knows what that will look like. "You're resourceful enough to figure it out. I'll help."

"You can only help me from the outside. I have to get out of this fortress first—with a crying baby, no less."

"Pick a time when he's sleeping."

"And what about the rest of it, Leo?" she asks. "I can turn off a camera for twenty minutes, but what about the guards? Not to mention the fact that Spartak is here most of the time. And when he is, he wants me with him."

"I know it's a bold plan."

"It's not bold; it's reckless. I have a higher chance of getting caught if I take Pasha and leave. I can try and smuggle him to you but—"

"No," I snap immediately. "Too risky."

"For whom?"

"For you. If Belov finds out you got Pasha out, but you're still in his control… You're as much a part of my family as Pasha is. I won't lose either of you."

She goes silent for a second, and I know she's touched. She just doesn't know how to process sentimentality anymore. It's because she believes that if she leans into it, she stands a chance of being hurt. And she can't take anymore hurt. The next one might kill her.

"My mission will end when Belov does. Not a moment before."

"Leave Belov to me," I say. "I'll end the *mudak* one way or the other. You don't have to be chained to his side when I do."

"But I want to be."

"Ariel—"

"I want to see him die, Leo. After everything I've been through, I deserve to be the one to kill him."

And I realize one thing: she's fucking right. If anyone deserves to rob him of his worthless life, it's her.

"Okay. I'll make sure that happens."

"Really?"

"Yes. You can murder the fucker. You have more than earned that honor."

She mulls that over for a moment. "Okay."

"Okay what?"

"Okay, I'll try and find an escape route out of here," she says. "With Pasha."

I smile. "It'll be good to have you back, Ariel."

She snorts. "That's what you say now."

"You know I have property all around the world. You can take your pick."

"See?" she says. "Trying to get rid of me already."

I laugh. "My gift to you."

"And to yourself, no doubt," she says sarcastically.

I hear my son gurgle again, and I feel that strange warmth spread through me. Is this what it means to be a father? Does that feeling last? And if it does, will I ever get used to it?

"I have to go," she says abruptly. "I'm hearing movement downstairs."

"Stay safe."

"Back atcha."

The line goes dead in the middle of one of Pasha's cries, and I feel an overwhelming sense of determination settle over me. I don't know how, but I know this is going to end soon.

"She okay?" Jax asks. I'd forgotten he was even in the room.

"I heard my son today for the first time," I rasp.

For a change, he looks solemn and respectful. "What did that feel like?"

"It made me feel… infinite," I say.

Jax frowns, and I know immediately he doesn't understand. Then again, before becoming a father, I wouldn't have understood that statement either.

Wisely, he decides to leave that alone. "How's Ariel? Is she okay?"

"No," I reply honestly. "But she will be. We all will be."

32

WILLOW

"Jax."

"Eh?" he grunts. He's been sitting to the side watching me train for an hour. He must be freezing, seeing as how he's wearing just a t-shirt and thin sweatpants, but he shows no signs of discomfort. I still haven't decided if that's because he's tough or because he's dumb. Probably a little bit of both.

He also hasn't offered to help me train again. He seemed so eager before, so enthusiastic. Now? Not so much.

"Come spar with me."

"I think I'm good," he grumbles.

"Don't tell me you're scared."

He bristles. "Do I look like I'm scared?"

He stands up, and if I didn't know any better, I'd be the one who was scared. He's a big man. Leo is big, too. But Jax looks like the poster boy for an ad campaign about steroid abuse.

"I can't think of another reason why you wouldn't train with me," I say innocently.

"I can think of one really big reason."

I roll my eyes. "So you *are* scared of something."

He smiles and—I can't believe I'm actually seeing this—*blushes*. "Okay, maybe I'm scared of one thing."

I'm surprised he admitted it all. "You guys are supposed to be friends. Isn't it weird having to take his orders?"

"You trying to drive a wedge between us, Willow?" he asks, raising an eyebrow.

"Just curious."

"That killed the cat, you know."

"Might kill me, too, if Leo has anything to say about it. But you didn't answer the question."

He laughs and leans against one of the mossy boulders lining the edge of the training area. I walk over and hop up on the rock next to him.

"He is my friend always," Jax explains quietly. "But he's my don first."

"Sounds confusing."

"Not really. It's the way it is." He says it simply, in a matter-of-fact way that makes me wish I'd been born into this world. Try as I might, I still struggle to understand parts of it. This, for instance. How can someone so proud and defiant be so willing to follow another man's orders? And not just follow them, but live by his every word. Go to war for him. Kill for him. Die for him.

That kind of loyalty just does not compute.

"I don't think I could ever take orders from him," I say honestly.

Jax smirks. "Shocking."

I nudge him with my elbow. "I spent my early twenties with a man who controlled everything about my life. I've changed since then. I don't think I can settle for another man who does the same thing."

"He's not trying to control you, you know—"

"Don't say he's trying to protect me. For God's sake, say anything but that."

"Well," he shrugs innocently, "he is."

"I cannot roll my eyes hard enough."

Jax pivots to face me, suddenly serious. "Every choice you make can affect another person. Sometimes, it's the difference between life and death. He's just trying to minimize the casualties."

"He treats me like I'm one of his men," I snap. "Little toy soldier Willow, at your service."

"That's because he doesn't know how not to be in charge," Jax explains. "He had to become don suddenly. No preparation, no warning. He didn't want the job, but he stepped up anyway. For his brother and his Bratva. Now, I think he feels like if he stops being in control, he'll relapse back into the person he was before Pavel died."

"And what kind of person was that?"

Jax smiles. "Fuck, if only you knew. We used to have *fun*."

I wrinkle my nose. "That doesn't tell me much."

"Pavel would send us out on missions," Jax reminisces fondly. "If there was a debt that needed to be paid or money that needed to be collected, the three of us would do it. And then afterwards, the celebrating was always the best part." His eyes are hazy with memory as he looks a decade into the past and sees a man I never knew. "There was this one strip club down Main Street. It was called—shit, what the hell was it called?"

"Oh, God," I groan. "I'm not sure I want to hear the grisly details, Jax."

He ignores me. "Vixen's Garden or Vixen's Palace. Some shit like that. But lemme tell you, the girls were great. And willing. I never had to pay extra to get a—"

He breaks off when he notices the look on my face.

"Sorry," he says with a sheepish smile. "Forgot who I was talking to."

"I'll bet you did," I say. "So at this strip club, what did Leo enjoy?"

The smile drops off his face. "It was long before you."

"That's not what I asked."

"You hear that? I think I hear Gaiman calling me."

I grab his arm. "Jax!"

"Sorry, gotta go." Laughing, he pushes himself off the rock and starts ambling off in the opposite direction.

"Coward!" I yell. He just laughs as he disappears into the trees.

Sighing, I turn back to the mountains and try to enjoy the silence. When I first got here, it was calming. A moment of respite after a lifetime of chaos.

But there's no comfort in it anymore. Not when I know my son is Spartak Belov's prisoner and there's nothing I can do to get him back.

The smile Jax left behind dies on my lips. Grimacing, I stand up and head back to the main cabin.

When I come through the trees, I see Leo outside in the other training yard. He's got his sweats on, but otherwise, he's naked from the waist up.

He hasn't noticed me yet, so I stand and admire. It's impossible not to. His body is all muscle. But where Jax is bulky, like a garbage bag full of ribeyes with a twelve-year-old's sense of humor, Leo is lean and toned and serious.

He squares up with the punching bag. A roundhouse kick, followed by three jabs. The first punch makes the bag shiver. The second sends it swinging. The third knocks it clean off the hook.

It lands on the snow a few feet away, kicking up a white dust cloud.

The man is a machine. When he turns to me, he's barely breathing hard.

"Enjoying the view?" he asks.

Maybe he noticed me after all.

I try not to be affected by how intense his gaze is today. Stormier than usual. I keep my head down as I walk over to the porch steps and sit down on the top stair.

"Something bothering you?" I ask.

"Always. Why do you ask?"

"You beat that bag up like it owed you money."

He shrugs without even a hint of a smile. "Needed to let off a little steam."

"Fucking me in the snow didn't do it for you?"

That almost draws a smile. "Maybe I just need to try it again."

My skin heats instantly. My attempt to set him off balance backfired. I don't know why I'm surprised—Leo always has a comeback ready.

He saunters over and sits next to me on the porch steps. "Ariel called."

My face goes ghost-white. "What?" I gape at him. "When? What did she say?"

"This morning."

"That's why Gaiman came and got you."

Leo nods.

"Why didn't you come get *me*?"

"It was a short call. She didn't have much time."

I grit my teeth in frustration. I'm always on the outside, looking in. I'm getting very fucking sick of it. "What did she say?"

"She said that Pasha was safe and doing well. He's being looked after. Spartak has a nanny carrying for him."

Relief floods through me. I know from experience that it's probably going to be short-lived—nothing good in this world lasts long—but at least it's something.

"Wait," I say, thinking fast. "This means that Belov probably wasn't lying about wanting to make Pasha his heir."

"I don't think he was lying about his impotence either," Leo agrees. "No man would lie about that. Not to his enemy's face."

"So the deal he offered me was for real."

He looks me right in the eye. "Tell me you wouldn't actually take him up on that."

"To protect my son?" I say. "I'd do it in a heartbeat."

"You don't know what you'd be walking into. You still don't understand."

"I'll take my chances."

I expect to be met with anger, and I'm gearing up for a fight, but he just sighs and doesn't say anything more. In fact, he doesn't even seem angry. He just looks… thoughtful. Pensive.

"What else did Ariel say?" I prod gently after a moment has passed.

"She was with Pasha when she called me," he admits. "And I… I heard him…"

The hair on my neck stands on end and guilt tugs at me. I can't imagine being denied all the memories I have with Pasha. Holding him, kissing his cheeks, smelling him. The tiny little moments that confirmed that he was real, that he was mine, that he was beautiful.

Leo has had none of that.

"I wish you could have been there," I whispered. "When I gave birth to him."

"Were you alone?"

"Apart from the doctors, yes. But I preferred it that way. Anya wasn't exactly interested."

"I can't imagine she would be."

I run a hand through my hair as I think about my mother. "In her own way, she tried to be there for me. She tried to mold me into this other person. A Bratva princess, the person she thought I had to be to survive everything that was coming for us. She wanted me to be prepared for anything. But she had no idea how to connect with me. How to be a person. A parent."

"She wasn't made to be a mother, Willow," he tells me. "She was meant to lead a Bratva."

"Yeah, I got that," I grumble. "Not exactly comforting."

"Do you want to speak to your parents?" Leo asks suddenly.

I glance at him with one arched eyebrow. "I've been thinking about them a lot lately."

"But?"

"But… I want all this to be over before I see them again," I say. "They've worried about me enough. I don't want to reconnect with them now, only to tell them that their grandson is the hostage of a madman. There are just too many questions I can't answer. More importantly, there are too many questions I don't *want* to answer."

He nods, and if I didn't know better, I'd almost say he was impressed by my restraint. "I understand. You should know I've told them that I got you back."

"You did?"

"They deserved to know, Willow. They've been beside themselves with worry the last year. I wanted to give them some peace of mind."

I do a double take at him. He looks the same as he always has—gorgeous, but brutal and unapproachable, like a famous statue in a museum that you aren't allowed to get near.

But there's life beneath that surface. I used to only see that cold, heartless exterior. Underneath it, though, I'm starting to see just how much more there is.

A heart, maybe. A heart that can hope and love.

If he lets it.

"What have you told them?" I ask.

"That I found you, but it's complicated. I told them that once it's all over, I'll give them a proper explanation."

"And they were okay with that?" I ask.

"They trust me," he says, as if those three little words don't gloss over the messiest backstory in history.

"Wow."

"Does that surprise you?"

"I mean… a little."

He shakes his head and laughs softly. "I don't know why you insist on underestimating me. Surely you're starting to get sick of being wrong."

I giggle, and when it fades, we sit in the easy silence. I almost don't want to break it because of how calm and comforting the energy between us is right now.

But I can't ignore the nagging in the back of my head.

"Leo, we need to come up with a plan to get Pasha back."

"You don't think that's what I've been doing all this time?" he asks.

"I think we need to discuss *my* plan," I suggest delicately. "Accepting Belov's terms and—"

"We're not doing that," he interrupts. "You are my wife, and I'm not sending you directly into the lion's den. If something happens to you..."

"What other option do we have?"

"We have Ariel."

"That's news to me. I thought she was undercover."

"She is. But that can't last forever. Now is the time to pull her out—with Pasha."

"But... but... if she tries, won't Belov suspect her?" I ask. "She's the only one who has that kind of direct access to him. Aren't you abandoning the mission to kill Belov if you pull her out now?"

He leans back, one elbow on the porch behind us, eyes raking the frozen horizon. "In my eyes, she's completed her mission. She'll still be fighting. Just not from the inside anymore."

I actually find myself smiling. If anyone deserves retirement, it's Ariel. "That's great news."

"Don't celebrate just yet," Leo says. "She still needs to coordinate the escape. That'll take time. And risk."

"How much time?" I ask urgently.

"At least a few days. This has to be executed perfectly. If not…"

He tapers off, and I'm glad he does. I don't need to hear him say what Belov will do to her if he catches her.

"What happens in the meantime?"

"We wait for her call. If nothing comes in the next forty-eight hours, that means there's no plan in place and no way for her to leave safely."

My heart sinks at the very thought. "Do we have a backup plan?"

He looks at me and smirks. "Always."

"Which is…?"

"We go in, guns blazing."

I gawk at him. "Is this the part where you say, 'Just kidding'?"

"I never kid. That's the plan."

"Leo," I say, standing up and starting to pace nervously. "A full-on attack is risky, to say the least."

"Any plan at this point is going to be risky."

"But… but he could kill Pasha the moment we attack."

"We won't give him time to," Leo says confidently. "In any case, Ariel will still be on the inside if we have to resort to that. She'll make sure he's safe."

"I don't know about this."

"This is how we do things here, Willow."

I groan. "Jesus. 'The fucking Bratva way.' I don't know how you can live with this constant weight on your chest. God knows I'm sick of it. No wonder you murdered the punching bag."

He smiles. "I was seeing Belov's face every time my fist struck."

"If only it were really him."

"I would love to gut the bastard myself. But I promised that honor to Ariel. She deserves the closure."

I pause and consider that. "You're probably right. But will she get it?"

"Your guess is as good as mine. Some days, I fear she's gone too far down the rabbit hole to ever come back."

I shudder, remembering how dead and flat her eyes looked when Belov smashed her face into the table at the meeting. "Don't say that."

"Avoiding hard truths doesn't help anyone, Willow."

"Maybe not, but for once, can't you just pretend?" I ask. "Can't you just pretend that everything's going to work out and we're going to have a happy ending?"

He smiles. "Okay. Let's pretend."

I groan. "Why do I feel like you're about to make me regret this?"

"Let's have dinner tonight," he continues. "For one night, we can pretend that all this is behind us. We can pretend everything is fine, and we're happy."

"You're taking this further than I thought you would."

He holds out a hand to me. "Is that a yes?"

I sigh. This isn't exactly what I had in mind, but I know enough to know this: Leo Solovev always gets what he wants.

So I take his hand and we go inside.

33

LEO

Willow is late for dinner.

The food has been out for five minutes. The crab legs in curry leaf leche de tigre are starting to get cold.

Then I hear footsteps on the stairs.

I look up. Sky-high black heels give way to long, gorgeous legs as she rounds the spiral staircase.

She has on a slinky silver dress with the thinnest straps imaginable. The neckline is deep, highlighting her gorgeous breasts.

The hem falls below her knees, but it follows the curves of her body closely, leaving little to the imagination.

She's brushed out her hair and left it loose around her shoulders. It falls in rich, silky waves.

As she walks towards me, I'm transfixed by the way her hips are moving. I blink and pull myself together before I can start to drool.

"Sorry I'm late," she murmurs.

I force my eyes up to her face. We may be pretending tonight, but I don't have to fake my reaction. "It was worth the wait. You're a fucking vision."

Her lips turn up in a shy smile, and color blooms on her cheeks. She tries to hide her pleasure as she sits down gracefully next to me.

"Thank you. You look pretty dapper yourself."

I haven't taken as many pains as she has, but I know I pass muster. I've gone for fitted pants and a black button-down that hugs my biceps closely.

Still, she seems as preoccupied with my appearance as I am with hers. She hasn't even looked at the intricately set table and food.

"Hungry?" I ask.

She shakes her head slowly and gnaws at her bottom lip. "Not for food."

Our eyes meet, and the heat that passes between us is raw and palpable.

"Come over here," I order huskily.

Instead of arguing back like she usually does, she obeys with an alluring lowered gaze that makes my cock spring to attention. She rises from her seat slowly and struts around the table, coming to a stop between my parted legs. Her fingers graze over my shoulders and down my biceps.

I want to tear her gorgeous dress off with my teeth.

But I resist.

Because tonight, I want to take my time. I want to savor her body.

"Sit down."

She doesn't straddle me. Instead, she tucks one leg under the other and sits down daintily on my lap.

I like this position, though. I run my hand under the slit of her dress, smoothing my palm up the length of her thigh. With the other hand, I cup her cheek and run a thumb across her plump lips.

She keeps her eyes fixed on me. This whole moment feels like a fever dream. Every sensation is heightened to the fullest and beyond.

"You dressed up for me," I point out with a wry smirk.

"We're pretending we're normal, happy people tonight, right? I figured getting dressed up was more normal than coming down stark naked."

I chuckle at the memory. "I wouldn't have minded either way."

She reaches up and runs her fingers through my hair slowly, brushing it away from my face and sighing softly. "I've always wanted to do that."

"Always?"

She nods. "Since the first night I met you in that restaurant. You have amazing hair."

"Why haven't you?"

She shrugs. "It's too intimate, isn't it? Too gentle. That's never been our thing. But tonight… I'm pretending it is. Let me lie to myself."

She leans in and places her lips over mine. The kiss is light as a feather. It makes me crave more.

The beast inside me roars for the heat of her thighs. It wants to devour her.

But I wrench him back.

Slowly. Slowly. Tonight is about moving slowly.

My hand dances higher up her smooth thighs. Her legs part in silent invitation, and I let my fingers delve deeper.

The moment I reach her heat, I raise a brow. "You skipped a few layers, *kukolka*."

Willow's eyes burn with intensity to match mine. She shrugs innocently. "Oops."

Then she leans in again and kisses me. This kiss is soft and deliberate, but there's a new urgency lingering underneath.

She's holding herself back just like I am.

Slowly. Slowly.

I run my fingers up and down her slit, teasing her. I part her open gently and probe inside, massaging until she breaks away, her breathing hot and heavy against my neck.

I pull my fingers out and raise them to her lips. "Taste yourself."

She pulls two of my fingers in her mouth and sucks on them. Her moans vibrate around my fingertips deliciously. When she lets her mouth fall open, I return back to her pussy.

This time, my fingers slide in easily. Deeper. Her spine arches and she faces the ceiling. I take the opportunity to kiss the elegant curve of her neck. When she looks back down at me, desire burns deep in her eyes.

Slowly is starting to be really fucking difficult.

With my free hand, I slide the straps off her dress off her shoulders. She's not wearing anything underneath, so the material pools at her waist, leaving her top half deliciously naked.

I lean down and capture her nipple between my teeth. She sucks in air and stiffens while I nip at her. After a moment, I send my tongue in. All it takes is one flick before she's moaning on my lap.

"Oh, fuck, Leo. Like that… that feels good…"

As my tongue works over one nipple and then the other, I start finger fucking her a little faster. Her body rolls against mine and her hands flutter uselessly at my shoulders.

I don't think I'll ever get tired of turning her into a whimpering puddle.

I pull my fingers out at the same time I stop sucking her nipples. "Stand," I tell her. "And lose the dress."

Breathlessly, she does as I say.

It's ironic how obliging she can be when it comes to sex, but the moment I give her a command outside of it, she fights me tooth and nail. She's a study in contradictions, this little wildcat.

She stands and shimmies her hips until the dress drops around her feet. She steps out of it and walks back in between my legs wearing nothing but heels and a silver necklace. I grab her hips and press a kiss to her toned stomach.

Then I spin her around so I'm faced with her perfect ass. I lean in and sink my teeth just enough to draw a yelp. She gives a little gasp, but I hold her in place.

When I slap her ass hard, she yelps again, but she still doesn't pull away. Instead, she arches closer.

"I want you inside me, Leo," she pleads. "I need to feel you inside me."

"Then what are you waiting for, *kukolka?*" I ask. "Sit down."

I unzip my pants, pull out my cock, and position myself at her entrance. She eases herself over my cock, hands on my thighs for balance, and swallows it whole.

I enter her with a satisfied sigh. Soul-deep. Bone-deep. She feels even tighter at this angle. And as she starts to bounce up and down, picking up speed as she goes, I feel my grip on the reins of my self-control getting dangerously loose.

She grabs the edge of the table and uses that to secure herself as she bounces on my cock. I pull her back into my embrace, her spine against my chest, and capture her earlobe between my teeth.

"Faster," I breathe.

She rides me like that, moaning and trying not to lose it, one hand encircled around the back of my neck as she holds on for dear life. I watch her ass bounce on my cock, committing every deep thrust to memory.

Once I notice her legs begin to shake, I stand up while still inside her and bend her over the table. She upends half of our meal in the process, but neither one of us gives a shit at this point. Only one thing matters.

Release.

I slam my hips into her again and again. Her ass cheeks shiver with each thrust.

She grips the tablecloth in her fists. "Please, Leo…"

I wrap a hand around her waist and find her center. The moment my thumb whispers over her, she cries out. Her orgasm syncs with mine perfectly, and we come together. Once I've emptied inside her, I stand there, admiring the smooth lines of her back and the beaded sweat like a row of jewels on her neck.

Then, with a mournful sigh, I pull out. I watch with a fierce sense of ownership as she straightens herself shakily. She grabs a napkin off the table and wipes herself off before reaching for her slip dress.

"Jesus," she gasps, falling back into a chair the moment the dress is in place. "I don't think I'll be able to walk right for a week."

I smirk and reach for a piece of bread.

"You don't have to look so proud, you know," she adds teasingly.

In response, I look her dead in the eye while I tear off a hunk of bread with my teeth. So much for table manners. She let the savage out of the cage, and it has no interest in going back in.

"Hungry?" she asks, trying to fill the silence.

"Yes, but I'd rather be eating you."

Even after what we just did, she still blushes. She breaks our heated eye contact and reaches for the wine.

"Do you think she'll call?" she asks after a long sip to steady herself.

"Willow," I say gently. "We're pretending tonight. Normal. Remember?"

She sighs. "It's easier said than done."

"It was your idea."

She takes a deep breath and sips her wine thoughtfully. "Okay. If we're pretending… tell me where Ariel is right now."

"She's in France," I say without hesitation. "She's living in a villa in the south, deep in the countryside, no one around for miles. She goes down to the beach and swims in the ocean on the weekends."

"And during the week?"

"She gardens, when the mood strikes. Paints, too."

"She paints?"

"She used to," I say. "In another life. Back when she was with my brother and she smiled all the time."

"Does she have someone?" Willow asks tentatively. "Is she happy?"

"I want her to be happy," I say. "But I know she'll never love anyone like she loved Pavel. It's more likely she has dozens of lovers dotted all over the continent. One for every day of the week with plenty to spare."

"Sounds like the life," she says, giving me a coy smirk. "What about you?"

"What about me?" I ask.

"You've spent your entire life as don chasing after revenge," she points out. "What do you do now that you have it?"

The smile drops from my face. Some things cannot be imagined. They must be lived.

Revenge is one of those things.

"I don't stop being don just because I killed Belov," I growl. "In any case, I have two Bratvas to run instead of one."

She frowns just like I am. Just like that, the spell of normalcy withers. We both drop the pretense of our fantasy. "So you plan on taking over after Belov?"

"It makes sense. Our son will inherit both," I say. "I might as well make the transition easy for him."

She studies me carefully, a curious look passing over her face.

"Tell me what you're thinking," I say.

She takes a deep breath. "What if I stake my claim on the Mikhailov throne?"

I weigh it for a moment, but there isn't much to truly consider. The answer is simple. Straightforward. "Then I'd hand over the reins to you."

Her eyes go wide. "Are you serious?"

"Yes."

She frowns, suspicion narrowing her eyes. "Are you only saying that because you know I have no real interest in leading a Bratva?"

"I don't know that."

She sighs. "You know exactly that. I just want to live a normal life, Leo. Somewhere quiet where I can raise my children."

"Children?"

She looks away from me awkwardly. "I just meant—forget it. It was a slip. I didn't mean anything by it."

"Are you sure about that?"

She rolls her eyes. "You didn't answer my question."

"I thought I did. I'm going to continue to be don. I still have a Bratva to run, and I still have ambitions where the Solovev dynasty is concerned."

"Ambition," she repeats softly. "Every man's undoing."

"I disagree. It's what raises us up. Ambition is a good thing."

"So the Solovevs will grow?"

"In size and power," I confirm.

"And Jax and Gaiman?"

"They'll be by my side while I execute my vision."

"What if one day they want to leave?"

"To do what?"

"I don't know. What if one of them meets a girl? What if they get married and have children of their own?"

"They can do all that and still be by my side."

"And if they choose not to?" she presses.

"Then they're free to go. They're not my prisoners, Willow. They're my Vors. And more importantly, they're my friends."

She nods. "Right. Friends. Maybe the three of you can reinstate old traditions."

She's going somewhere with this, I'm just not sure where. She doesn't make me wait long, though. Silence has always been her undoing.

"Tell me," she says, running tentative fingers over her silverware, "when's the last time you went to Vixen Pond? Or was it Vixen Palace?"

I sigh and press my head to the table for a moment. "That's why I tell Jax to keep his mouth shut."

She smiles. "I'm glad he opened up to me."

"We were young," I tell her. "And horny. It was the best way we knew how to celebrate. In fact, Jax still celebrates like that from time to time. Gaiman got tired of the scene a few years ago."

"And you?"

I smile. "What is the answer you want from me, Willow?"

"The truth," she says. "That's all."

"I enjoyed myself when I was a young man. That's all I'll say."

Her face sours just a little, though she doesn't say anything.

"But after Pavel's death, things changed for me," I say. "Indulging in alcohol and women wasn't as fulfilling anymore. Things changed for good. They've never gone back."

She looks relieved, but a ghost of worry still lingers over her face. "Well, that's... interesting."

I lean over and grab the arm of her chair. In one swift movement, I pull her over so she's sitting right next to me. I place my hand on the slit running up her dress so that I'm touching her bare skin again. She's got goosebumps.

"Jealous again?"

She frowns. "I'm not jealous."

"Really?" I ask. "Because you did a brilliant imitation of it before you knew who Ariel really was."

"What about you?" she demands, blatantly changing the subject. "You get jealous, too."

"Give me one instance."

She arches a brow. "When I walked down here naked and you practically beat the waiter for looking at me."

She isn't wrong. I'm still tempted to gouge the man's eyes out. "That was quite the stunt you pulled."

"You thought I wouldn't do it," she says. "So of course I had to."

"Stubborn as ever."

She smiles. "What about me?"

"What do you mean?"

"In our game of pretend," she says. "Where am I? What am I doing?"

"You're right here, of course," I tell her. "Leading the Bratva with me. Raising our children."

Now it's her turn to pick out that one little word. "Children?"

"We'll have more, of course. A dozen, maybe. I've always wanted to be able to field a whole sports team of my own."

"Oh, is that so?" she laughs, trying not to smile too much. "And was I consulted about any of that?"

"Sure, but it was hardly necessary. I know exactly what you want."

"And you think that what I want is more children?"

"No, what you want is me," I say slowly, meeting her eyes. "Go ahead… deny it."

She stares at me, her expression growing serious. I can see the whirlwind of emotions running around inside her head. She's an overthinker, and right now, her brain is on overdrive.

"Leo… I can't be the wife you want me to be."

"You'll learn."

"That's just it: I don't want to learn to be a doormat. I did that once and I vowed I'd never do it again."

"I don't want or expect you to be a doormat wife, Willow," I tell her. "I want the opposite. I want a queen."

She frowns. "Okay, sure, that sounds very nice and flattering and all. But I know why you married me. And I want to be with a man who's madly in love with me. Who wants me as much as I want him. This relationship we have… it's always going to be one-sided. And I'm not sure I can live with that."

"That's what you believe?"

She sighs. "We don't need to beat around the bush. You married me for my last name. But I can't just be in a marriage of convenience, Leo. That's not me. I want something real."

I open my mouth to tell her just how wrong she is. How she might have started as a pawn in a game, but she's become so much more. Something I dream about. Something I crave. Something I can't see myself living without ever again.

"I—"

"Boss."

Gaiman walks into the dining room from the kitchen. I'm about to kick him out again when I notice the look on his face.

I stand up fast. "What is it?"

"We just received a package at a Bratva outpost down south," Gaiman informs me.

"And?"

"There was a note that came with it claiming it was urgent. So the men sent it up here to you. They checked it thoroughly, no explosive residue anywhere. I went over it myself. But…"

"But what?"

"It's here." Gaiman jerks his head toward the door to indicate. "Outside. I didn't want to bring it inside. The package, it… it smells."

My blood curdles in my veins. "Willow, why don't you go upstairs to your room? You don't need to see—"

"Not a chance," she retorts, moving past me and Gaiman before I can even get out of my seat.

"Fucking hell," I growl, following her. As I pass Gaiman, I mutter to him, "You couldn't have called me out and told me all this privately?"

"Sorry, boss," Gaiman says, but his voice sounds strange. I've never seen him like this. He looks lost.

"You know what's in the package?"

"I have my suspicions," he confesses. "I don't think it's good."

The box has been placed on the porch, right at the edge of the steps. It's big, maybe the size of a basketball. Willow stops short and turns to me expectantly. Her nose crinkles up as she picks up on the stench.

"Jesus," she coughs. "It's horrible."

The thumping of blood in my temples worsens. I feel like I'm dreaming again, but this is a nightmare. "Willow… step back."

"I'm not being dismissed," she argues.

"Just… back."

She must hear the catch in my voice, because she frowns and obeys. She moves towards Gaiman as Jax comes into view from the other side. He doesn't bother climbing the porch steps. He just stands in the snow, waiting solemnly.

I pull out the knife I keep in my right boot and slice the edges of the package open. With every second, I'm frowning more confident I know what's inside.

There's only one thing that smells like that: rotting flesh.

I pull open the lid and then stand back. There's something that happens to the body when you die. Especially the face. Every muscle relaxes, sags with the weight of gravity. The person looks almost unrecognizable. Almost.

"Leo…"

"Willow," I say firmly. "Get inside. Now."

"What is it? I can't see…" She grabs my arm and pushes past me.

But she stops short once the box comes into view. She goes ramrod straight for a moment as she tries to make sense of what her eyes are seeing.

The cut at the base of the neck is sharp and clean. Belov knew what he was doing. He was careful. It's almost surgical.

Everything else looks the same as the last time I saw her. The long blond hair, as vibrant as ever, even in death. The chipped front tooth, broken from where it hit the table.

The fantasy we had withers on the vine.

No more hoping. No more pretending.

Willow claps a hand over her mouth. "Ariel…"

Then she collapses.

34

WILLOW

I keep seeing her face.

Both of them. The one from when she was breathing and walking and living, and the one from after.

I can't quite believe that what I saw in the box was real. It looked more like doll parts, like a prop from a cheesy horror movie. Stripped to something inhuman. Disassembled like plastic.

I haven't eaten for two days. I haven't slept, either.

Every time I try, I see Ariel's head in that box. Then I either throw up or wake up screaming.

Leo holds me as often as he can. He whispers things to me that I don't hear. Things I can't hear. Because all I hear is the thrumming of my pulse telling me I'm still alive.

And Ariel is dead.

This is the third day now. I'm getting better at avoiding that image of the bloodstained box in my mind. I'm getting better at dealing with the insurmountable weight that's settled on my chest. God knows if I'll ever be free of it again.

"Willow?"

Leo walks to the bed in the darkness. But I know it's morning. Flickers of light come through the blinds every time they move in the breeze of the fan.

He sits down on the edge of the bed and I turn to him. "Have you eaten anything today?"

"Bread," I lie.

He raises a disbelieving brow.

"Fine. Nothing. I can't eat," I tell him. "I'll just throw up."

"The funeral is today."

"Funeral?" I ask, sitting up. "You're having a funeral for her?"

"Of course. She deserves a proper burial."

"But you don't have… all that's left is…" The image rises up like bile, and I swallow it back down.

"It's something," he says. "And she needs to be honored. She earned a warrior's send-off."

I press my forehead against the back of his hand. He's warm to the touch, and comforting. "We need to kill him, Leo. He claimed to love her, but he…" I clap a palm to my mouth to keep in a sob. "He has our son."

"He's not going to touch Pasha," Leo says confidently. "I won't let him."

And even though I know he can't make those kinds of promises, it feels good to just believe him. His strength, his confidence, his unassailable self-assurance… it's all easy to cling to.

Matter of fact, it's the only thing I have left to cling to.

"There's no one on the inside to protect him," I whisper. "There's—"

He grabs my hand and pulls it to his heart. "Listen to me: we cannot afford to crumble now. Pasha needs our best."

"How can you be so calm?"

"I'm the don, Willow. I don't have the luxury of breaking down. I have to keep it together. All the fucking time. No matter what."

He knew Ariel better than I did. If either of us should be falling apart, it should be Leo.

"I'm sorry," I say. "I shouldn't be—I should be here. With you. For you. I should be able to keep it together, like you are."

He pats my hand. "You don't have to keep it together. That's why you have me."

I give him a shaky smile, but it falls off my face almost immediately. "I don't know if I can make it to the funeral," I admit. "I… I won't be able to hold it together."

He squeezes my hand. "Willow, this is what we do."

"I'm not Bratva."

"Ariel wasn't Bratva either," he tells me. "Until the day she was."

It hurts almost as bad as any pain I've ever felt. But I know he's right.

I nod slowly and pull myself out of the bed. Leo doesn't help me. He just stands back and watches me as I stumble achingly towards the bathroom.

I manage a quick rinse in a cold shower. When I walk back out, there's a black dress laid out on the bed. Leo's nowhere in sight, but I know he's the one who picked it for me. It screams of his influence. Sleeveless, tasteful, with a modest hem and a sweetheart neckline. I slip it on and pull my hair up into a severe knot.

When I'm dressed, I sit myself in front of the mirror and stare at my bare face. I look the way I feel: burned out and hopeless. I have dark circles around my eyes and caved-in cheeks. I apply just enough foundation to make me look presentable and then I head downstairs.

Leo is standing in a loose circle between Jax and Gaiman. All three men turn to me.

Gaiman stays where he is, but Jax moves towards me. "Need a hand?" He offers me his arm.

I take his elbow gratefully, and we proceed down the forest path towards the column of vehicles.

"Where are we burying her?" I ask Jax.

"There's a cemetery in the area, just down from the village. Leo handled arrangements with a pastor. It's a fitting place for her. She…"

He trails off, and I chance a glimpse at his face. His usual bright smile is gone.

"Were you close with her?" I ask.

"We had our moments," he says. "I didn't know her that well. Her mission kept her away a lot of the time. But I respected her."

I nod. "She was probably the bravest woman I've ever known."

"You and me both."

We get into the jeeps. I'm glad when Leo takes the wheel. He said he'd be strong for me, that he'd protect me, and God, how I need that. I need to be close to him so I can absorb some of that strength.

But I've learned how to be strong on my own, too. Maybe that's what he means by a queen: someone who can accept help as often as she gives it.

The drive down to the cemetery is quiet. Just the thrum of the engines and the crunching of rocks beneath our tires.

When we arrive, Jax helps me out of the car and we turn to survey the area. Gravestones dot the frozen ground, but the space is wide open. The mountains are visible all around, a hedge of protection against a gray and unforgiving sky. The village is just down the hill. Smoke rises from the chimneys and swirls overhead.

It's a beautiful location. Austere, remote, but then again, she was also those things. And even though Ariel isn't in a position to care either way, I feel better about it.

Jax walks me to the burial site. The brass coffin is already set up and ready to be lowered into the ground. I don't have the faintest idea how they managed to dig six feet into this icy rock, but I don't ask. Leo proved long ago that he is capable of regular miracles.

Speaking of Leo, I don't see him. I turn and look around, but his face isn't among the rows of Bratva men waiting at quiet attention.

"He just likes to keep busy," Jax says, interpreting my confusion correctly.

"How's he doing?" I ask. "Really?"

"I think he's feeling everything. Grief, sadness. Guilt. Not that he's said a word, of course. That's never been his way."

"So he doesn't talk to you guys, either?"

"No. He keeps his emotions pretty close to his chest."

"Has he ever opened up to anyone?"

"Once. Then he died."

The way he says it tells me everything I could've ever known about Leo.

I stare at the coffin, wondering if Ariel is really in there. The part of her that was sent to us, at least. My stomach twists again as the memory rushes back to me in vivid detail.

My hand tightens around Jax's arm as I struggle to stay on my feet.

"Are you okay?" he asks.

"I… I… I will be…"

"You look pale."

"I just—"

I turn and see Leo walking towards us. He looks so handsome in his black suit and his slicked back hair, but his eyes are a million miles away.

"I'll take it from here," he rumbles.

Jax transfers my hand from his arm to Leo's. I expect him to stand beside me, but instead, he pivots me around and starts walking in the opposite direction.

"Where are we going?"

"The pastor isn't here yet," he says. "We have some time before we lower her down. I thought we could take a walk."

I know the walk is for my benefit. Leo knows everything. He could tell I was close to losing it.

"I'm trying," I whisper. "But how do you get used to it? All this… death?"

"You just do," he says. "Ariel always knew that it might end like this. So did I." He shakes his head. "But there's no point going back, Willow. No point playing and replaying what happened. What we could have done differently. What's done is done."

"I am grateful to Ariel," I say softly. "And I respect and admire her. But… I can't stop thinking about Pasha. That he's alone in there. Does that make me a bad person?"

"No," he tells me. "That just makes you a mother."

"Do you feel that way, too?" I ask, almost hopefully. "Like a… like a father?"

"All the fucking time," he says.

I turn around to face him. His expression gives nothing away. It might as well be a normal day. We may as well be a normal couple out for a normal walk. The fantasy from our dinner the other night lives on, as sick and twisted as it's become.

"Is this how you handled your brother's death?"

He laughs bitterly. "Not at all. I was out of control when he died."

"And now?"

"I'm older," he says. "I'm wiser. I know that raging against fate never changes anything. So I choose to focus on what I can change. I can't bring Ariel back, but I can save our son. I can avenge her death. I can avenge Pavel's death."

"I'm surprised you're taking the time to bury her. I figured you'd be on the warpath already."

"Ariel believed that death was the end. She never much cared what happened to her body after she died." He shrugged. "I may not be raging, but we all have to figure out a way to say goodbye. This funeral is mine."

I reach out and curl my hand around his arm again. "I'll give you one thing: she has a great view."

"She deserves it," he says. "She deserves so much more."

We stand silently for a while, surveying the valley opening up below us. The village is clustered on the side of a steep mountain, clinging on for dear life. The horizon looks like it goes on forever.

"I have to go in, Leo," I say softly. "I have to give myself to Belov. At least on the surface. I have to—"

"Enough."

He doesn't raise his voice. In fact, he seems to get quieter. Yet the command in that one word stops me immediately.

"You are not going in. Especially now. I won't let you put yourself in danger. Don't bring this up again."

"Then what do I do, Leo? Do I just sit back and do nothing?"

"No. You just trust me."

I do trust Leo. And he told me once that fear can be a powerful tool. It can cause you to freeze in place, to falter and die.

Or it can drive you to act.

I believed him when he said that. I trusted him. And it's how I know that, right now, my fear is pushing me to act.

With or without him.

35

WILLOW

I'm wide awake when Leo gets into bed beside me.

The moment his weight sinks into the mattress next to me, I turn towards him and curl myself into the crook of his arm. I can tell he's surprised—we haven't done this since before I was taken. He tenses and I wonder if he's going to push me away.

Then he relaxes, curls his arm around me, and gives me his warmth.

"It was a pretty funeral," I tell him, the darkness making it easier for me to speak. "She would have liked it."

"She wouldn't have cared either way," Leo corrects. His voice is raspy, his breath tinged with alcohol. "But I'm glad you thought so."

"Do you think about death a lot?" I ask.

"Not really."

"But you see it all the time, in a way not many people do. Up close and personal."

"Exactly," he says. "I see enough of it that I don't want to spend the rest of my time thinking about it. In any case, death doesn't scare me."

The funny thing is, I believe him. If there's one man alive that Death itself is probably terrified of, it's Leo Solovev.

"Well, it scares me," I whisper.

"Why?" he asks. "Death has to be better than life."

I glance up at him. For a man who is masculinity personified, he has such long, pretty eyelashes. They brush across his cheeks as he blinks.

"Has anyone ever told you you have a very morbid view of existence?"

"Occupational hazard." He shrugs and then turns to me. "You seem to be doing better, by the way."

I nod, hoping that my face gives nothing away. I don't want him to see something in my expression and stop my plan before I can even set it in motion.

"I wouldn't say that," I say mildly. "I'm just trying to survive. For Pasha."

"I will get him back, Willow. I know that won't stop you from worrying. But trust that I will keep him safe."

I do trust Leo. But he won't believe that once I leave.

I'm not even anxious about walking into Belov's territory. I'm anxious about leaving Leo. I'm worried that he'll think I doubted him. Betrayed him.

And I'm worried I won't make it out alive.

It makes me want to say things to Leo that I've never had the courage to say before. The irony is that if I say them now, he'll suspect something. He'll know that what I'm really saying is *goodbye*. So I shut my mouth and cling to the feeling of being in his arms and try to let that be enough of a farewell to last me through the hell I'm about to wade into.

"When all this is over," I whisper to him, falling back into our game of pretend, "I want to visit Europe. I've never been before."

"I'll take you," he says simply.

"Will you have the time?"

"I'll make the time."

I smile so hard it makes me want to cry. Because I know he's playing pretend, too. I rest my hand on his chest and stroke back and forth for a while.

His muscles are as hard as they look. I support myself on one elbow as I look down on him, admiring the contours of his body. All this time and I've never stopped thinking that he is the most beautiful man ever to walk this planet.

"Do you think this will ever be over?" I ask. "I've only been a part of it for a fraction of the time and it still feels like forever. I can't imagine how it must be for you."

"It does feel like forever," he admits. "But you learn to cope."

"How?"

"Just keep going."

"You make that sound so simple." I shake my head. "I wish I could be more like you."

He looks at me with his intense, confident gaze, and I imagine that for a man like Leo, enduring is just par for the course. He's the kind of man who can make the oceans move if he chooses to.

But me? I've always moved with the waves. Let the current lead me.

Starting tomorrow, that's going to change.

But tonight, I'm still playing pretend.

I rest my hand against his face and lean in to press my lips to his. I'm not sure if he knows I need the distraction or if he needs it just as badly. But his kiss is deep and reassuring. And so I let myself be comforted.

I slide onto his body, straddling him. I sit up and pull my t-shirt over my head in one move, flinging it to the floor beside the bed.

Leo runs his hands up my sides, tightening around my waist. His thumbs brush the undersides of my breasts before his warm, rough hands palm me. My nipples pebble under his touch.

Then his hands slip down my body. I lean forward, our bodies pressed together inch for inch. I kiss his neck, his chest, his abs. I roam his body and just like always, it takes my breath away.

I go further south, tracing over his tattoos and the sharp-sloping V of his lower abs, until I reach the hard length of his cock. He springs to life in my hand.

I circle his shaft with my fingers and massage him gently. As I do, I move lower and run my tongue over his balls.

He lets out a contented sigh. I suck on one ball and then the other while my hand pumps at his cock. As his groans deepen and multiply, I run my tongue up his shaft. I linger at the tip, sucking on his head.

I take my time. I let him fill my mouth slowly until I'm able to welcome him deep into the back of my throat. His hand curls in the hair at the back of my head, but it just rests there gently. He lets me control the speed and depth. I take him to his base three times before I finally pull out, unable to ignore the throbbing in my pussy any longer.

I climb on top of him and press his cock against my opening. With my hands planted on his chest, I slide down onto him. I stretch around him slowly, taking his length inside in one smooth move.

"Fuck," I moan, my eyes rolling back in my head. We've gone to bed God only knows how many times now, and every time still feels as good as the first.

Leo grabs my hips, and I start to grind up and down on his cock. His eyes are dark and focused. He watches me move on him with singular focus, but I feel too good to be self-conscious. I'm lost in it already. I roll my hips, pleasure zinging through me with every movement. Heat pools low in my belly and my body begins to tremble.

"Leo," I breathe. I say his name like a prayer. Like a plea. "Leo…"

"Come for me, *kukolka*," he says.

With that, my body gives in to the pleasure. I clench my thighs around him and arch my back. I cry out as I spasm around him so many times that I start to wonder if this orgasm will ever end. I'm lost in a haze of lust and need and sensation, and a warmer, deeper emotion that swims beneath all of that. I grind against him until I have nothing left.

When I collapse on his chest, Leo wraps his arms around me and rolls me onto my back.

I'm sure I'm completely spent, but as usual, Leo knows better. He drapes my legs over his shoulders and wrings more pleasure out of me. His thumb circles my center, and before I've fully come down from the last orgasm, I'm crying out again.

This time, Leo falls with me.

Afterwards, we lie together in silence, staring at the ceiling and immersed in our own thoughts. We wait just long enough to catch our breath, and then we fuck again.

Four times that night, I lose myself to orgasm. Four times, he comes, marking me in every possible way. I fall asleep naked on top of him, exhausted and spent.

∽

When I wake up, he's gone.

Secretly, I'm relieved. I take a bath, wash my hair, and dress carefully. Jeans. A long sleeved, tight-fitted white sweater. A thick jacket to stave off the cold. I take a satchel with me, but there's nothing inside it apart from a little cash and an extra change of clothes, just in case.

I tie my hair back and head downstairs. I know the staff's movements now, so it's easy to avoid them and slip outside.

The vehicles are parked off to the side of the gravel drive that winds up to the cabin. I hide in the brush and watch to see if they're being manned yet. I wait through fifteen minutes of frigid stillness before I approach.

Some of Leo's men head into the village for supplies most mornings. When I'm sure they haven't yet disembarked from the warmth of the cabin to the jeeps, I climb into the first car in the line and hide underneath the same tarp I used last time I pulled this stunt.

Another fifteen or twenty minutes of silence passes with me mummified in the back of the car. I can't feel my nose, my fingers, my toes, and every breath hurts like an ice pick in my throat.

At long last, I hear the thump of oncoming footsteps. The doors crank open, men chattering to themselves in Russian and English as they load up.

A few more agonizing breaths later, the engine roars to life, and blessed warmth fills the cabin.

I close my eyes during the drive to the village, absorbing every bump of the unpaved roads as softly as I can. When the car stops and the engine dies, I wait for the slamming of car doors.

Once everything is quiet again, I remove the tarp and peer outside. I don't see anyone around, so I get out of the jeep and make a run for it.

I head into the nearest café and order a coffee that I don't plan on staying long enough to drink. While I'm waiting, I scan the people sitting at the small tables. There's a couple at the window table and an elderly man reading a newspaper in one of the center tables. I can see his car keys dangling against the waistband of his belt.

I pretend as though I'm heading to the bathroom and then I make a detour around his table. I have to dip low to retrieve the key, but I manage to snag it without him noticing.

I get a look from the couple as I head out the door, but I don't turn back to see if they suspect anything.

When I press the unlock button on the fob, the headlights of a small blue car flash only a few feet away.

If the owner is paying attention, he'll see me climb into his car and drive away. I have to move quickly. I start the engine and rip out of the street parking, not daring to check the rearview mirror.

I drive fast, speeding down mountain passes, listening for a siren that never comes.

The car doesn't have navigation, but I don't need it. I know where I'm going.

It takes me almost three hours to get there. I make a stop halfway to switch cars, more for peace of mind than anything else. And then I keep going.

After a year away, being back in the city—and free—feels strange. But I move through the streets like I never left.

I pass by all my old haunts and head to a bar I know is tied to the Mikhailov Bratva. It was part of my training with Anya. *Know the land. Know your enemy.*

And so long as Belov is leading the Mikhailov, they're the fucking enemy.

I park the car right outside the pub and walk inside as confidently as I can.

"We're closed," a man rasps from behind the bar..

I walk up to the counter and plunk myself down on one of the swivel barstools. "Tell Spartak Belov I'm here to see him. And get me a drink while I wait. Something strong."

The man snorts. "And who the hell do you think you are, little missy?"

I raise a brow and fix him with an icy glare. "Viktoria fucking Mikhailov," I say. "Call Belov. I'll wait."

36

LEO

Gaiman and Jax aren't sure what to do with my rage.

Truth be told, I'm not sure what to do with it, either.

My hands clench. The urge to lash out, to destroy something, to punish someone, is strong. But I need to save this rage for the man who deserves it.

"We don't have a full security system set up here," Gaiman says cautiously. "It covers a lot, but—Shit, Leo, we didn't think Willow was a flight risk anymore. She didn't even have an assigned guard."

"Why the flying fuck did she make a run for it?" Jax interjects. "She seemed fine."

"She's not running from me," I grit out. "She's running towards *him*. Towards our son."

Jax's eyes go wide. "You mean… she's taking Belov up on his deal?"

I turn my back on both of them. "Get the men ready. We're going in."

"Are you sure?" Gaiman asks. "Preparations aren't—"

"We can't wait any longer. Willow has forced my hand. It's time to move forward and let the chips fall where they may."

"But Willow and Pasha," Gaiman warns. "They'll be at risk."

"He'll use them," I say. "Undoubtedly. But Willow is more capable than I've given her credit for. She'll have to hold her own. At least until I can get close enough to Belov and snap his neck myself."

My fingers flex, imagining the satisfying crunch of his spine. I told Ariel she could be the one to kill him. But now I'm all that's left.

I don't mind doing the job.

I'm moving to the door when my phone starts ringing. It's a private number. "It's him," I say immediately. Willow must have given him my number. It's the only way he'd have my private cell. "He's requesting a video call."

Gaiman rushes towards the monitor on my desk. "I'll transfer the call to the computer."

He takes my phone, taps some buttons on the screen, and hands me my phone. I press *Accept*.

At first, all I see is part of a room. White walls, shelves stuffed with books I know he's never read. Generic. Unthreatening.

Then Belov steps into the frame.

I wouldn't be surprised if he has a director standing behind the camera. The man loves putting on a show.

"Thanks so much for answering my call, old friend," he croons. "Your dear wife gave me your number. I hope you don't mind."

"Where is she?" I growl.

"Right here." Belov waves his hand and the camera pans around. "Catching up with her grandfather."

The camera lands on Semyon first. He's in his wheelchair with his nurse standing right behind him. For the past several years, I've never seen one without the other. She's the old man's shadow. You get the feeling he'd die if she took too many steps away from his side.

In the chair next to Semyon is Willow.

She seems to be unharmed. She's not even tied down. She's sitting calmly next to him, if somewhat stiff and vacant-eyed.

"Willow."

She looks off to the side, and I know she's looking at me on the screen. "I'm sorry, Leo," she murmurs. "I had to do it."

Belov steps back in front of the camera, but I can still see both Willow and Semyon on either side of his monstrous head.

"I owe you many debts," he says. "The first of course is the beautiful mole you planted by my side."

"Did you never suspect her?" I ask. "I'm sure you didn't. If you had, she would've died years ago."

"It was clever, I must admit. Was she always yours?"

I clench my jaw tight, remembering just how far back we went. "From the very fucking beginning."

"Then it's a shame you didn't get her back in one piece," Belov says with mock sympathy. "Unfortunately, I had to play with her one last time before she left. And I play a little rough."

Willow shivers behind him.

"You will pay for what you did to her," I promise. "I'll see to that myself."

"Really?" Belov asks. "It seems a little late for threats. Because as far as I can see, I've already won."

"Then you're delusional."

The smile slides off his face. I can see just how much Ariel's betrayal has lit the flame of his mania. It's a nauseating glimpse into the chasm where his humanity should be. All I see is poison.

He spins around in a circle, arms wide. "Am I imagining all of this? I don't think so. I have your son. I have your wife. I've had Semyon for years, but the old man is pretty much useless now that I have Viktoria Mikhailov."

He moves towards Semyon's wheelchair. I know what's about to happen. Can feel it in my bones.

But I'm not sure Willow does.

"I had to put up with this old sack of shit for years. Despite what you seem to believe, Leo, I do know how much the men value the bloodlines," he says, sitting between Willow and Semyon. "But you were right about one thing: he stopped calling the shots a long time ago."

Belov looks to the nurse and gives a quick nod. In a flash, she pulls out a knife.

I watch as she slits the old don's throat with one swift slash.

Willow gasps, but before she can truly respond, Spartak yanks her out of her seat and pulls her to her feet. He spins her around so that her back is pressed to his chest. Then he walks her over to the camera.

I lean forward instinctively. I want to jump through the screen and tear his hands off at the wrists for even daring to lay a finger on my wife.

"For every mark you leave on her, I will return the favor a hundred times over," I growl. "That's a fucking vow, Belov."

"If only that threat scared me, Leo," he tuts. "But you see, I'm don now. And this is my queen. Isn't she a beauty?"

He presses his lips into her neck as Willow trembles. Her body is shaking, but her expression is almost eerily calm.

"Don't you worry, though," Belov says as he resurfaces. "I don't plan on hurting her. As a matter of fact, I plan on fucking her until she forgets all about you."

He twists Willow's face around so she's forced to look right at him. Then he presses his lips to hers, and I'm forced to watch as he steals a kiss that was never meant for him.

Willow stiffens under his barbaric hold. She's not returning the kiss, but Belov doesn't seem to care. It's enough for him that he's able to gloat. This is a display of what he thinks is power.

But he doesn't know the first thing about real power.

I intend to show him.

Belov breaks away and smiles maniacally at the screen. "Are you ready for the last act, Leo? It's time we finished this."

"I couldn't agree more."

He nods. "It will be so much more satisfying watching you die knowing that I'll be fucking your wife every night. Knowing that your son will grow up calling me *Otets*."

"Keep dreaming," I tell him calmly. "When I'm done with you, endless sleep is all you'll have left."

He smiles.

The line goes dead.

Black clouds of anger roil through me, but I take a deep breath. I focus the rage into action. Into one thought.

This fucker is going to die today.

I head downstairs where Jax and Gaiman are rallying the troops. Men are running around, gathering their weapons and trying to get in the headspace for battle. I know I haven't given them a normal amount of time to prepare, but it doesn't matter.

I know each one by name. I know what they're capable of doing. And I also know Belov's men are as unreliable as mine are deadly. It is about to be a motherfucking slaughter.

~

By the time we get to Spartak's compound, I'm so pumped up that I can practically taste the adrenaline on my tongue. The building rises up before us, squat, concrete, and fortified.

In a few short hours, it will be reduced to rubble.

"Gaiman," I bark as we get out of the jeeps, "find Pasha and Willow. Make sure to get them out safe. Take however many men you need. They're going to be well-guarded."

Gaiman nods and pulls out his guns.

Jax does the same. "I'll lead the charge."

"No," I say. "*I* will. I want that fucker to see death coming for him. You get the explosives ready."

A few minutes later, the ground beneath us shakes as our explosives are detonated around the Mikhailov gates. The metal screams in protest, but it's no match for the bombs. Once the dust settles, the path is clear.

I give the command for my men to drive through. "Stay in the jeeps until you have them on the defensive," I instruct.

The line of cars is swallowed by the lingering smoke from the explosives. Before we clear the area of reduced visibility, the gunshots begin.

And I make my move.

I head inside with Jax at my back. He covers me while I look for a way into the massive mansion.

My men in the jeeps are picking off Mikhailov soldiers like fish in a barrel. There doesn't seem to be any effort at a coordinated attack. Just flailing chaos in every direction.

Belov had to have informed the men we were coming, but they still look like amateurs on their first day of work.

And then I realize why.

None of them have the Mikhailov mark. They're not Belov's men. They're the mercenaries Belov paid for.

Best fucking news I've heard all day.

Smiling, I jump onto one of the jeeps and hoist myself onto its roof to get a vantage of the battle unfurling all around me.

Belov's men litter the ground, their blood soaking into the cold earth. In comparison, only two of my men look injured. We have no one dead on our side.

"You're outmatched!" I yell, calling everyone's attention. "In both numbers and skill. If you continue to fight, you will die. And I will show you no mercy. But lay down your weapons now and you might have a chance to fight again. To fuck again. To live."

The mercenaries hesitate, not lowering their weapons, but no longer shooting. I don't know how much Belov is paying them, but it can't be enough.

My men tighten around the remaining mercs.

"What do you choose?" I ask. "You want to fight and die, or surrender and live?"

The first one to put down his gun is older. A long scar runs down his face and burn marks pepper his other cheek and shoulder.

He looks like a man who has seen it all. If he is laying down his weapon, it's because he knows the battle is already lost.

Just as I suspected, the moment he gives up, the others follow suit. A dozen men drop their weapons, followed by a dozen more.

That's how far loyalty gets you when it's paid for in cash.

The only currency that matters is blood.

The only men left standing, clasping their weapons stubbornly, are ones I recognize as true Bratva. The ones who wear the mark of their leader. Who would die for him.

I look at all of them in turn. How many in total? Fifteen, maybe twenty?

"I know who you are," I tell them. "I respect it. But the man you follow is not your don. He stole the title from a man who was born to it."

One of the men still standing speaks up. "Don Mikhailov picked Spartak Belov to lead us."

He's slight in comparison to the others. Fine-boned, almost delicate. But I can see the steely-eyed resolve in his face. He's a man who'll fight to the death for what he believes in.

"No, he didn't," I say, making sure to raise my voice just in case Belov is listening from his fortress upstairs. "He didn't choose Belov. He was fooled by Belov. And by the time he knew better, it was too late."

"You don't know that."

"I know more than you think," I say. "I wouldn't be here today if I didn't. Belov is not Bratva. You all know that. So why do you still follow him?"

"We follow Semyon Mikhailov."

"Semyon is dead," I say. "Killed by the man you claim he chose."

A murmur goes up through the crowd. Confusion. Uncertainty. Good—I can use that.

"Don't believe me?" I press. "Go inside. You'll find him in his wheelchair with his throat slit."

"Why would Belov kill him now?" the man asks.

"Because he has my wife," I snarl. "He has Viktoria Mikhailov. And he believes you will follow him because of that. Is he right?"

The determined ferocity on their faces is starting to wane a little. They're beginning to question the path they're on, the leader they've chosen to follow.

"What's the alternative?" the slight man asks. "Follow you instead?"

"I will not ask any of you to follow me," I say. "If your loyalty calls you to follow Viktoria, then I will welcome you as brothers. If your loyalty compels you to walk away from the Bratva life completely, I will respect that."

"Why should we believe you?"

"I am not the fraudulent don that Belov has pretended to be," I say. "I have the loyalty of my men because I've earned it. Do you imagine that would have happened if I didn't keep my promises?"

"I'm not making a decision until I see Don Semyon's body," one man shouts.

The others yell in agreement, and I nod. "Very well. But in order to give you proof, I'm going to need to enter the house."

The slight man gestures towards the door. "None of us will stop you."

I nod and jump down off the roof of the jeep. I land on my feet and straighten immediately. Jax and Gaiman approach from both sides.

As the three of us step through the bullet-marked doors of the Mikhailov compound, I listen for sounds.

The sounds of my wife.

The sounds of my son.

But all I can hear is the pumping of adrenaline through my body. It sounds like a drumbeat. It sounds like a dirge that's playing me home.

"That had to be the shortest fight in history," Jax complains.

"Disappointed?"

"Of course I am! We've been waiting for this moment for eight years. That was anticlimactic, to say the least."

"Calm down, Jax," I tell him. "It's not over yet."

37

WILLOW

Somehow, he's not dead yet.

I stare at the old man. My grandfather, though it's still hard to think of him as that. His eyes lull sightlessly in his head. Against all odds, he's still in there.

I know he doesn't deserve it. But in his last moments of life, I decide to do the only humane thing. I kneel down beside his wheelchair and take his hand.

"He would have married you off to a powerful fuck with a lot of money and the ambition to match," Spartak says, watching me intently. "Be thankful I got rid of him for you."

As if on cue, Semyon's head slumps forward. His hand goes limp in mine.

He's gone.

"Right," I say, releasing the old man's hand and stepping away from his body. "And in contrast, you've done so much for my benefit."

He shrugs. "In a way, I have. I've restored a crumbling Bratva. And one day, I will deliver it to your son. He will have my name, but what will it matter?"

In a way, I'm relieved. He *is* planning on keeping Pasha alive.

I glance towards the woman who killed Semyon. I'd always thought she had a kind face. Guess I was wrong.

"You took care of him for years," I say softly. "Why waste your time keeping him alive only to kill him in the end?"

She looks at me with a bewildered expression, like the question simply does not compute. "I was hired to obey."

Spartak laughs and moves forward. "You see, my beauty? That's how you survive in my Bratva. You obey."

There's so much more I want to say to him, but I bite down on my tongue until the combative words retreat. I didn't come here to argue with him or prove myself.

I came here for one reason only: to protect my son.

"I did obey," I point out. "I came here. I accepted your deal. I will obey. But only so long as my son stays safe."

He rolls his eyes. "I've already promised that."

"I want to see him."

"Jesus," he mutters. "Fine. You can see him. Come on."

I head to the door as Belov gives the killer nurse instructions on what to do with Semyon's body. In the hallway, he takes the lead.

The house is a labyrinth. The last time I was here, I spent a week trapped in one dank, dark little room with no one but a blonde nightmare for company.

It's strange that I find myself back here now, longing for that blonde nightmare to be at my side again.

When he finally stops at a door, I rush forward. But Spartak throws out a hand and stops me before I can even touch the handle.

"Not so fast, my pretty girl," he says with a sickening smile that makes my insides twist with disgust. "After you finish squealing over your fat baby, I expect to see you in my… *our* bedroom. Is that understood?"

I stiffen immediately, as much as I try to avoid it.

"Did you or did you not promise to obey?"

"What do you want from me?"

"I want to fuck Leo Solovev's wife." His eyes spark with cruelty. "The next time I see him, I want to be able to tell him how you felt clenched around my cock. I want to tell him how you tasted."

I now perfectly understand the expression *"made my skin crawl."* Because standing in front of Belov now, I feel like I'd rather skin myself alive than be touched by him. My entire body revolts at the fact that I'm even standing next to him, let alone discussing having sex with him.

"I said I'd obey. I never said I'd make you happy."

The smile slides off his face, and his expression turns intense. He takes a step forward until we're nose to nose. I want to back away, but I know that if I do, he'll make me pay for it.

My son is on the other side of this door. If I can hold my ground for long enough, I just might see him.

"Do you want to know what I did to her?" he hisses.

He doesn't say her name, but he doesn't have to. I can see the fury in his face. The anger he's suppressing at being duped.

"No."

"No?" he repeats. "That's too bad. Because I think it's important that you know what I did to her when I found out she wasn't working for me. You see, I had special cameras installed in the baby's room. Cameras no one but me knew about. Imagine my surprise when I came home, sat down in front of my monitors, and heard her talking to Leo Solovev on a burner phone."

"Enough," I say.

"No, it's not enough," Spartak lashes out. "It was the worst betrayal I've ever experienced. She was with me for years. Fucking *years*."

"She was good at her job."

He shakes his head, still dumbfounded. "She fucked me like she meant it."

"She did mean it," I tell him. "She meant it because she needed to convince you of her loyalty in order to kill you one day."

"Is that your plan, too?" he snarls in my face.

I flinch away from him and try and look as scared as I possibly can. "I'm no spy," I say. "And despite what my birth name suggests, I'm not Bratva either. I'm just here for my son."

"Does that mean I won't have any more trouble from you?"

I nod and look away.

"And what about when I present you with your husband's head?" he ponders. "What then?"

I stiffen again, but don't say anything. It's too horrible to think about, even though I don't believe that will ever happen.

Leo is far too stubborn to die.

Belov tips his head to the side. "Do you love him?"

I stare at this monster in front of me. This question, I have no trouble answering. "Yes," I rasp. "I love him."

"Even after all he's done to you. He plucked you from your life and threw you to the sharks."

"You can't choose who you love."

He nods. "It's true. I know the feeling."

"You?" I scoff. "You know nothing about love. You claim to have loved Ariel, but if that were true, you would never have been able to kill her."

He laughs. "This is the Bratva, princess. Love means nothing after betrayal. I would have killed my own mother if she'd dared to cross me."

"That's because you're an evil piece of shit."

"Spare me the theatrics. You don't think your shining prince would do the same?"

"He's harsh when he needs to be. Brutal, even," I say. "But he's not like you."

He grabs my jaw suddenly, pulling me towards him so his breath fills my nostrils, rancid and strong. I try to break away, but his grip is so tight that I'm forced to stay still.

"He is *exactly* like me," he snarls. "Exactly. And once I've fucked the fight out of you, you'll see that."

I cringe away from him, and this time, he releases me.

"Never forget who you belong to." Belov turns away. "You have half an hour with your brat. Then I expect to find you naked and ready in my bed. Understand?"

I nod, but my eyes are fixed on the door. When Belov opens it, I fly through.

It's not a huge space, but it's comfortable. Natural light streaming in through the bay windows, illuminating a crib pushed into the corner.

A woman is rocking in a chair next to the crib, her face cast in shadow. She's in her early thirties with long blonde hair. She stands up when she sees me.

"Who are you?"

"I'm his mother," I snap. "Move."

I walk forward and look into his crib.

For a terrifying moment, I actually imagine finding nothing there. That it'll be empty, that this nightmare story will have a nightmare end.

But then I see him.

I see his dark, beautiful eyes and his dark, fuzzy hair.

I see the features that are slowly starting to take shape just like Leo's.

"My boy," I sob. "My baby boy."

He raises his little fists and bats at the air. I reach down and lift him into my arms. It feels so amazing to feel his weight sink into the crook of my arm.

He coos softly, and I plant tear-stained kisses all over his face. "My boy," I cry. "My beautiful boy. I'm so sorry I left you. I'm so sorry."

The woman watches us for a moment, and then sits back down in her chair and opens a book.

Pasha has gotten so much bigger the last few months. I ache at the realization of how much I've missed. I'll never get those moments back. They're lost to time forever.

"I'll never leave you again," I promise him.

I bend down and press a kiss to his cheek. I want to tell him that I'll get him out of here. That I won't let him grow up thinking that monster, Belov, is his father.

But I can't risk saying it out loud.

So I just say it with another kiss. I press my lips to his chubby cheeks. "I'll take care of you," I whisper.

Then, in the distance, I hear an explosion.

Followed by gunfire.

The woman jumps to her feet and rushes to the window. I follow, Pasha still in my arms.

We both watch as smoke billows from the far right of the compound. Then, black jeeps appear through the smoke like the four horsemen of the apocalypse, raining bullets as they approach. Mikhailov men fall dead on the grass.

"Jesus," the woman breathes.

Wrong, I think to myself. *Leo*.

He's come for us.

A few minutes of chaos and gunsmoke pass by. It's hard to make out anything, just the vague, thrashing silhouettes of men doing violence to one another.

Then I see him.

Tall and confident, he fights his way through a line of men. To my surprise, he veers left and jumps onto the roof of one of his own jeeps.

The men before him stop fighting and turn to him, enamored with him the way I am. He was born to be a leader. Born to the power he wields like a deadly weapon.

I strain to hear what he's saying, but I can't make out his words. Whatever it is, it seems to get through to the men fighting.

When I see Leo jump down from the jeep and walk into the house, I want to flee the room and run to him. I want to meet him at the front door.

But this fight isn't over.

Not yet.

The door clicks open, and I pray it will be Leo, even though I know it's too soon for that. My heart drops when I see the nurse enter the room. She is still wearing the blood-speckled uniform she had on when she slit Semyon's throat.

Pasha's nanny rushes forward. "What's going on? Where are our men?"

"Dead or deserted," the nurse says coolly. Her eyes flicker to me.

"Oh God… they're going to kill us…"

"Don't worry, dear. They won't kill you," the nurse says calmly. "I will."

Then she pulls out a gun and shoots the nanny in the head.

I barely have time to turn and shield Pasha. When I look back, the nanny is on the floor, a pool of blood growing around her.

I face the nurse. I don't even know her name "Please…"

But before I can finish my thought, we hear footsteps approaching. The nurse turns the gun to me. She closes the distance between us and presses the muzzle to my head.

I squeeze my eyes closed, say a silent prayer, and kiss my son's forehead.

Whatever happens next is out of my control. I can only cling to my son and think of Leo.

38

LEO

I find him in a boardroom.

"Watching your legacy go up in flames?" I ask. "Seems a little masochistic, even for you."

Spartak turns to me, his gun lying casually in his hand. "You think this is the end?"

He's sitting at the end of a long table. The room is empty apart from him. His men have either abandoned him or died.

"I know it is." I brandish my gun. "It's time for your final speech, Belov."

He gives me a smile. "You think because you've got me cornered, I'm done? You don't think I have a contingency plan?"

"I'm sure you do," I say. "I never thought you were stupid. Merely misguided."

His eyes narrow as he tries to brush off the insult. "I have your wife. And your son."

"They'll be fine."

"How can you be so sure?"

"Just show me where they are," I say. I don't want to play any more games. I'm ready for this to end.

He smiles. "It would be my pleasure."

Belov rises slowly and leads me out of the room and down the hall. He heads up a flight of stairs, seemingly unconcerned that his back is to me and I'm armed.

On the way, we run into Gaiman and Jax.

"Go back down and make sure everything is under control," I tell both of them.

"What about you?" Jax asks.

"I can handle this."

"Cocky," Belov murmurs thoughtfully. "Every don's downfall."

Jax and Gaiman hesitate, but when I glare at them, they sigh and do as they're told. Spartak leads me down a long corridor and stops in front of a plain door with a golden handle.

"After you," he says.

I shake my head. "You first."

He exhales impatiently and walks in. I follow him into the room and find Willow standing there, clutching a small bundle in her arms.

"Leo…" Her eyes go wide when they land on me.

And so do mine…

When I see that Semyon's nurse has a gun pointed at her head.

"Don't worry," I tell her. "Just trust me."

"Trust you?" Spartak laughs. "Trusting *you* is going to get her killed. Trusting *me* is going to make her a Bratva queen. Now, unless you want Marika here to blow your wife's brains out, lower your weapon."

Without hesitation, I drop my arm. Belov gives a satisfied smile and relaxes.

"See, my dear? I'm the horse you should have tied your wagon to," he says. "Any last words to your dearly beloved husband?"

"Don't kill him," she begs. "Please."

"My beauty, don't make this harder on yourself than it has to be. Say what you need to say while you still can."

She says nothing, but I can see tears start to pool in her eyes.

"Very well," Belov says with a shrug.

He turns to me and raises his gun. I stare at the barrel calmly.

As I expected, he doesn't pull the trigger. He can't bear ending things so unceremoniously. He wants the whole fucking dog-and-pony show.

If only he knew how this was really about to end.

"Let's clear up a few mysteries first, shall we?" Spartak asks. "How did you find out about Willow in the first place? By the time I learned of her existence, you had already married her."

"Let's just say I had a friend on the inside."

"And they found out about Anya's secret bank account for Willow?" he guesses.

"Exactly."

"Okay, I'll bite," Belov says. "Who was this friend on the inside?"

I glance towards Willow. I planned on doing this part differently. I planned to sit her down and explain the whole story, from beginning to end, so she could finally see just how all the puzzle pieces fit together.

But circumstances change. Plans shift. Life interferes.

"Semyon Mikhailov."

Willow's eyes go wide.

I turn to Belov, and he's wearing the same shock. He shakes his head. "It can't be."

"Why would I lie now?" I ask. "He knew the monster to whom he had handed over his Bratva. He regretted it. When he found out about Anya's secret account, he traced it back to Willow and surmised that she was his granddaughter. That's when he made the decision to reach out to me."

Belov's surprise is shifting to rage. "He reached out to you?"

"This is going to be tedious if you insist on repeating everything I say," I sigh. "Yes, he reached out to me. That's how I knew about Willow."

"I monitored the old fuck," Belov spits. "I watched him like a hawk. He didn't leave the fucking compound without my say-so. Without my being there."

"He didn't leave the compound," I say. "He sent me a letter."

"He would have needed help to get a letter to you," Belov says, trying to connect the dots. "He would have—"

He stops short. "Of course," he whispers. "Of course… Brit."

I shake my head. "She wasn't the go-between. We'd placed her too close to you. I couldn't risk her identity being compromised if you happened to catch her with a letter from Semyon that was addressed to me."

Belov is starting to look nervous now. I can see the fear quickly replacing his confidence.

"Do you really think that Ariel was the only mole I planted?" I press. "I planted someone even before Ariel. Someone no one would ever suspect. A person who could hide in plain sight. Except that Semyon was a lot more perceptive than I gave him credit for. He discovered my mole early on. He made it clear that he had no intention of fighting against the Solovevs any longer. The only person he wanted destroyed… was you."

Belov's face has gone dark with rage. "Who was it? Tell me who the fuck it was!"

The nurse pulls the gun away from Willow's head and aims it at Belov.

"It was me," she says.

Then she shoots.

Willow curves her body over Pasha and runs to the corner of the room, away from the action.

Belov is lying on the ground, clutching his bleeding leg. The nurse shot to wound, not to kill.

In the excitement, he dropped his gun. I kick it out of his reach.

"Surprise, motherfucker," I whisper, enjoying the way his expression is twisting between rage and fear.

"It… it can't be…"

"Luda," I say, gesturing for her to come forward. "Why don't you come and introduce yourself?"

She walks over and stands at my shoulder. The gun is still in her hand, steel in her eyes. After almost a decade of lying in wait, she's seething with rage.

"My name is Luda Yolkin," she says. "My son's name was Petyr Yolkin. Do you remember him?"

Belov stares at her blankly, his eyes shifting from her face to the gun in her hand.

"Petyr," Willow breathes from where she's crouched in the corner. "He was your brother's second in command."

I nod. "Pavel's closest friend and his most trusted Vor." I turn to Belov. "You killed him along with my brother the day you decided to spit on the Bratva code of honor."

Spartak's eyes go wide as they veer between Luda and me. "You... you're his mother?"

She gives him one curt nod. "I have been waiting for the day when I could stand before you and watch the life drain from your eyes."

He shakes his head. "I can... I can offer you money..."

"Money?" she asks in disgust. "You think money can make me forget how you murdered my son? My only child? Money can't bring him back. And it won't save you now."

I glance back over my shoulder. "Willow," I say, "take our son to the next room."

She frowns. "But—"

"I'll be there in a minute."

Our eyes meet, and she nods. Once she slips through the adjoining door into the next room, I turn back to Belov.

I squat down in front of him, savoring this moment.

"Do you know who Brit was? Who she really was?" When he doesn't answer, I continue as though he had. "Her name was Ariel. She was Pavel's fiancé. Their wedding day would have been a month after that meeting."

"I killed the bitch," he snarls, still twitching with anger and agony. "I don't need to hear her fucking sob story."

I nod. "She should have been here for this. But in her honor, I'll make your death as painful as she would have."

"You motherfucking—"

I pull out my knife. "This blade belonged to my brother. I carry it with me always."

A single slash downward is all it takes to split his stomach open. He groans, but it all happens so fast he doesn't have time to cry out.

I hand the blade to Luda. "I owe you a great debt, Luda."

"I was the one who came to you, Leo," she reminds me, taking the blade from my hand. "You owe me nothing."

"Take your pound of flesh. But make sure he stays alive."

"Don't worry," she assures me. "I am a nurse, after all. I know how to keep a man from dying."

I savor the fear on Belov's face as Luda descends on him. But I don't need to stay and witness his pain. It's enough to know that he will suffer.

I leave Belov with Luda and move into the next room.

Willow is standing by the window, but she's ignoring the view and staring at the door. Waiting for me.

"Leo," she breathes.

I shut the door and walk towards her. "Did you ever doubt me?"

"There were moments," she admits. Then she smiles. "But never again."

"Good."

"Is it true?" she asks.

"Every word."

"So, Semyon… he was working with you?"

"He was."

"He wanted you to take over the Mikhailov Bratva?"

"So long as I took care of his granddaughter," I say.

"I thought he was a monster."

"He *was* a monster," I tell her. "But he died an honorable man. This was his attempt at making amends."

A tear falls down her cheek. "I wish I knew, before…"

"He wanted to die, Willow," I tell her. "He'd had enough of life by the time he wrote to me. But he hung in to make sure it ended properly."

"So Luda…?"

"Luda gave him a quick and painless death. He asked her to kill him long before Belov gave the order."

"You knew this would be the outcome all along?"

"It was all part of the plan," I say simply. "Ariel's death was the only thing that was never supposed to happen. But even a don can't play God."

"At least not all the time, huh?"

I smile, and Willow takes a deep breath. "I think it's about time you meet your son."

She takes a step forward and pulls the baby blanket aside to reveal the face of the plump, little baby in her arms.

"He looks like you," she whispers.

I lift my son in my arms for the first time.

"No. He looks like the future."

EPILOGUE: WILLOW
ONE YEAR LATER

"I can't believe he's one already," Mom says affectionately.

Pasha stands up only to fall back on his butt almost immediately. I offer him a hand, but he ignores it and tries to stand again.

"Stubborn," I tease with a smile. "Just like your papa."

"Whereas his mother accepts help so graciously?" Dad asks, chuckling in my direction.

"Very funny." I roll my eyes. "So maybe he gets that from both of us."

"That'll make life fun for you two when he's a teenager," Mom chimes in.

I wave her away. "I'm not thinking about that until I have to."

Right now, Pasha is still a chubby little baby who needs me. There are some days when I feel like it's going to stay this way forever. I wish it could.

I rest my head on my mother's lap and she strokes my hair. I've let it grow out the last few months so it falls down to my middle back.

I mentioned cutting it ages ago, but Leo gave me a wicked grin. "But what will I have to hold onto?"

People say it's impossible to find alone time with your partner when you have a little one, but Leo and I manage it. Frequently. And he makes full use of my long locks every time we do.

"It's so lovely to spend quality time with the two of you," Mom sighs.

"But where is Leo?" my dad asks. "I thought he was supposed to be here, too."

I smile, thrilled that my parents want to see my husband. Apparently, the year I spent with Anya saw the three of them grow quite close.

"Business meeting." I roll over and turn my face up to the sun.

I love the gardens at this time of year. It's cool enough that you don't sweat and warm enough that you can spend hours lounging in the grass, watching fluffy clouds drift by overhead.

"Shouldn't you be in there?" Dad asks. "You're one half of the Bratva power couple."

I laugh. It took them a while to get used to the lingo, but now, it rolls off their tongues easily. *Bratva*, the same way he'd say *IBM* or *the water company*, as if it were merely another normal business doing normal business things. "I chose not to be there."

"Why?"

"Because I wanted to be here with you two and Pasha."

The truth is that, while I've grown accustomed to the Bratva lifestyle, I don't feel the need to be intimately involved in every detail of it. I trust my husband to handle the bulk of the work. I'm more like a silent partner.

Although I have no problem making my voice be heard if I feel strongly enough about something.

"What is it called now?" dad asks. "The Mikhailov Bratva or the Solovev Bratva?"

"Both," I say. "It's understood that they both have one don. And Pasha has both names, anyway, so we saw no need to change anything."

"Pasha Leonardo Mikhailov Solovev," Mom says. "That's quite the mouthful."

I sit up so that I can see both their faces. "Actually, you missed one."

"Dear Lord, you gave the boy another name?" Dad asks in alarm.

"He's strong. He can carry them," I say confidently. "You want to hear his whole name?"

They both nod.

"Pasha Leonardo *Powers* Mikhailov Solovev," I say.

My parents stare at me. Neither of them says anything, but their eyes look suddenly watery.

"What do you think now?" I ask, a teasing smile turning the corners of my mouth.

Mom presses a hand to her chest. "Sweetheart, are you sure?"

"I want my son to carry your name. Our name. My *real* name. Of course I'm sure."

"And Leo was okay with this?"

I shake my head. "He knew it was important to me. If there's anyone who knows the value of honoring where you came from, it's him."

Mom smiles. "He's a good man."

I nod and smile. "He's a complicated, but very good man."

I lie back again and think about my husband. The last year has been… different for us.

We've worked together to combine the Mikhailovs with the Solovevs. I expected nonstop bickering and squabbles for the right to decide things. But strangely, we were on the same page more often than not. It was exciting to be able to build something together.

Lately, I've been considering something else we could do together.

"Would you mind staying with Pasha?" I ask them, rising to my feet. "I need to talk with Leo."

They both look at Pasha fondly. They love alone time with him.

"Of course," Mom says. "Go right ahead."

I give her a kiss and head back into the house.

The door is shut, but I don't bother knocking. I push the door open and march inside. Leo is sitting with all his closest Vors. Gaiman and Jax, of course. But there are a few new faces, too, thanks to the Mikhailov alliance.

The men all stand as one the moment they see me.

At first, their respect made me uncomfortable. But now, I'm accustomed to it.

I've learned what it means to be a Bratva wife.

"Sorry to interrupt, boys," I say, moving towards Leo. "But I need a moment with my husband."

Immediately, they start filing out. Jax and Gaiman are the last two out of the room. Jax makes a subtle, but crude gesture suggesting that my husband and I are charting a collision course with some adult activities. I ignore it for his sake. Leo wouldn't be pleased if he saw.

The moment the door clicks shut, Leo stands up. "Is there a reason you interrupted my meeting?"

"I have something important I want to discuss with you."

"Tell me."

I move forward and place my hands against his chest. "You look really sexy right now."

He's still in business mode, but his eyebrow arches. Desire darkens his eyes. "Willow…"

I tug on the collar of his shirt, popping a button off. "I want another baby, Leo."

Both eyebrows jerk upward now. "You want another baby?"

"Pasha's almost a year and a half," I say. "And we weren't together during my pregnancy or his birth. You missed so much. We both did. And I want to do it all again… with you by my side this time."

He puts his hand over mine. "I like the sound of that."

"You do?"

He nods. "When do we start?"

I drag a hand down his chest and palm the crotch of his pants. "Now."

Leo stands up, taking me with him, and walks me back to his desk. He sits me on the cool wood and pushes my legs apart with his knee.

I undo his pants and pull his cock out while he yanks down the zipper of my dress. Every movement is faster than the one that came before it. Heat builds, spreads.

"I need you. Now," I breathe. There's no time to disrobe completely. I wrap my legs around his waist and pull him close.

He lifts my hips with one arm and thrusts into me. I arch into the delicious pressure, tipping my head back and moaning at the ceiling.

Leo bends and presses kisses to my collarbone as his hips crash into mine relentlessly. He nips at the slope of my neck, the spot that always turns me liquid in his arms.

"Fuck me, Leo," I moan. "Please… don't stop…"

He angles my hips higher, and every thrust sends a new sensation through me. I lean back and grip the desk, writhing in pleasure. He increases his speed and pushes me to the brink.

"Right there," I cry. "Keep going. Don't—"

But just before I come, Leo pulls back.

I sit bolt upright, ready to scream in frustration. "What are you doing?" I shriek, eyes wild, totally undone with lust.

"Just having a little fun," he smirks.

I wrap a hand around his neck and bring his face close to mine. I narrow my eyes. "Make. Me. Come."

Edging makes me... edgy. I need Leo. *Now.*

His smirk irons out into that lusty, way-too-serious look that always makes my toes curl. "Your wish is my command."

With that, he slams back into me, rendering me immediately mute. He amps up the speed until I can no longer form coherent sentences. Hell, I can't even get out a proper word. All I can do is cling to him and try not to scream loud enough for my parents to hear.

The orgasm hits me like a freight train. My entire body clamps down. I pull him close, refusing to relinquish even a fraction of him, as I eke out every possible ounce of pleasure.

And as I contract around him, Leo groans. I feel the rhythmic pulsing of his pleasure inside of me. The beginning of our next chapter, starting now.

I lay my head on his shoulder until he's done, both of us breathing heavily and slicked with sweat.

Leo lays me back gently on his desk and slides out of me. He wipes himself off and then moves to clean me, as well.

I slap his hands away. "I need that inside me, remember?"

"It's already running down your leg," he points out.

"Damn it." I twist around and lift my legs up in the air.

He chuckles. "It's probably going to take a few attempts before you get pregnant."

"I don't know about that. That felt like babymaking sex, didn't it?"

"It was as good as any time before," he admits. "But I also don't mind if it was just the practice round."

His eyes flash with mischief, and then he sweeps me off the desk and carries me to the sofa by the fireplace. He sits down and settles me on his lap.

"I know you want this. And I do, too. But we'll have our baby when the time is right," he says. "No pressure."

I rest my head against his chest. "I just really want to do it all over again. With you."

"Well, you'll have to give me a few minutes," he says, glancing down at his waist. "I'm not sure I'm ready for another go just yet."

I laugh and slap his chest. "Not what I meant."

"I'm excited to have a baby with you, too, *kukolka*. But it'll happen when it happens, and you won't even have to lift your legs into the air like a crazy person." He blocks another one of my playful slaps and snags my hand out of the air. He presses a kiss to my knuckles. "It'll happen. You trust me, right?"

I smile and look up at his strong face, his simmering eyes. Sometimes, it stuns me how we got here. How we ended up together. But not only that, how lying in Leo's arms feels safe. Comfortable.

How being with him feels like home.

"I trust you," I whisper. "Always."

EXTENDED EPILOGUE

Thanks for reading RAVAGED THRONE—but don't stop now! Click the link below to get your hands on the exclusive Extended Epilogue and take a glimpse five years into the future to see Leo and Willow's family, a new adventure for Jax and Gaiman, and more!

DOWNLOAD THE EXTENDED EPILOGUE TO RAVAGED THRONE

MAILING LIST

Sign up to my mailing list!
New subscribers receive a FREE steamy bad boy romance novel.

Click the link below to join.
https://sendfox.com/nicolefox

ALSO BY NICOLE FOX

Solovev Bratva
Ravaged Crown
Ravaged Throne

Vorobev Bratva
Velvet Devil
Velvet Angel

Romanoff Bratva
Immaculate Deception
Immaculate Corruption

Kovalyov Bratva
Gilded Cage
Gilded Tears
Jaded Soul
Jaded Devil
Ripped Veil
Ripped Lace

Mazzeo Mafia Duet
Liar's Lullaby (Book 1)
Sinner's Lullaby (Book 2)

Bratva Crime Syndicate
Can be read in any order!
Lies He Told Me

Scars He Gave Me

Sins He Taught Me

Belluci Mafia Trilogy

Corrupted Angel (Book 1)

Corrupted Queen (Book 2)

Corrupted Empire (Book 3)

De Maggio Mafia Duet

Devil in a Suit (Book 1)

Devil at the Altar (Book 2)

Kornilov Bratva Duet

Married to the Don (Book 1)

Til Death Do Us Part (Book 2)

Heirs to the Bratva Empire

Can be read in any order!

Kostya

Maksim

Andrei

Princes of Ravenlake Academy (Bully Romance)

Can be read as standalones!

Cruel Prep

Cruel Academy

Cruel Elite

Tsezar Bratva

Nightfall (Book 1)

Daybreak (Book 2)

Russian Crime Brotherhood

Can be read in any order!

Owned by the Mob Boss

Unprotected with the Mob Boss

Knocked Up by the Mob Boss

Sold to the Mob Boss

Stolen by the Mob Boss

Trapped with the Mob Boss

Volkov Bratva

Broken Vows (Book 1)

Broken Hope (Book 2)

Broken Sins *(standalone)*

Other Standalones

Vin: A Mafia Romance

Box Sets

Bratva Mob Bosses (Russian Crime Brotherhood Books 1-6)

Tsezar Bratva (Tsezar Bratva Duet Books 1-2)

Heirs to the Bratva Empire

The Mafia Dons Collection

The Don's Corruption

Printed in Great Britain
by Amazon